Jeremiah leaned closer

Not a lot. Just enough that the equation between them changed and Lucy's better sense was drowned out by the sudden clamoring demands of her body.

"I might be wrong, but I'm sensing that perhaps you're interested in breaking a certain rule you've given us."

"It wasn't just me," she whispered, looking at his lips, the lushness of them. Gorgeous. "You agreed that anything between us would be a mistake."

"Well..." He sighed. "Maybe we need different rules."

His finger brushed against her hand. He tilted his head as if to get a better look at her.

She touched his hand, the roughness of his skin. Her imagination roared as she pictured his body. The perfect sculpture of it. The flex of muscle.

"Lucy."

She looked into those endless blue eyes filled with fire. His lips fell across hers. Light and warm and sweet, and she melted into the moment, into him. He breathed out and the earth stopped rotating.

"Hey, Uncle J." Aaron, the oldest boy, charged onto the deck, ~~breaking them~~ them apart.

She c_____ _____ ____ __ _____ _k Aaron or curse ___ _____ _____ ___ ___ed away.

"Lucy?___ __ _____ ___ _____ "We're not done."

They wer_____ _____t.

Dear Reader,

My family had the most incredible opportunity to tour around New Zealand this fall. It was seven weeks of amazing. Rugby— go, the All Blacks!—hiking natural wonders of every variety, beautiful, welcoming people often offering us beautiful, delicious food. There were some lowlights. Seven weeks in a camper van with a two- and a five-year-old—things were bound to get ugly. But from the moment we arrived until the moment we left, the trip surpassed every fantasy I had going in.

Part of what made everything so memorable was being at the New Zealand RWA conference. The first night of the conference Harlequin editors took the published authors out for dinner. It was a great time and, as you can imagine with a group of like-minded women, things got personal very quickly. I had the pleasure of sitting next to Sandra Hyatt, who was one of the most gracious and enthusiastic women I've ever met. She invited our entire family to visit her and she offered the use of all her kids' travel things. I was blown away by her kindness and generosity. Tragically, that night Sandra took ill suddenly and died. She was young. She had a husband, two kids and a wealth of writer friends who were left shocked and grieving (with a conference in full swing).

I urge you all to pick up any of Sandra's Harlequin Desire books. Her last novel, *Lessons In Seduction,* is amazing!

I hope you enjoy my latest Harlequin Superromance, *Unexpected Family,* and find everyone's happy ending as satisfying as I did. Please drop me a line at molly@molly-okeefe.com to let me know what you think!

Happy reading!

Molly O'Keefe

Unexpected Family

MOLLY O'KEEFE

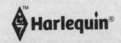

TORONTO NEW YORK LONDON
AMSTERDAM PARIS SYDNEY HAMBURG
STOCKHOLM ATHENS TOKYO MILAN MADRID
PRAGUE WARSAW BUDAPEST AUCKLAND

Recycling programs
for this product may
not exist in your area.

ISBN-13: 978-0-373-71783-5

UNEXPECTED FAMILY

www.Harlequin.com

Printed in U.S.A.

ABOUT THE AUTHOR

Molly O'Keefe grew up in a small town outside Chicago, and while she and her husband and two kids now live in Toronto, Canada, there is something about Rochelle, Illinois, that will always be home. However, every time she brings up moving there her husband reminds her of the lack of sushi restaurants and she quickly changes her mind.

Books by Molly O'Keefe

HARLEQUIN SUPERROMANCE

*The Mitchells of Riverview Inn
**The Notorious O'Neills

Other titles by this author available in ebook format.

Don't miss any of our special offers. Write to us at the following address for information on our newest releases.

Harlequin Reader Service
U.S.: 3010 Walden Ave., P.O. Box 1325, Buffalo, NY 14269
Canadian: P.O. Box 609, Fort Erie, Ont. L2A 5X3

For the attendees of the 2011 New Zealand RWA conference, in particular those in my Conflict and Character workshop.

Thank you for such an inspiring weekend and for getting me out of the mess I had written myself into.

CHAPTER ONE

No one was going to stop the train wreck at the end of the bar. Lucy Alatore stopped listening to her sister describe the house she and her husband were going to build and looked around for Joey, the bartender, who was supposed to stop train wrecks like the one the drunk cowboy at the bar was courting as he searched for his car keys.

"You're not listening to me, are you?" Mia asked.

"Sorry." Lucy stood, only to find Joey flirting with the margarita girls at the end of the bar. "I'm trying to—"

"Find someone to take that cowboy's keys, I know." Mia stood and shrugged into her denim jacket. "It's just as well, Jack's going to be waiting up."

As she spoke, Mia—usually as reserved and quiet as a nun when it came to sex—couldn't keep the womanly smile from curling the corners of her lips.

Lucy refrained from doing anything as childish as pretending to gag. But if her sister didn't stop flaunting her sex life all over the place, Lucy was going to have to resort to name-calling just to vent her envy.

Lucy hugged her sister, holding her closer for a moment, longer than what might seem necessary even between two sisters who dearly loved each other.

"I've been sitting here for two hours waiting for you to tell me what's bothering you," Mia whispered.

"Bothering me?" Lucy leaned back, making sure her

smile was bright. "Nothing bothers me. It's a rule of the universe."

But Mia's amber eyes drilled right into Lucy's head and it took every weapon in her arsenal to keep her smile in place. Beyoncé's "Single Ladies" ringtone blasted from deep in the purse on the chair beside her for the tenth time that night.

"You going to answer that?" Mia asked.

"Nope."

Mia sighed, defeated. "You're okay to drive?"

"Good as you." They both glanced down at the plate of nachos and light beers on the table. Both beers were half-full. Growing up around an alcoholic had ingrained a certain caution around booze.

Mia squeezed Lucy's shoulder and left, winding through the tables and out the door of the Sunset Bar and Grill. Lucy took a deep breath and turned toward the bar, pulling down the jersey Armani shirt she had bought at a resale shop. She wanted to give the girls a chance to do the convincing for her as she stopped a drunk train from leaving this particular station.

"Hey there, cowboy," she said, stepping up to the man digging through his pockets for his keys while fighting to stay upright.

He yanked his keys free of the beat-up denim coat. "Found 'em." He sighed, as if he'd been satisfied on some deep soul level by the appearance of those keys. He turned and she shifted into his way.

"Where you headed?"

"Home." He glanced up and did a drunken man's double take. Slow and sloppy. "Unless you want to have a drink with me?" His smile was charming despite the booze behind it and she smiled back.

"I think you've had enough. Why don't you let me call someone to come pick you up?"

"No one to call." He narrowed his eyes. "Don't I know you?"

She looked back at the man. At first glance he looked like every man under thirty who walked through this bar, with cowboy boots, a tan, weathered face and strong chin. But those brown eyes...

"Holy crap," he muttered, listing toward her slightly. "Lucy Alatore. You showed me your boobs at the state football game."

Oh, Lord. Reese McKenna. "One of my proudest moments."

"I won that game."

"Yes, you did."

"Your boobs were pretty." He stared down her shirt and she reached to hike her pewter jersey shirt up higher on her chest.

"Still are."

"Can I see?"

"Nope. But how about I drive you home?"

"Well, now, I like an aggressive—"

"You're drunk, Reese. And you can't drive. Not like you are right now."

He stared down at his keys as if he were waiting for their input. As if the two of them were old friends who had been in this situation before.

"Come on," she said quietly. "I'll take you home."

"I don't...I don't want to bother you, Lucy." His smile was embarrassed, and she saw a sweet glimpse of that luck-kissed boy she went to high school with.

"You and I know there aren't any cabs around here, Reese." She patted his arm, strong and thick under his shirt, while lifting her palm up for the keys. After a moment he dropped them in.

Lucy led him out into the cool, clean air of Wassau, California, population: Podunk. In city limits, there were about twice as many cows as people. Main Street stretched down toward the Sierras, lit up for a few blocks by four streetlights.

Her beat-up Civic sat in all its rusted glory to her left. But Reese's keys had a fancy foreign emblem on the key chain and out of curiosity she hit the lock release button.

The lights that flashed belonged to a slick sports car crouched in the far corner of the parking lot, sticking out like a sore thumb surrounded by dirty pickup trucks.

Let's see, she thought, *beat-up Civic or fancy sports car?*

It wasn't even a question.

"We'll take your car," she said, the heels of her Prada-knockoff boots grinding into the gravel.

Please, God, don't let that car be stick shift.

Reese climbed into the passenger seat and tucked his hat down over his eyes, looking like a man about to sleep it off.

"Hold up, Reese, where do you live?"

"Staying out at Jeremiah's place."

"Jeremiah Stone?" Well, well, well, this night just keeps getting better. Playing chauffeur to a drunken Reese got a whole lot more appealing with Jeremiah Stone at the other end. "I didn't know he was back in town."

"Yes, ma'am," he muttered, and then, shifting deeper into his bucket seat, he seemed to pass out.

Stone Hollow was the ranch next to the Rocky M, the ranch where she grew up and was currently calling home. It was currently her home while her life in Los Angeles fell to pieces.

Jeremiah, five years older than her and Reese, had been a local legend in Northern California. A rodeo stud, he left town to make it big in the arena when Lucy was a freshman. Last she saw Jeremiah, he was on the front page of a grocery store tabloid and on his arm was a gorgeous country music star.

The car's engine roared to life when she turned the key, the reverberations rumbling up through her body, and she felt as if she were sitting on top of a wild creature. She put the car into Drive—not a stick shift, God had been listening for once—and a familiar reckless thrill flickered through her chest as the powerful vehicle rolled onto Main Street.

She opened the window, letting the mountain air comb fingers through her hair and blow kisses across her cheeks. The neck of her shirt gaped and the air slid down into more intimate places.

Glancing sideways at the sleeping man, she grinned and gunned the engine, racing through the night up into the mountains.

Twenty minutes later she pulled to a stop in the paved parking area in front of the sprawling, two-story ranch house that sat in a pretty pocket of land just west of Rocky M. Fields were made silver by the bright moonlight, horses took on a mystical look as they shook their manes, their breath fogging slightly in the cool night.

Funny how things worked out. When she was growing up here, all she wanted was out. Away. She wanted adventure and culture. Excitement. Not dust.

But in Los Angeles for the past five years she found herself missing the smell of sun-baked junipers. In a city where wearing a cowboy hat was an ironic statement, she'd longed for the real thing. And after dating a bunch of cynical men in skinny jeans, she'd nurtured a yen for the kind of cowboy who would squash a guy in skinny jeans like a bug.

The front door opened, a rectangle of golden lamplight spilling out into the darkness. It had to be Jeremiah who stood there, judging by the long lean size of him, blackened against all that light. She was glad to see those wide shoulders of his because she had a feeling Reese was going to have to be carried out of this car.

She got up out of the car and waved.

"I have Reese," she said. "He was too drunk to drive home."

Jeremiah didn't say anything, just plugged his feet into his boots and stepped out onto the porch and down the steps to the car.

Once he cleared the shadows, the silvery moonlight highlighted his black curls, the icy blue of his eyes.

Jeremiah Stone hasn't changed a bit, she thought, her body still humming from controlling that car. Or maybe it was Jeremiah. He was the sort of man to make a girl's body hum.

The devil was in that man's smile and she found herself smiling back. Honestly, Jeremiah could seduce a saint with that mouth of his. And remembering his reputation, he'd probably already given it a shot.

"Thanks for bringing him back," Jeremiah said, opening the passenger door. Reese spilled out like all that whiskey he'd been drinking at the bar and Jeremiah grabbed him easily. He half marched, half dragged him toward the house. Reese's hat tipped over into the dust and Jeremiah paused for a second, as if trying to figure out how he could pick it up.

"I got it," she said, and grabbed the hat, following the men into the house.

She'd been in the house a couple of times growing up. The last time was when the husband of Jeremiah's sister, Annie, died about five years ago. But the big open living room didn't look anything like she remembered. It looked more like a Laundromat and sporting equipment store had a baby right there on the couch.

Jeremiah kicked a stack of laundry down to the floor and dropped Reese onto the long denim couch.

"That's Lucy." Reese pointed at her. "She showed me her boobs."

Jeremiah's dark eyebrows hit his hairline.

"Fifteen years ago. And it was for luck."

As if that made it reasonable, she thought.

For lack of a better place, she hung the cowboy hat over a hockey stick that was jammed into the cushion of a chair.

"It was the state football game," she added.

"It must have worked. He won that game, didn't he?"

"Apparently my breasts have powers even I don't understand."

Huge points to Jeremiah, who didn't glance down at her breasts, didn't in any way ogle her or joke. In fact, he didn't even look at her. He jerked a faded red, white and blue quilt off the back of the couch and draped it over his drunken houseguest, whose face was resting on a clean pair of little-boy superhero underwear.

"Thanks for bringing him back," Jeremiah said.

"I couldn't let him drive."

"I shouldn't have let him go."

Lucy glanced around the house, waiting for his sister to come out, wrapped in a robe, to give them all hell for being too loud. "Where's Annie?"

Jeremiah cleared his throat, bending down to pick up the laundry he shoved off the couch. His T-shirt slid up his back, revealing pale skin dotted with freckles over hard muscle. Just at the edge of his shirt she saw the snaky tail end of red scar tissue—a healed wound she didn't want to think about. The faded denim of his jeans clung to that man like a faithful lover, and she had to wonder if the hallelujah chorus didn't ring out every time he bent over.

"She died. Last spring."

"What?" She tore her eyes away from his body, feeling like a degenerate. "Oh, my God, Jeremiah…what happened?"

He stood up with a stack of small blue jeans in his hands.

"Cancer." He threw the jeans in the overflowing laundry basket. "It was fast."

"I'm so sorry, Jeremiah. I didn't know—"

"It's all right, Lucy. I don't expect the world to keep up with all the Stones' tragedies."

"Where are your nephews?" she asked.

"Sleeping," he said with a wry smile. "It's ten o'clock at night."

"Are you…" It was just so weird to think of Jeremiah Stone as the guardian of three small boys. Jeremiah Stone was a cowboy sex symbol. He got interviewed on ESPN, and that footage of him getting trampled by a bull had been a YouTube sensation. He dated beautiful country music stars, and did not, definitely did not, fold superhero underwear.

He sighed and smiled as if he couldn't believe it, either. "…in charge of the boys? Yep."

Jeremiah ran a hand through those ebony curls and then set it on his hip, looking around the room as if it were the sight of a national disaster and he just didn't know what to do next.

"I'm so sorry for your loss," Lucy murmured, not sure what else to say.

"Yeah. Me, too."

The silence pulsed for a moment and she opened her mouth to make her exit just as Beyoncé started singing in her bag.

"Is that your phone?" Jeremiah asked.

"It's really more of an anthem," she said, avoiding the question and the phone call.

He laughed and the somber mood was broken.

"You want a drink?" he asked, cutting through the melancholy like a knife. He was smiling again and a smiling Jeremiah Stone was a difficult temptation to resist. Like saying no to chocolate-covered potato chips, or a clearance sale at Macy's. And it's not like she had better things to do.

"I'd love a beer."

"Great." He took a big step over the laundry. "Let's hope Reese didn't drink them all."

She followed him into the kitchen, which was in about the same shape as the living room. Not dirty, really, just very cluttered. Plates filled a drying rack and cups littered the sink. A round table on the far end of the room was covered in backpacks and schoolbooks. A plate with half a peanut-butter-and-jelly sandwich sat on a chair.

Jeremiah was a daddy. The sexiest daddy on the planet, which she still couldn't get her head around.

"Here you go," Jeremiah said, handing her a beer. "Let's have—" He turned to look at the table and winced. "It's nice out, let's sit on the porch."

"Sounds good," she said.

He slid open the sliding glass door and she tried not to

notice the casual nature of his strength, the way the worn T-shirt flowed like water over muscles that bunched and released every time he moved.

"Lucy?" Her eyes jerked to his and she caught him laughing. At her. *What the hell,* she thought, grinning back at him, the man had to be used to being stared at. Men who looked like him got stared at. It was a rule. "You coming?"

"Right behind you."

The porch was a wide patio filled with more sporting equipment. Jeremiah sat down at the table and she sat next to him. The air was cool and found her skin under the thin jersey, but sitting close to Jeremiah was like sitting next to sun-warmed rock.

"So, Lucy Alatore, what brings you back to the Rocky M?"

"A girl can't long for the scent of cattle poop in the morning?"

"Not girls like you."

She felt him eyeing her feathered earrings, the bangles on her arms, her leggings and high-heeled boots. Around here she was exotic. Freaky almost. Not that it bothered her.

"That is true, Jeremiah. That is true."

"How long are you staying?"

She shrugged. "We're not in any rush." No rush at all to get back to the mess she'd made.

"We?"

"Mom and me. She moved to Los Angeles with me when I went."

"Your sister says your jewelry business is doing great. You're the toast of SoCal." Jeremiah smiled at her.

My sister has no idea what she's talking about, she

thought, but what Lucy said to Jeremiah was, "She's proud," and left it at that.

"I bought a girlfriend one of your necklaces," he said, and she nearly spat out her beer.

"Really?"

"Those pretty little horseshoe ones? I liked 'em."

Those pretty little horseshoe necklaces had been her Waterloo. Her Achilles' heel. The snake hidden in tall grass. "Well, I should have gotten you to endorse me."

"You didn't need me. Those necklaces were all over Hollywood."

There was no way she was going to ruin this moonlight by talking about those necklaces. She looked at him sideways and changed the subject. "I have a hard time imagining you in Hollywood."

"That's where the pretty girls are." He waggled his eyebrows but then stared at his boots. "I was only there for a while. The relationship didn't last much past that necklace I gave her."

"You didn't like it?"

"No, I really liked your necklace—"

She laughed. "Los Angeles."

"Good God, no." He shuddered. "Not my scene at all."

"That city must have loved you, though." With that hair and those eyes, the way he moved, part cowboy, part cat, but all man. Casting agents must have fallen over themselves to get to him. To say nothing of the women.

"What about you?" he asked.

"That city does not love me." If there was one thing she could be sure of it was that Los Angeles barely knew she'd been there, which was such a bitter disappointment when she'd gone intending to light the streets on fire. And she'd been close. So damn close.

She spun the bottle between her hands. Her chest

ached as if there was someone standing on her rib cage. *I guess that's what failure feels like.*

"Hey." His shoulder nudged hers, his heat a wave through her body that shook her out of her musings. "This is the closest I've been to a date in months so please don't cry. If you do, I'll probably start, and I've sworn off crying on dates."

Charmed, despite her crap mood, she smiled at him. "Does that get you laid?" she asked. "Crying on dates?"

"No, actually. It's a very effective birth control."

He was watching her, a strange smile on his face. It was as if he'd turned around and found a treasure sitting on this porch next to him and for a long moment she got lost in the blue of his eyes.

I'm going to kiss him, she thought, delighted by the idea. Drunk on the notion. Before leaving his house tonight, she was going to taste this man.

She was a serial monogamist—hadn't had a one-night stand in fifteen years. For her, it was one long-term relationship after the other. She didn't just date, she contemplated marriage over dessert. But she did like to kiss.

Her life hadn't been very easy the past few months. Stress and worry and regret and fear had worn her down to the bone and she'd grown so used to the sensation that sitting here, contemplating kissing a gorgeous cowboy in the moonlight, seemed like the sweetest relief.

He lifted a finger and brushed back a long strand of dark hair that had fallen over her eye.

Her skin sizzled at his touch and the rest of her body cried out in jealousy.

"You remind me of Hollywood," he murmured.

"What do you mean?" she whispered, so lost in his eyes that if she was being insulted, she didn't care.

"Beautiful and sad, all at the same time."

She cleared her throat and looked away. It was one thing to kiss a handsome cowboy in the moonlight. It was another thing to have him see her so clearly.

"So how did you end up with a drunk cowboy on your couch?" She rolled the bottle between her hands, liking the click of the glass against her rings. The sound was loud and chased away her thoughts of kissing handsome cowboys.

"Reese? He showed up yesterday. He won big down at the rodeo in Fort Worth and was looking for some help spending the purse."

"And the guy in charge of three young boys was the logical choice."

His smile was thin and drawn. "He didn't know. Nobody really knows. I just faded away after my accident."

"I saw that footage!"

"YouTube?"

"It was awful. You were like a rag doll."

"I know." He laughed. "I was there." His lightheartedness amazed her; she could only gape at him.

"How can you laugh? Didn't you think you were going to die?"

"I did. But somehow I didn't." He finished his beer and set it down beside him. "But that's part of the job. A rare part of the job, but there isn't a rider out there who doesn't watch that gate get thrown open and know that he might be living his last seconds on earth."

"That's crazy."

"That…" His eyes sparkled, his grin widened. Her breath caught at the danger that glittered around this man, the thrill. It was like breathing in sparks. "…is the beauty of rodeo."

"You miss it." It wasn't a question because it was all

too obvious the man lived and breathed that kind of excitement.

"You have no idea," he whispered, staring up at the large moon that hung over the junipers at the edge of the lawn.

Oh, no. She set down her beer bottle and put her hands between her knees. If there was one thing she loved more than a handsome man in the moonlight, it was a sad, handsome man in the moonlight. It was a sickness, she knew that—one more weakness in her already weak character.

She liked to think she could save men. A doomed proposition every single time, but it didn't stop her from trying.

She stood and turned to face him. He looked up at her, his eyes alight with interest, with a sexual speculation that made her entire body hum and purr. It had been so long since she'd been touched and stroked and she planned on being noble right now, and walking out of this house without having removed her clothes. But not without taking a little something for herself.

"Stand up, cowboy," she murmured, feeling that same reckless thrill that spelled disaster.

The moonlight danced in his hair and the corner of his smile where it tipped up toward heartbreaking. Toward devilish and risky.

When he stood, his chest brushed her breasts and she gasped slightly at the pleasing pain of her nipples getting so hard so fast. They had barely touched and she was panting.

But so was he and that was about the sexiest thing she'd ever seen.

"What are you going to do with me, Lucy?"

"I'm still deciding."

"Take your time."

Her hand found the hard curve of his biceps, the soft cotton of his T-shirt brushing the back of her hand as she reached under it. Her palm embraced the soft skin of his arm.

"I've decided."

"Thank God."

"I'm going to kiss you."

CHAPTER TWO

ONCE, A LONG TIME AGO, Jeremiah had been a gentleman. It was a point of pride in his life. He could afford to go slow, or take his time. Or even refuse if the moment didn't quite feel right.

And not just women and sex. He could turn down advertising contracts, another cup of coffee, a role in a movie. It didn't matter. He could be a gentleman because he was never desperate.

But then his brother-in-law died and then his sister died and now he craved, every day, every minute, for just a taste of all the things he turned away in his old life.

There was no abundance in his days right now. Every bone was rubbing up against another bone, his stomach growled, his body hurt, and he went to bed every damn night hungering for what he used to take for granted. And now he had the current superstar, Reese, on his couch reminding him of everything he no longer had.

If this beautiful, sexy woman wanted to kiss him, he wasn't going to say no. When maybe he should.

He should.

There was no maybe about it.

He was too old for one-night stands. And these days with his three nephews inside and the work involved in running this ranch, he had nothing left over. There was no time, no energy, no feeling, to give Lucy except whatever she was going to take.

But there was no way in hell he was going to open his mouth and tell her all of that. Not when she was about to kiss him and he hadn't been kissed in months.

When he last saw her, Lucy Alatore had been a skinny girl on the edge of womanhood. But the sparkle, the dare, in her eyes was still there—that was what he could not resist.

Her long, elegant arms twined around his neck and the sensation of her soft wrists made him ravenous for more. Ravenous for something sweet and soft and tender, just for him. Something he didn't have to share or reject or postpone because three boys needed him.

That beer on her breath went right to his head and he waited, patient but burning for the silken graze of her lips over his. When it came, it was like the chute had been thrown open and he was holding on for dear life.

The kiss rocketed up out of control and ran whole hog into the wild in two seconds. She gasped against his mouth as if she was just as surprised.

Trying for gentle, but falling miles short, he pulled her closer, the rough calluses of his fingers catching on the soft material of her fancy shirt.

She opened her mouth under his and pulled him as tight as she could into her body until he was curved over her, holding her against the curl of his body so that not even a breeze could pass between them.

It was wild. Hot. The lush curve of her hips under the tight black leggings she wore was too much a temptation to resist and he slid both palms over her, squeezing as he went, listening to her groan.

Her fingers tugged on his hair, the pain an electric bliss down his back, across his skin, through his blood, waking him up. Bringing him back to life.

The growl, like the lust, the fire, rolled up through his

gut, obliterating his brain, and he spun slightly, ready to drag her into the house, ready to do whatever it took to take off her clothes, to find the secrets of her skin.

"Yes," she groaned, lifting herself into him, the sweetest arch, the sweetest capitulation. He grasped his hands over her hips, taking all her weight and, like every teenage fantasy of what a woman should do, she slipped those long legs around his waist.

Ready to take her into the house, he turned toward the screen door, but immediately tripped over Casey's scooter and then backed into Ben's baseball bat—both of which clattered to the ground. The sound was like gunshot in the quiet night.

He tore his lips from Lucy's and focused his gaze on Casey's window just above them. He held his breath, waiting for the light to come on, for the five-year-old to come looking for him like he did every night.

But the window stayed dark.

Thank God.

He sighed, resting his head against Lucy's.

Under the relief that Casey hadn't woken up, he felt something awful, a black tidal wave of anger. A tsunami of resentment.

A kiss. One goddamned kiss in the moonlight! Couldn't he just have that? Couldn't he just have this one thing for himself?

He didn't ask for any of this—the ranch, the work and the boys who stared at him with their hearts in their eyes.

I don't want it! I don't want any of it!

The scream gagged him. His miserliness shamed him. Those boys didn't ask for him, either. In a heartbeat they'd take their mom and he'd give Annie back to them if only he could.

Lucy pressed her lips to his and he wanted—more

than anything in the world right now—to get right where he'd been in that kiss. But the moment was gone.

There were three kids in that house. A drunk cowboy. And three days' worth of work to get done all before he could go to bed.

That was his life and the truth was he was terrified of what would happen if he forgot that, even for an hour. How much of his resentment and anger would slip through the cracks of the control he'd had to build up over the past year. How many days would it take for him to look those kids in the eyes again? How many nights of staring up at the ceiling and forcing himself not to run away?

The answer was *too many*.

He kissed her, a tender, reluctant goodbye kiss. And she must have read it in his lips because she unwrapped her legs from around his waist and slipped her arms from his neck.

"Well." She patted his chest, her fingers so hot through his T-shirt he had to step back to get some distance. Some clarity. She blinked at him, her fingers suspended in the distance between them, and he had to look away. He hoped she wasn't hurt, but he didn't look at her to find out and he sure as hell didn't ask, because he was such a mess. Everything was a mess.

Looking at her was like looking at everything he once had and could no longer have again.

"Thanks, cowboy," she said.

"Sorry."

"No sorry about it." The teasing, the sauciness, in her voice made him smile, allowed him to look up at her. Allowed him to breathe.

"Thanks," he said. "For Reese and for…"

"Rocking your world?"

He laughed. "It needed rocking." Which was a lie. His life had been taken by its heels and shaken until everything he knew and recognized had vanished. He'd been rocked enough and what he needed was to be left alone so he could figure out how to handle it.

"Good night," she said, and then she walked across his porch.

It was rude. Bad-mannered in the extreme but he did not follow. He did not yank open the sliding glass door for her, even though he knew it stuck. He just stood on that porch and stared up at the moon until he was numb enough to go back inside.

LUCY TOOK THE LONG WAY back to the Rocky M. Opening up Reese's car over the pass, the engine roared and the world slipped by like a ribbon. The wind blasting through her open window wasn't enough to cool her fevered skin and her damaged pride, so she hit the controls to roll down every window until it was a cyclone inside the car. Her hair whipped around her head and still her skin burned, her heart ached.

Stupidly, she felt like crying.

Don't care, she told herself, slowing down to take the first curve down the mountain toward the ranch. *You've got enough shit to worry about, without worrying about Jeremiah Stone.*

The smart move would be to leave. To pack up her mother and face the mess in Los Angeles.

But the thought made her panic and a cold sweat formed around her hairline. She wasn't ready. It had only been three weeks since she'd let go of her employees and closed up the shop.

Couldn't she have some time to grieve? To lick her wounds? To hide?

Such a coward.

The Rocky M ranch slipped in and out of view through the pine trees until she turned left up the long driveway. The brown ranch house sat under a granite overhang. As a kid she'd prayed more than once that the mountain would fall down on that house. It baffled her that Mia could call this place home.

Mia and Lucy had grown up on here as the children of ranch employees. The McKibbons, Walter and his wife, owned the land while her father, A.J., had been the foreman and Lucy's mom, Sandra, the housekeeper and cook. Mia and Lucy's childhood hadn't been unhappy, but it had never been secure. Not a moment had passed that they'd been unaware of their status. Every tie they had to this home and this land could be severed. And almost had been.

That this was where Lucy chose to lick her wounds was even more strange. But beggars couldn't be choosy. Broke didn't even begin to describe her financial state.

She parked beside her sister's old pickup truck, rolled up the windows and turned off the engine. The quiet echoed and boomed like a heartbeat. Like the house was alive and waiting for her.

Exhausted by the roller coaster of the night, she finally pulled herself out of the car and into the house through the side door. It was midnight and the house was silent.

Mia and Jack were living a mile up the road, using the house Mia and Lucy grew up in—the little two-story that their mother, Sandra, had cared for so passionately—until their new house up in the high pastures was finished. Walter, Jack's father, still occupied the ranch house. And for the past three weeks, Lucy and Sandra had been staying in the rear guest rooms of the house;

they smelled like mothballs and had beds like hammocks.

She unzipped her boots in the mudroom, stepped back and looked at her gray high-heeled Prada knock-offs next to the filthy work boots. She saw it as the perfect example of how she didn't belong here. Had never belonged here.

Just a little bit longer, she thought. *Just until I formulate a plan. Get my feet under me.*

Through the dark she walked right to her mother's bedroom and knocked softly on the door.

"Mom?" she called, and she heard the bed creak.

"Come in, Lucy," her mother said, and Lucy walked into the small bedroom. Mom pushed herself up in bed, her black hair a cloud around her shoulders. The white of her nightgown glowed in the dark. "Are you okay, sweetheart?"

Knowing she needed no special permission, she crawled into her mother's bed, the warmth under the covers immediately banishing the chill of the evening.

She curled up on her side and stared at her mother's still-young face. They needed to find her a life. A man to take her dancing. A church group that would keep her young.

"Fine," Lucy whispered, and Sandra turned on her side, her hands under her chin, mirroring Lucy's position.

"It's time for us to go home," Sandra said.

"What? Why?"

"I thought it would be easier coming here," she said. "But it's difficult—"

"Because of Walter?" Lucy practically spat the man's name.

"Not just Walter, he doesn't help. This place used to be happy and now…now it is haunted."

"But Mia's here—"

"And married. Settled." She blew out a long breath, looking at her hands. "There's nothing for me to do here. No way for me to be useful." Lucy could not understand her mother's driving need to be needed.

"But, Mom…" She grasped at straws, finally settling on the truth she hadn't wanted to face in the five years they'd lived in Los Angeles. "You don't like the city."

"That's not true."

She gave her mother a wry look.

"Well, I don't like it here so much, either." Sandra sat up. "There's nothing for me to do here. I'm useless."

"You're cooking—"

"Cooking!" she cried, and then shook her head, as if biting her tongue.

Lucy wrapped her fingers over her mother's fist. Her father had died five years ago and, in the grand scheme of things, that wasn't all that long. Sandra was still grieving.

Yeah, Lucy thought, *and you're the ungrateful daughter keeping her someplace she doesn't want to be.*

"What about your jewelry?" Sandra asked. "You've been gone three weeks—aren't you needed back at your studio?"

Her heart was a rock in her chest. Lying to her mother made her sick, but Lucy couldn't give her mother more grief. Couldn't give her a failure as a daughter. "I'm the boss, Mom. And I haven't had a vacation in years. I'm… I'm burned out. I haven't had a new design in months."

Sandra stroked back Lucy's hair. "This is true. You work so hard. A few more days, then? And then we go back."

Lucy wished she was rich, and not for the first time. Wished that she could take her mom on vacation, whisk her away to Rome. But she was more than broke. And they couldn't go back to Los Angeles, nor could they stay here much longer.

Talk about limbo.

Lucy forced herself to smile. "Sounds good."

"Sleep, sweetheart," Sandra murmured, and Lucy let her eyelids shut, pretending to sleep so her mother wouldn't worry.

LUCY STARTED AWAKE at the sound of her mother's snores. Hard to believe, but Saint Sandra snored like a merchant marine. Her father had always joked about it, saying sleeping next to his wife was like being back in the navy—no one thought twice about it when they found him asleep on the couch. Chased out of his bed by his wife's deviated septum.

"Oh, man, Mom," Lucy muttered, swinging her legs over the side of the bed. "We gotta get that fixed."

The moon in the window was so bright she could read her watch—3:00 a.m. It would be a battle getting to sleep again. She'd never needed a lot of sleep, but in the past year she'd flirted with insomnia. It was as if her brain was a giant hamster wheel, and every hamster in the world wanted a turn. She just couldn't turn off her thoughts.

She followed the moonlight that lay across the floor in big sheets, heading out the door of the room. But instead of going to her own room, she went to the kitchen. And to whatever dinner leftovers might be in the fridge.

The carpet of the hallway changed to stone as she walked into the dining room and she rounded the counter that separated the kitchen from the eating area. Then she stopped dead in her tracks.

Walter, owner of the Ranch and Mia's father-in-law,

sat on the floor in a puddle of moonlight, small orange pills scattered around him. His face unnaturally pale in the bone-white light.

"Hey," he said, trying to brace himself against the floor so he could move. But she could see he was in too much pain.

"What happened?" she asked, crouching beside him. She smelled booze on his breath and she stood back up. "You're drunk."

"I fell." His hard face cracked into a grimace. "I think I hurt my leg."

His ankle, which jutted out from beneath the frayed edge of his light blue pajamas, was swollen and purple. Damn it, it had to be sprained and who the hell knew how long he'd been sitting here.

"You fell because you're drunk."

He sighed, looking down at his body as if it had betrayed him.

"I dropped a pill and bent down to get it…. I just lost my balance."

"Because washing down Parkinson's medication with whiskey improves balance?"

"Could you…could you just get Jack? Or Mia?" he asked.

Anger popped and pulsed inside of her. "No." She went back into the mudroom and jammed her feet in her boots, then she grabbed the keys off the counter, calling Walter all the names under her breath that she was raised too well to say to his face. Stomping back into the kitchen she glared down at him.

He stared down at his hands. Ashamed. *Good.*

"Sandra—"

"Everybody is sleeping and I'm not dragging them

out of bed because you were too drunk to stay on your feet. You're stuck with me."

He nodded slightly, his white hair picking up the moonlight and glinting silver. Walter was still handsome, a big masculine man, but all she saw when she looked at him was ruin.

"You're going to have to help me a little," she said, crouching beside him and flinging his arm over her shoulder.

He grimaced. Sweat bloomed across his forehead but he didn't groan. Nope, not Walter. Just like he'd sit here all damn night rather than scream for help.

All that pride wasted when it came to drinking. It's a shame.

With a lot of effort she got him to his feet and when he shifted his body to go toward the living room she steered him instead to the mudroom.

"What are you doing?"

"I'm taking you to the hospital."

"I'm fine—"

She shifted her weight away from him and he stumbled, catching himself on the counter that split the kitchen from the dining room. Tentatively he put his foot onto the floor and cursed when he couldn't put any weight on his ankle.

When he glanced at her she shrugged. "It's sprained at least, and you've been sitting there for how long?"

He shook his head. "I'm not sure."

"Right, then, we're going to the hospital."

Hopping and stumbling and then begrudgingly accepting her help she got him out to the sports car.

"Where's your car?" he asked.

"It turned into a pumpkin." Carefully, she eased him

into the passenger seat and then walked around to the driver's side.

She backed the car up, gravel spitting out from under her tires. He didn't say anything and she drove into the night, the moon's watchful eye hovering over the car.

"I'm…I'm sorry," Walter said, his chin up, his shoulders back. Clinging to the pride he had.

"Tell that to my mother."

She stopped, realizing what had just happened. Walter had a sprained ankle. At least. Combined with the drinking, the Parkinson's…he'd need help. And Sandra needed to be needed. Lucy couldn't help but laugh out loud.

"I don't see what's so funny," Walter said.

"No. You wouldn't." But, oh, Lord, it was funny. The Fates could not conspire to help her business, but they could conspire to keep her on the ranch.

But at what cost to her mom?

"Not three hours ago Mom was saying she wanted to leave." Her fingers curled into talons around the steering wheel. "And I had to convince her to stay. And now you have handed us the perfect reason to stay and I can't…" She stopped at a stop sign and glared at him. "And I can't abide by the thought of her taking care of you."

"I haven't asked her to. I wouldn't."

"It doesn't matter. You need her. I couldn't drag her away if I tried."

She pushed the accelerator, too hard, and Walter winced as his foot hit the car door. In his silence the past rushed back, drowning her in bitter memories.

"Your wife—"

"Is gone. Divorced."

"Too late. You don't win any points for that, Walter! And she tried to kick my mom out of her home after Dad died. My dad, who was your best friend!" She threw the words at him like grenades lobbed across the car. "He was your most loyal employee. And what did you do to stop your wife? Nothing. Just like you did nothing when she was beating up Jack." He flinched at that and her stomach turned.

This isn't you, she thought, but she couldn't stop. The bitterness was out of control.

"You stood by while your bitch of a wife ruined everyone's lives and I can't just shrug my shoulders and let my mom take care of you like nothing ever happened!"

The sound as he shifted in his seat was loud and she glanced over at him, furious.

"Don't you have something to say?"

"I can't forgive myself, either. And as for your mom...I don't want her to stay. Not for me."

She laughed, dark and resentful. "Well, at least that we can agree on. Not that it will do us much good."

"What do you mean?"

"I mean, like it or not, we'll be staying."

CHAPTER THREE

AFTER A FEW HOURS of sleep Lucy woke up, got dressed in her favorite jeans and loose white T-shirt, pulled her hair back in a sloppy ponytail and contemplated her jewelry.

Everything was too light, she needed something heavy. Something dark. But her designs never leaned that way. Finally, she settled on the beaded silver hoops.

Sandra was already up, humming as she put scrambled eggs onto a blue plate. She glowed with a grim purpose, which was entirely expected.

Careful what you wish for, she chided herself.

"Hey, Mom," she said, grabbing the keys to Reese's sports car from the dish on the counter where all the keys sat. She opened her purse and pulled out her cell.

Meisha had called four times this morning.

She turned off her phone.

"You're up early." Her mother's voice, softened and textured by her Spanish accent, was still the best sound in the world. And the sight of her in a kitchen was like seeing an animal in its natural habitat. Sandra ruled the kitchen, every kitchen. It didn't matter where she was, in ten minutes she would have food and drink to end your hunger and soothe your soul. She was magic in a thin, five-foot package. And this morning all that magic was ignited.

"I've got to take a car back over to Stone Hollow."

"You want some eggs?" Sandra put a fork on the plate.

"I'll take a bite." She reached for the fork, but Sandra moved the plate out of the way.

"These aren't for you. I'll make you some, though."

"Walter?" Of course she would already be waiting on Walter.

"It was good what you did, getting him to the hospital."

"Yeah, well, you know what they say—no good deed goes unpunished."

"Lucia Marie—"

"Mom." She took a deep breath and fanned her hands over the counter as if finding, by touch, the argument that was going to work. It was time to get her head out of her own misery and take care of her mom, the way her mom had always taken care of her. "I get it, he needs you, but don't let him take advantage of you."

"He hasn't even let me into his room, honey."

"You wanted to leave…remember? One more week."

"He's going to have that cast for at least three."

"Jack's not poor, Mom. He can hire someone to take care of him."

"And how will that work? Walter—"

"I don't think Walter gets a vote on the subject anymore."

"Everyone is allowed their pride, sweetheart."

Lucy put her head down on the counter. Lifted it and thunked it again. "Mom, he's a drunk. He will always be a drunk. Caring for that man will bleed you dry."

"Not if he quits."

"And you honestly think that will happen?"

"I pray for it."

Like a true sinner, she wondered what prayer's success rate was against alcoholism, but she kept her mouth shut. There was no arguing with her mother when she was all hopped up on playing the nursemaid. And Walter was like an amusement park of need.

"Have you forgotten what he did to us after Dad died?" Lucy hated saying the words, bringing the memory up front like this. It made her stomach hurt. It made her want to do over last night and let Walter sit in pain on the kitchen floor for another couple of hours.

"I have forgotten nothing." Sandra's tone of voice made her seem a foot taller. "But the man has a sprained foot, Lucy. When did you get so hard-hearted?"

"Me?" Lucy gaped at her mother. "It's not like I'm saying let's leave him in the mountains to die. I'm saying you've done enough, Mom."

"How about this," Sandra said. "We stay until they hire someone Walter can live with to take care of him."

"That will be forever."

And that suits your purposes just fine, a dark voice said. *Three more weeks of not having to face up to the mess you made in Los Angeles. Why are you fighting this?*

Sandra licked her lips. "I'll…I'll do what I can to hurry it along."

"What does that mean?"

"Walter doesn't want me here, not really. And when reminded of that, he'll…" She shrugged. "He'll agree to have someone else help him."

Lucy wasn't going to ask for more information. She had enough problems of her own without digging into Walter's issues with Sandra.

"Okay, three weeks. That's as long as we're staying. I swear, Mom, if I have to drag you—"

Mom lifted a hand, her face unsmiling.

Right, Lucy thought, *Mom didn't get dragged. She went willingly or not at all.*

"Three weeks should be sufficient," Sandra said.

"I'll be back in an hour," Lucy said. "And then I'll talk to Mia and Jack about getting a nurse." She grabbed her bag and headed out into the sunny morning.

Once in town, she used what money she had left in her wallet to get gas. She was going to have to get a job soon. Or sell the condo, but she needed to talk to Sandra about that, since she helped put down the deposit, and that was a conversation she wasn't quite ready to have.

Then she drove by her Civic at the bar just to make sure it was still there. It was. Dusty and red and old. Reese could drop her off here after she returned the car.

She stared at her car for a while, stalling for time, reluctant to go up to Stone Hollow and pretend like that sad desperate kiss had never happened with Jeremiah. Because that was really the only thing to do.

Life sure has gotten complicated in the past twenty-four hours. She sped out of town, opening the engine up over the pass in a fond goodbye.

She could use a car like this to outrun all the problems after her. Hell, a car like this she could sell and solve most of her problems.

The parking area in front of Jeremiah's house was empty and she nearly sang a little song of relief. No brooding cowboy problem. *Huzzah.*

Once out of the car, she knocked on the door to the house and waited. A long time. She cupped her hands around her eyes and peered through the glass, trying to see signs of life.

Suddenly, there was thump that shook the door. Wary, she stepped back and a small face covered in what looked like grape jelly appeared in the window. A little boy with brown curly hair. His blue eyes not unlike Jeremiah's.

"It's a girl!" the boy yelled over his shoulder, the sound muffled by the door. Someone over the boy's shoulder must have said something because he nodded and turned back to face her.

"Do we know you?" he asked.

"I'm your neighbor."

"No, you're not. Mia is our neighbor."

"I'm Mia's sister."

The boy seemed to process that and he turned to yell something over his shoulder.

"What's your name?" he asked when he turned back around.

"Lucy."

His face split in a wide grape-jelly smile and Lucy felt herself smile in return. *Heartbreaker.*

"My friend Willow has a dog named Lucy," he yelled through the glass.

"That's great, buddy, is your uncle here?"

"No."

She blinked. "Are you here by yourself?"

The door thumped again and the little boy vanished only to be replaced by a slightly older boy. Under his dark hair, dark eyes narrowed in an attempt to be threatening. It was oddly effective. *Troublemaker.*

"I'm going to need to see some ID," the boy said, and she laughed before she realized he was serious. She pulled her driver's license out and pressed it up to the glass.

The boy studied it and then looked back up at her with his simultaneously young and old eyes. "You here to rob us? 'Cause there's nothing here to rob. Not even a video game or computer."

She shook her head.

"You going to kidnap us?"

"What? No!"

"Because you don't want to kidnap Casey," the boy said. "He wets the bed."

"I do not!" a little voice yelled, and the boy jostled and grinned down at Casey, who hit him.

"I'm not kidnapping anyone."

"That's the sort of thing a kidnapper would say."

Perhaps it was the lack of sleep, but she had no comeback. This boy totally had the better of her. Instead, she held up the keys. "I'm here to give Reese his car back."

The boy looked down, presumably at his brother, and she had to admit this was the strangest, yet most thorough, interrogation she'd ever been a part of.

There was another thump and the older boy vanished seconds before the door opened.

The two boys stood barefoot in the doorway and somehow the sight of those small pink toes on the edge of the welcome mat brutally reminded her of their situation. *Orphans.*

"Where's your uncle?"

"He's picking up Aaron from hockey practice," Casey said, and the older boy punched him in the arm.

"You're not supposed to say that sort of stuff, remember? We're supposed to say he's in the shower."

"Sorry." Casey's lower lip started to shake. "I forgot. There are so many rules now."

"I'm Lucy," she said quickly, holding out her hand to the little boy, who grabbed it and shook using his whole body.

"I'm Casey. I'm five."

"Wow," she said, putting on a show of being impressed. "Big boy." She turned to the older boy, who still watched her with suspicion. Which she supposed was a good thing in this situation, but it made the boy look disturbingly old. "Who are you?"

"Ben." He crossed his arms over his chest, effectively ending that discussion.

"Well, it's nice to meet you guys. Is Reese here?"

Casey shot his brother a panicked guilty look but Ben just jerked his thumb over his shoulder.

Lucy stepped past the boys into the living room, which no longer looked like the love scene between a Laundromat and a sporting goods store. Reese was still there, a quilt-covered blob on the couch. But he wasn't just covered by a quilt anymore.

Balanced all over his body were toys, glasses and plates. Stuffed animals. A hockey puck.

He looked like an altar.

She glanced, wide-eyed, at the boys. Casey at least had the good sense to look guilty.

"It's a game we're playing," he said.

"It's a pretty strange game. Some of those glasses look heavy."

"It's none of your business," Ben said.

Reese shifted and a full glass of water that had been balancing on him fell to the ground, spilling water everywhere. A stuffed bear followed and so did a storybook and half a peanut-butter-and-jelly sandwich.

"Uh-oh," Casey muttered, running forward to clean it up.

Lucy stepped forward to help. She grabbed what looked like a dirty towel from the coffee table, but Ben snatched it out of her hands.

"You don't use that," he said, handing the green towel over to Casey, who quickly shoved it under the couch.

Ooooookay. "How about you go grab another towel from somewhere."

"I'll get it," Casey said, darting off into the kitchen. Lucy cleaned up what had fallen off Reese and eyed what was still stacked on top of him.

Careful not to look at Ben, who radiated tension like a nuclear reactor, she picked up a glass plate and replaced it with a throw pillow and on top of that she stacked the stuffed bear and a bunch of Lego pieces.

"See," she whispered, "you have to put your big things on the bottom so that there's better balance. And things made out of glass don't stack as well." She grabbed a coffee mug from off Reese's feet and replaced it with three race cars she stacked one on top of the other.

She glanced over her shoulder to see Ben watching her, his neck all red. His body held so taut she thought he might snap right in front of her eyes, as if all the pressure inside of him were pulling him to pieces.

It seemed natural to hug him; it seemed, in fact, like that was exactly what he needed—she would be a heartless monster not to hug him—but when she reached out he jerked back so hard he bumped into the coffee table.

The juice cups and coffee mugs shimmied and toppled. A glass plate broke on the floor.

"What the hell?" Reese yelled, and sat up, knocking all the toys and pillows off.

Casey ran back around the corner and, seeing the mess and his brother's furious expression, burst into tears.

"Now, look what you did!" Ben shouted. "You made Casey cry!"

"Oh, my God, please stop yelling," Reese muttered.

So, of course, that was the moment Jeremiah walked in.

JEREMIAH HAD COME TO EXPECT a certain amount of disaster when he walked back into the house from picking up Aaron every other Saturday morning. He wasn't a father but even he understood leaving a nine-year-old in charge of a five-year-old for an hour wasn't the best idea. Or maybe it was okay for other kids…but for Ben it was like an engraved invitation to trouble.

Not that the kid needed much of an invitation.

But he and a few of the other parents carpooled to hockey practice and he couldn't take Ben and Casey because there just wasn't any room in the truck. And he couldn't beg off because he'd done enough of that. Yeah, things were hard here, but it was time to handle it and stop taking every handout that came his way.

So every other week he walked in the front door wondering what it was going to be this time. Shaving the dog? Casey tied up in the closet? The kitchen the scene of a breakfast cereal war?

The last thing he expected was Lucy on her knees in front of Reese with Casey—holding every kitchen towel they owned—crying in the corner.

Ben, with his arms over his chest, glaring daggers at Jeremiah was, however, totally expected.

"What's going on?" Jeremiah asked, throwing his keys on the ledge by the door.

Aaron bumped into him from behind with his hockey bag. "Take all of that stuff into the laundry room, Aaron," he said. "I'm tired of washing clothes that have been sitting in that bag all week. It's gross."

Aaron nodded and stepped toward the laundry room in the back but stopped when he saw Lucy. Jeremiah had to admit, she looked just as gorgeous as she did last night, even without the feathers and boots and moonlight.

"Hey." Lucy lifted her hand in a little wave.

"Hey." Aaron's voice broke over the word and he got

so red the tips of his ears lit on fire. He vanished down the hall to the laundry room.

"I came by to do a car exchange, but Reese wasn't up yet."

The lump on the couch groaned and pulled the quilt up over his head.

"Still isn't." Jeremiah sighed and rubbed his hands over his face. "Casey, buddy, could you stop crying?"

Like a faucet was turned off, the whimpering stopped.

"Are you mad?" Casey whispered.

"Of course not," Lucy answered for him.

"Yes, he is," Ben said, always ready for a fight, and Jeremiah sighed again—bone-weary of these fights he never won no matter what he did.

"Come on, Casey and Ben," Lucy said, "let's get this stuff cleaned up."

"You don't have to do that," Jeremiah said, stepping forward to take one of the towels in Casey's hand.

She smiled at him, sympathetic and perhaps a little pitying, which was exactly the opposite of the way he wanted her to look at him and it pissed him off. He wanted her to look at him the way she had last night. He wanted that little bubble of time to be unbroken, unsullied by reality, so he could think about it alone in his cold bed. But having her here, in the unflinching light of day, robbed him of the fantasy.

"I'll just take you home." He was way gruffer than he intended and he saw Casey look over at him full of anxiety.

God, I just cannot get this shit right.

"Don't worry about it," Lucy said, picking up toys and stacking them on the coffee table.

"You don't have to clean this up." He stepped forward, taking the toys from her, trying to get her to stand.

Trying actually to get her out of here, but she was stubbornly reluctant.

"It's almost done, isn't it, Casey?" She winked at Casey, who'd thrown all the kitchen towels over the lake of water next to the couch. *Great, just great. Now, I'll have to dry all of them.* But Casey beamed at her and it was the last damn straw.

"I said stop!"

Everyone halted and turned to stare at him. Casey's lower lip started to tremble. The front door slammed shut and he figured that was Ben running out to the barn, which is what he did every time Jeremiah yelled.

"Okay." Lucy stood and dropped the car keys on the coffee table. "Don't worry about the ride, I'll just call Mia and wait for her outside." She gave Casey a big grin and the little boy stared after her with his broken heart in his eyes.

"See you," Lucy said without making any eye contact, and Jeremiah knew, he totally understood, that he was the biggest asshole in the world. Yelling at kids and a woman who were just trying to help.

The front door shut and in the silence Casey's big five-year-old eyes damned him.

"Hey." Aaron came back in the room reeking of that deodorant all the preteen boys wear, convinced the smell made them irresistible to girls. "Where's Lucy?"

"Jeremiah scared her away," Casey said.

"Uncle J." Aaron sighed and then walked into the kitchen for something to eat.

"I was a jerk, wasn't I?" he asked Casey, who nodded.

"I should apologize, shouldn't I?" Casey nodded again.

Swearing under his breath, he grabbed Reese's keys from the coffee table and headed outside to apologize to Lucy.

MIA WASN'T PICKING UP her phone. Probably because she and Jack were having wild monkey sex while Lucy stood here getting barked at by a man she'd almost had sex with just a few short hours ago.

She snapped shut her cell phone and looked up at the sky wishing there was some kind of prayer for teleportation. Mom hadn't shared that one with her.

"Lucy?"

She spun at the sound of Jeremiah's voice. He stepped down the steps to the asphalt and she opened her phone and quickly pressed Redial.

"Look, Jeremiah, I get it, things are tough for you, but frankly, my life is no picnic right now. So, why don't you just go deal with your mess and I'll deal with mine?"

He ignored her, stopping a foot from her. "I'm sorry, Lucy."

Mia's voice mail came on and she snapped the phone shut.

"Your sister's not around?"

"No."

His smile was a variation on his million-dollar grin, more devastating because it was tarnished at the corners. "I can take you home."

Past caring about his feelings, she looked him right in the eye and didn't bother mincing words. "I think you have bigger problems to deal with."

She watched him bristle, his blue eyes dark.

"Where's Ben?" she asked.

"Probably in the barn."

"He do that a lot? Run away?"

"Enough that I know he's in the barn."

"Are you—?"

"I'm giving him and me a chance to cool down," he interrupted. "I appreciate your concern, but I've been doing this for a year, Lucy. You met these boys five minutes ago." He held up Reese's keys. "Take Reese's car. He'll come and get it when he gets off the couch."

There was more she wanted to say. Plenty more. But what was the point, really? She grabbed the keys. "Thanks."

"See you."

"Yeah," she snapped, remembering the way the touch of his hands turned her inside out, the way he kissed her like she was the best thing he'd tasted in years. She felt duped by that man in the moonlight last night. "See you."

She got back in Reese's car and peeled out of the driveway, leaving Jeremiah Stone in her dust.

Good riddance, she thought.

CHAPTER FOUR

JEREMIAH WAITED UNTIL he could no longer see the dust plume behind Lucy's car.

Not your finest showing, Stone. Not at all.

If his sister were alive she'd take him by his ear and give him a good shaking. But the truth was, he'd suffered through months of women with the best intentions coming through this house with their casseroles and sympathy and he'd watched the boys run roughshod all over them. Using that well-meaning sympathy to their advantage.

Eating pie for dinner, sleeping all together in Aaron's room, playing video games for hours at a time, not doing their homework. The last babysitter he'd hired had let Casey walk around with Annie's favorite green towel, like it was a baby blanket. And Ben... Christ, that kid's temper had grown out of control the past few months. He was like a lit bomb and Jeremiah never knew when he was going to go off.

It's not that he didn't think the boys needed sympathy, but they also needed rules. He needed rules. He needed some boundaries and Ben needed to know that he couldn't just run off to the barn every time he felt like Jeremiah was being unfair.

Jeremiah mentally braced himself and headed into the barn. Usually Ben sat in the empty stall at the back, burying himself in the clean hay. But he wasn't there.

"Ben?" he yelled, and then listened for a rustle or a creaking board. Nothing. He climbed up into the hay-loft and only found the cats snoozing in the sunlight.

The nine-year-old wasn't in the arena, or feeding any of the horses in the paddocks.

He tried; he really did, not to jump to the worst possible conclusion. But the worst possible conclusion was the kind of thing that happened to this family time and time again. And he couldn't stop himself from imagining him running off along the fence line toward the creek and the high pastures and all kinds of trouble. His heart, feeding on worry and anger, pounded in his neck as he stomped toward the house.

He threw open the front door and stepped into the living room where Reese was finally sitting up, his head in his hands. Aaron and Casey were eating peanut-butter-and-jelly sandwiches and watching ESPN.

"We got a problem," he said.

"Could you not yell?" Reese groaned.

"Ben's run off."

"What else is new?" Aaron asked, not taking his eyes off the TV and the baseball highlights.

"He's not in the barn."

Aaron glanced over. Annie's eyes were in Aaron's man-boy face, and it brought Jeremiah up short every damn time he looked at the kid. Aaron put down the sandwich and stood. "Casey and I will take the ATV," he said.

"I'll saddle Rider and check out the creek."

"What can I do?" Reese asked.

"Stay here in case he comes back."

"Oh, thank God," he muttered, and flopped backward on the couch.

"It will be okay, Uncle J.," Aaron said as he and Casey put on their boots. "He always comes back."

Grateful for the help and the optimism, Jeremiah clapped his hand on the eleven-year-old's shoulder, wishing things weren't they way they were. Wishing these boys could just be boys, and he could just be an uncle and that every situation didn't have the capacity for disaster.

LUCY DROVE UP to the small house she grew up in. She was happy to see the red climbing roses her mother had cultivated through the years still creating a green canopy over the south end of the house. It wasn't warm enough for blooms yet, but every summer the scent of those flowers filled the air that came in through the window of her old bedroom.

Rose was the scent of her childhood. Of a warm, safe home. It was the scent of her family all together. In Los Angeles Sandra grew roses in pots on the balcony of their condo. But they weren't the same. The scent had to combat exhaust and smog and Mr. Lezinsky's cabbage rolls. And they didn't bloom with the same wildness, the same gorgeous display of excess, as they did here.

Sort of like Mom, she thought.

Lucy stopped the car in front of the yellow house with white shutters and a bright red front door. For the hundredth time this morning, she called her sister.

"Jeez, Lucy," Mia finally answered, lewdly out of breath. "Take a hint, would you?"

"Oh, for crying out loud. I'm outside. Stop whatever it is you two are doing. We need to talk."

By the time she got out of the car and past the roses, Mia had the door open and was kissing Jack as he walked out the front.

"Your shirt is buttoned wrong," Lucy pointed out, and Jack's hands flew to fix the buttons on the black shirt he wore, in the process revealing pale skin and muscle.

"Stop staring at my husband," Mia said.

"I'm sorry, I can't stop. I didn't think hydro-engineers were supposed to have bodies like that."

"Mine does. Now git." Mia pushed Jack down the porch steps. "I'll meet you and the architect in an hour."

"Wait," Lucy said, stopping Jack from walking down the steps. "We have a situation up at the ranch house." She filled Jack and Mia in on Walter's sprained ankle.

"How long was he sitting there?" Jack asked.

"Doctors said according to the amount of fluid in his foot at least two hours."

"Stubborn son of a bitch," Jack muttered.

"Well, he's on an air cast and is supposed to stay off it for at least three weeks. And that's best-case scenario. And now Mom is talking about staying until Walter gets on his feet."

"Well, that's handy, isn't it?" Jack blinked at Mia and then Lucy, as if the problem were solved.

Men are so dense.

"I'm not going to let our mom care for your dad. Not after what he did," Lucy said.

"I agree with Lucy," Mia said when it looked like Jack was going to argue. "We should just move back to the house," Mia said. "I can—"

"No!" Jack said quickly. "I mean, I will move back if we have to, but…"

Mia ran a hand down his arm. That house didn't have a whole lot of happy memories for Jack.

God, what a mess. Lucy didn't want to go home and she didn't want to stay. She didn't want Mom taking care of Walter, but it was utterly unfair to ask these two to do it.

Mom wants to do it, she reminded herself.

"Mia," Lucy said. "You guys deserve a little time alone. You've been caring for that man for five years."

Jack and Mia shared a look and then Jack nodded. "We were just talking about this. Getting a 'housekeeper' who could act as a nurse."

Mia pushed away from the white door frame to cup her husband's cheek. It was too bad they were going to move out of this little house. It looked pretty on her sister. Sweet.

"It won't be easy to find someone to take Walter on, much less get Walter to agree to it," Mia pointed out.

"Well, Mom seems to think she knows how to get him to agree to a caregiver sooner rather than later."

"How?" Mia asked.

"I have no idea, but Mom wants to stay for three weeks. By then he's off the cast and the worst of it should be over. If I can't get Mom to leave after three weeks, then I'm never going to get her leave."

And three weeks should be enough time for me to figure out a plan for the rest of my life.

"You know," Mia said, "if you need to get back to Los Angeles, you can. It's not like Mom needs a babysitter."

"You've done your time, Mia." She smiled over at Jack, hoping she sounded convincing. "The two of you are building a house, starting a life. You don't need to play referee between Mom and Walter."

Mia sighed and put her hand on Lucy's shoulder as if she could discern what was wrong just by touch. And she probably could. Lucy felt uncomfortable being so naked to anyone—even her sister. She fought the urge to shake off Mia's fingers.

"Hey, Lucy?" Jack asked, his eyes focused on something past her head. "Who's the kid in your car?"

She whirled in time to see Ben climbing out of the backseat of Reese's car into the driver's seat. The boy barely saw over the steering wheel, not that he was looking at them. Nope, the kid was focused on the steering wheel. The ignition key.

"Oh, Jesus," she muttered, running down the steps of the porch just as Ben started the car.

The engine roared to life and she heard Jack and Mia charge down the steps after her.

"Stop!" she screamed, her heartbeat deafening in her ears. "Ben!"

The boy looked up, his dark eyes barely clearing the steering wheel. And then the car rocketed into Reverse and spun out, kicking up clouds of dust that choked and blinded her.

Frantic, she waved the dust away but it didn't do any good, so she simply ran after the sound of the engine.

Oh, God, please don't let him hit anything big.

Just as she sent the prayer skyward there was a sickening crunch and the terrifying sound of breaking glass. The dust cleared and she stopped at the sight of the back end of the car buried in the green roses on the side of the house.

She skid to a halt just as Jack ran past her and threw open the driver's side door. She was a coward but she knew her heart couldn't take seeing that boy hurt in the driver's seat of that car. The blood and broken little bones.

Please, please let him be okay. Please.

"He's fine," Jack said, glancing at her over the roof of the car. "A little banged up, but fine."

"I'm going to go see if the inside of the house is okay," Mia said, and she ran back inside.

Ben, looking so small, so fragile, walked around the car and stopped in front of her.

"I'm sorry," he whispered.

She laughed, a wild gust of breath. It was impossible to process what had just happened in…had it even been ten seconds? Ten seconds of terror and relief. She was light-headed. "I think maybe you need to save that apology for Reese. Look at what you did to his car."

He glanced over his shoulder and hung his head, the black curls along his thin neck damp with sweat.

So small, so terrifyingly small.

"He scraped through a big patch of paint, but the structure of the house is fine," Jack said as he came up. "The roses, however, are toast. You dodged a bullet, son." Jack propped his hands on his hips and managed to look so disappointed even Lucy felt like apologizing.

"Does your uncle know where you are?" Lucy asked. She reached out to put a hand on Ben's shoulder but he jerked away before she made contact.

"No."

"Well, we're going to have to call him. He's probably freaking out."

"He's always freaking out."

"Doesn't make what you did okay," Lucy said.

"Not by a long shot," Jack said. "You could have been hurt. Or you could have hurt someone else. Badly. You should know better, Ben."

Ben's jaw, remarkably similar to his uncle's, set like concrete.

"I'll go call Jeremiah," Jack said, and stepped back toward the house.

"Do you have to tell my uncle?" Ben asked when

Jack was gone. For the first time in the few hours she'd known him, the little boy looked his age.

"Uh, yeah."

Ben stared down at his boots, which were beat up and dusty.

"What were you thinking, Ben?" she whispered.

He jerked a shoulder, trying so hard to be cool. An instinct she understood all too well, and she applauded his effort. Hard to act cool when you've just plowed a hundred-thousand-dollar sports car into someone's house, but he was giving it his best shot.

Things were bad at Stone Hollow, she thought, if a nine-year-old boy had to pretend to be so hard. Worse than she'd thought and she wondered if anyone knew it.

"He hates me," Ben whispered.

"Who?"

"Uncle J."

Lucy gaped at the boy, at the heartbreak and anger. This was bad, really bad. And she had no idea what the boundaries were. Or the rules. Jeremiah wouldn't like her interfering but Ben was a nine-year-old boy in a lot of pain who needed all the help he could get. "Oh, honey, no, he doesn't—"

"Yes, he does," Ben spat. "And I hate him, too. I do. I hate him. He's not my dad."

"Jeremiah's on his way," Mia said, coming around the side of the house. She glanced over at the car and winced. "So much for Mom's roses."

"I'm sorry," Ben whispered.

Mia laughed and handed Ben a glass of water. "Not as sorry as you're gonna be when your uncle gets here."

JEREMIAH STARED AT REESE'S sports car covered in slaughtered rosebushes and wished he had one clue about how to handle this. One single clue. A hint. He wished he could have a five-minute conversation with his sister for some guidance, because he was totally in the dark. He tried to think of what his own father would have done in this situation, a tactic that usually helped him in whatever parenting dilemma he was facing. But Jeremiah had never caused the kind of trouble Ben seemed drawn to.

So he stared at those rosebushes, the yellow clapboard house with the—*thank God*—cement foundation, and waited for the answers to come to him.

"The house is fine," Jack said, and Jeremiah nodded as if that was the much-needed answer to a question. But the truth was he didn't care about the house right now. He cared about the sullen, wild-eyed nine-year-old ball of anger to his left.

What about Ben? he wanted to ask. *Is he fine? Will he ever be fine again? Will any of us?*

Reese started up his car and slowly pulled it away from the house. Everyone breathed a sigh of relief as if they'd all been expecting the house to fall apart. The back of the car looked like an accordion. A broken and very, very expensive accordion.

"You," Jeremiah said through his teeth, unable to even look at his nephew, "will be working at the ranch until you've paid off repairs to that car. In fact, I think you're grounded until you're about thirty and if you even—"

Lucy cleared her throat and he glanced sideways at her, infuriated at her interruption.

"About that," she said. "What if he works off the repairs here?"

Ben looked up at that and his hope was palpable.

"Don't get excited, buddy," he muttered. "There's no way you're working here."

"Wait, Jeremiah, hear me out." She stepped toward him, the long dark locks of hair that had fallen from the messy knot on top of her head reaching out toward him on the breeze. The lines of weariness around her eyes didn't make her any less pretty and he felt like a jackass even noticing that.

"Ben, go wait for me in the truck." Like a criminal out on parole, the boy took off for the truck and Jeremiah watched him go, gathering up what was left of his composure. When he felt as if he could speak like an adult he turned back to Lucy and held up his hand. "The kid is in some kind of crisis," he said. "And he doesn't need to be coddled. He needs to understand he's done something wrong—"

"I'm not arguing with you, Jeremiah," she said. "But…look, something isn't working between you and Ben. It's obvious."

Jeremiah felt his ears get hot. She was right. So painfully right.

"You're not sticking around, why would you want to have Ben here?"

"Mom and I are staying at least three more weeks. And I'm just…I'm just offering you a chance to try something new with him. Something different. So, you know, you don't have to always be the bad guy."

"And you're going to be the bad guy?"

Lucy bristled at his sarcasm and took a step back.

"I'm just trying to help."

"Yeah, and I appreciate it, but this is family stuff. And we'll handle it."

Reese approached, looking like death warmed over in last night's clothes. "I think I'm going to have to get the car fixed here. There's no way I can drive it back to Fort Worth."

Jeremiah swore and kept on swearing.

"Come on, man," Reese said, his smile bright despite the black circles under his eyes. "It's not that bad."

"It is," he said, honest because he couldn't pretend anymore. "Because it takes time to fix this." Just saying that made him feel better, made him feel like he was pulling this family away from rock bottom. First, he had to get Reese off his damn couch. Life would be easier without this living reminder of the old days drinking beer and snoring in his living room.

And then, maybe, it would be time to break the family code of silence. Get Ben some help.

WALTER STARED AT the bright noon sky out the window of his bedroom and contemplated the long walk to the bathroom. Hard on a good day, impossible with the cast on his foot.

He rolled as best he could to the side of his bed looking for an empty bottle. Or a coffee cup. Anything. But Sandra's presence in this house was all too obvious these days.

Clutter didn't stand a chance against Sandra.

He pressed fists to his eyes. *And neither do I.*

A month ago he'd been so excited to have Sandra back in his house. Like righting a terrible wrong in the world, bringing Sandra back to the Rocky M was his best effort at repairing the mess he'd made years ago when A.J. died, his best friend, foreman and Sandra's husband.

All with the benefit of being able to see her every day. Being near her again—Sandra of the warm heart and the joyful laugh. Sandra, whom he'd always loved. Deeply. Secretly.

Yeah, and how did that work out for you?

"You are a sorry man, Walter. I thought I could come back here and feel nothing, but I have twenty-five years of living in these walls and if I'd had my way I would have died here and been buried right beside my husband, and you robbed me of that."

That's what she'd said two weeks ago, shattering all those delusions that he was doing Sandra a favor bringing her back here.

Her fury with him, rooted in disappointment, went deep. And he had no idea what it would take to change it. If he even could.

Damn, where was a bottle when he needed one? For being the room of a degenerate alcoholic, his room sure was devoid of the evidence.

No choice but to do this on his own.

Taking a deep breath, he swung his body up over the side of the bed and reached out to grab the crutch beside the bedside table. Carefully, holding his breath against the pain, he pushed himself up on his good leg and hopped slightly to get his balance.

Moving slowly, he made his way to the bathroom and—feeling pretty damn good—kicked the door shut behind him.

Once done, he washed his hands and hobbled back to the bedroom. Only to stumble at the sight of Sandra standing at the foot of his bed.

She wore black slacks and a bright red shirt, her long dark hair back in a ponytail that made her look like a girl. So bright, so lovely, he couldn't look directly at her.

He fell against the doorjamb, banging his knee, and then winced when his hurt foot hit the door. Sandra started toward him as if to help, as if to touch him, and he waved her off. Breathing through the pain, he made his way past her to the chair in the small window alcove. A chair he'd never in his life sat in. Why in the world, he often wondered, did you need a chair in a bedroom? But now he was grateful for it.

Sitting on his bed—the bed he'd shared with his wife—seemed an utterly wrong thing to do in front of Sandra.

"You haven't touched your eggs." She pointed to the plate of eggs long gone cold, sitting on the bedside table.

"I'm not hungry," he panted, rubbing his knee, wishing he could reach his ankle.

"You want some painkillers?"

He looked at her for a long time and realized he was at a crossroads of his own making. He'd been responsible for planting the idea in his son's mind. But now it was time for her to leave. And Lucy had been right last night—Sandra wasn't going to leave him when he was in need like this. Not unless he forced the issue.

"I want some whiskey."

"It's noon."

"I'm an alcoholic, Sandra. It doesn't much matter to me."

"I won't bring you booze."

"Well, then stop bringing me eggs."

She narrowed her eyes, an expression he'd seen on her stubborn, beautiful face more times than he could count.

"You should just leave, Sandra. There's nothing here for you anymore. Your husband is dead. Your girls are grown—"

"I'm not leaving you when you need so much help."

"I don't want your help."

"That doesn't much matter to me."

"A.J.—"

"Do not bring my husband into this," she said, bristling.

"He wouldn't like you being my nursemaid."

"He was your best friend, Walter." It was an accusation, a plea. The reason behind so much of their heartache. Walter had cared too much for his best friend's wife and his own wife had seen his secret shame. His favorite torture these days was wondering if Sandra knew. He would—without a shred of exaggeration—rather die than have Sandra know how he felt about her.

"Please," he whispered. "Just leave."

"If you want me to go, then get better. Stop drinking."

"Fine." He laughed, shaky and sick because he hadn't had a drink in fourteen hours. "I've stopped."

"Until the cast comes off. You stop drinking that long, I'll leave."

He laughed before he thought better of it. "Three weeks without a drink?" There was no way. No point.

She lifted her chin, her eyes sparkling with a challenge. "There's an AA meeting at the church on Sunday nights." She slipped a piece of paper onto his dresser. "I've written down the information."

"You're wasting your time, Sandra."

"If you love me like you think you do, stop drinking."

His heart stopped, blood pooled in his brain.

She knew. Oh, God. She knew.

CHAPTER FIVE

IF THERE WAS ANY EASE in Jeremiah's life, it arrived every Saturday afternoon with his dead brother-in-law's parents. Cynthia and Larry Bilkhead were going to be seventy this year, too old to care for the boys full-time. They never contested Annie and Connor's will, even when it was obvious that Jeremiah had no freaking clue what he was doing when it came to parenting.

But they came when he needed them as well as every Saturday afternoon, like clockwork. Like angels.

"Hi, Jeremiah, how are you doing?" Cynthia asked, stepping into the foyer to wrap him in her arms. She was small and round and smelled like cookies and pie. And there were times when he could have stood in her hug for a day.

"We're good." He lied, because really, what could they do with the truth? He kissed her papery, powdery cheek. "Some trouble with Ben—"

"What did that boy do now?" Larry Bilkhead stepped inside behind his wife. He was a six-foot-four-inch cowboy, who still carried himself like a man who'd won some rodeo in his day. His words might sound stern but Larry could not keep the love he had for his grandsons out of his eyes.

"I'll let him tell you," Jeremiah said, shaking Larry's hand. Jeremiah had always liked the rawboned man, who wore his age and his time in a saddle with pride. Now, Jeremiah loved him like family.

"The cooler is in the van." Cynthia put down her purse and kicked off her shoes to step into the family room. "Where are my boys?"

Upstairs there was a wild scream of "Grandma!" and the thundering of a herd of elephants running for the stairs. Casey was the first one down, followed by Aaron, who at eleven was too cool for a lot of things, but not too cool for Cynthia and Larry. Probably because Larry wasn't like other grandpas. And Cynthia was exactly what a grandmother should be.

Jeremiah eased out the front door to grab the cooler from the back of their minivan. Every week she showed up with some casseroles for the freezer and enough cookies and cakes and brownies for a hockey team. And bags of fresh fruit and vegetables from their greenhouse.

"Ben," he said, once he was back inside with the cooler. "You can unpack this."

The nine-year-old had the good grace not to argue, and followed him into the kitchen meekly. Jeremiah cleaned off the kitchen table while the boy put things away and then Ben took the cooler back out to the minivan.

"He smashed up a car?" Larry asked, filling the door frame between the kitchen and the living room.

Jeremiah nodded, carefully stacking some clean glasses in the cupboard.

"What's his punishment going to be?" Larry asked, and Jeremiah shook his head.

"I'm not sure."

"In my day—"

"I'm not going to spank him." Jeremiah turned to

face the older man. "I know how you feel about this, but I can't hurt that kid any more than he's been hurt."

Larry nodded, his cheeks red under the edge of his glasses. It was grief, not anger. Jeremiah knew Larry was just as at a loss for what to do when it came to Ben.

"I know," he murmured. "But what are you going to do?"

"I can make him muck stalls until he's eighty—but what good is that going to do? He's already working hard around here. Hell, I have the five-year-old doing fence work."

Larry just stared at him, his white hair lying smooth against his head. His blue eyes runny beneath his glasses. Larry was an old-world kind of guy. If Ben was his child, Jeremiah knew that Ben would have gotten the belt after this last stunt. Hell, maybe before then. But Jeremiah just couldn't.

As it was, Jeremiah made Casey swear not to tell Grandpa Larry that he allowed Casey to spend half the night sleeping in his bed. The poor kid was plagued by nightmares. Jeremiah let Aaron sleep with his parents' wedding picture under his pillow. Despite his tough words, Jeremiah was a total softy.

What these boys had been through couldn't be fixed by work. Or more violence.

They needed help—they all needed help. He ran a thumb over the chip in the counter. He'd put that chip there himself, when as a kid he tried to get the Pop-Tarts from the top shelf.

This isn't going to go well, he thought.

"I think Ben needs someone to talk to," Jeremiah said, anyway.

"What do you mean, 'talk to'?" Larry pushed off the door frame, his shoulders already tense because he knew where Jeremiah was headed. They'd been down this road before, when Ben first started acting out.

"A counsellor."

"He already has people to talk to. Us."

Jeremiah's laughter was bitter in the back of his throat. "He's not talking to me, Larry. He's never talked to me."

"I know, son, but Connor and Annie, they wouldn't like this going outside of the family. They were circle-the-wagons kind of people."

"I know." *But they're not here, are they? It's just me and I'm out of ideas!*

He didn't say it because it would only hurt Larry. It would only make them try harder to help and they were seventy years old. They did enough.

"Besides, he talks to Cynthia."

Jeremiah knew Ben talked to his grandmother. After these Saturday visits Ben always seemed better. Like the kid he used to be.

"Well, try to get them to talk tonight, would you?"

"Sure thing, son. I'll send them out for a yarrow walk."

Jeremiah smiled. Months ago, Larry had realized that Ben and Cynthia had a special bond so he made up this sudden need for the yarrow that grew wild along the driveway. He frequently sent his wife and troubled grandson out to pick armfuls of the stuff even though he burned all of it once back at his place. But the walks did Ben some good.

"Now." Larry's hand landed on Jeremiah's shoulder, heavy and warm. "You go have some fun. Don't try to take everyone's money."

"Isn't that the point of poker?"

"Well, no one likes a bad winner."

"You forget, Larry," he said with a smile, dropping out of reach only to pretend to land a punch to Larry's midsection, "I'm a great winner."

Larry laughed and put his arm over Jeremiah's shoulders, walking him to the door, past Cynthia on the couch with all three boys piled up around her. Aaron was telling her about his goal in practice this morning. Cynthia winked as he walked by.

"We'll be fine. Have fun," Larry said, and then, with one last step, Jeremiah was out of the house, the door closed behind him.

On his own. For a wild second every possibility open to him flooded his brain. He could be in Las Vegas in seven hours. Fort Worth in ten. Mexico in twelve. Women and drinks and sleeping in and no kids to worry about. No ranch. No house. Just him, the truck, the road and no worries.

When the second was over, he folded up those thoughts and put them away before checking his watch. Crap. If he didn't speed like crazy he was going to be late.

Speed like crazy, it was.

Forty minutes later he parked the truck in front of a small house in Redmen. To those who didn't know, it just looked like every other house on the street. Pretty redbrick with flowers along the porch. There was no sign, no indication, that it was more than a house.

When he stepped inside a bell rang out over the door and Jennifer, the receptionist, looked up.

"She's waiting for you," Jennifer said.

"Sorry I'm late." He took off his hat, patting down the more wild of his overlong curls. A haircut was one more thing to put on his list of things to do.

"We understand, Jeremiah." Her pretty smile held

no pity. Just the kind of firm understanding that he had come to expect from the women in this house.

He nodded in gratitude. Anxious because despite knowing how important these weekly meetings were, he still didn't like needing them. He didn't want to be here, but he was glad he was—a conflict that just didn't sit well.

Jennifer led him down the hallway to the back room.

"Dr. Gilman?" she said at the closed door.

"Come in," a voice answered, and Jennifer pushed open the door. The room was awash with end-of-day sunlight and Dr. Gilman, a sturdy woman in a denim skirt and long silver earrings, stepped out from behind a big oak desk to shake his hand.

Dr. Gilman had the firmest handshake of any woman he'd ever known. It was the handshake that convinced him to trust her six months ago when he came here desperate and worried for himself and the boys. Though at that point he would have trusted a paper bag if it promised to help him.

"Hi, Jeremiah," she said, her smile all earth-motherly and welcoming. Honestly, he loved this woman.

"Sorry I'm late," he said again, because he didn't know what else to say. All his charm and small talk were left in the truck; they seemed silly here. He hung his hat up on the rack beside the door. Briefly he wondered how many cowboys Dr. Gilman saw, if any. Getting psychological help was sort of against the whole code. Just ask Larry.

"It's all right." She held her hand out to the deep leather chair in front of the windows and across from a smaller chair where she usually sat. "Why don't you have a seat and tell me what's happened since last week."

Grateful, Jeremiah needed no urging. He sank into that chair and opened up like q box.

AFTER DINNER ON SATURDAY night Lucy slipped out onto the back deck with her cell phone. She'd been dodging her accountant Meisha's phone calls for two days—but it was time for her come-to-Jesus moment. She just hoped her come-to-Jesus moment wasn't going to cost her everything.

Taking a big breath for courage she turned and looked out over the decimated gardens that were overgrowing the backyard. It was surprising Sandra hadn't made her way out there yet to set things right. It was probably next on her list:

Save Walter

Do a little gardening

She was well aware her sarcasm was ugly. But at the moment it was all she had. A thin armor to keep out the cold.

Without allowing a chance to talk herself out of it, she hit Meisha's number on her speed dial and prepared herself for the worst.

"This is Meisha, sorry I missed you, leave a message."

"Oh, thank God," she breathed, collapsing with relief against the porch railing.

"Hey, Meisha," she said after the beep came and went. "I'm returning your calls. Sorry to be MIA, but I'm ready for the bad news. Call me when you get a chance."

She closed her phone and watched a bird—maybe a hawk, she wasn't sure—swoop along the ridgeline and ride the wind currents off the Sierras. Not a care in the world, that bird. Must be nice, she thought, totally aware that she was jealous of a creature with a pea-size brain.

Turning away, she walked down the rickety steps to the garden of ruin. Up close it wasn't nearly as bad as it seemed. At least not to her nongardener eyes. The strawberries were a lost cause, but the tomatoes just needed to be staked. Same for the peas. The lettuces were coming in and the feathery carrot tops were pushing their way up out of the dark soil. She had no idea if the other plants were weeds or vegetables.

But there was possibility here. A shot at redemption. These vegetables could be returned to glory, they just needed someone to care.

I could do it, she thought, though she had no idea how. No experience with…well, with anything but jewelry. *How sad is that?*

Since nearly the moment she could hold a pencil Lucy had been drawing. It had been her only hobby, besides boys. But even boys couldn't hold a candle to her love… her passion for art.

Her mother gave her a beading kit when she was eight and it was like the heavens opened. When she was thirteen she saved all her babysitting money for a soldering gun and some real turquoise stones. While other girls were trying out for sports and cheerleading she was buying silver wholesale and selling the cheerleaders her jewelry.

She took all her high school graduation money and went to South America to study tribal jewelry design and then to San Francisco to sell the pieces she made. From there it seemed like it was all meant to be. Every piece fell into place: the website, the orders from the boutiques in Los Angeles, finding the semiprecious stone importer. She earned enough money that she got comfortable.

Oh, come on, she thought, laughing at herself. *Comfortable? Hell, I got cocky.*

It all just seemed…fated.

But never in that dreamy beginning did she take an accounting class. Or a business class. And in the end that was what ruined her. Ruined everything.

Well aware that she wasn't the ideal candidate, but tired of feeling like a failure on all fronts, she looked at the garden of ruin and said, "It's not like I have anything else to do."

A hobby wasn't a bad idea. Perhaps it was time to see if she could do anything in this life other than making jewelry. Gardening might not be her first choice but it was the best option present.

She crouched to pull a weed.

And then another, but it was a parsnip, thin and ghostly. Far from ready for the light of day.

"Whoops." She tucked it back in its home and tried again until she got it right.

HOURS LATER THE RING TONE of her cell phone dragged Lucy out of a fitful sleep on the couch where she'd fallen asleep with a heating pad against her lower back.

Who knew gardening was so damn hard?

The living room was in shadows, and she reached for her cell phone where it rested on the end table by her head, but the cell phone's face was dark.

Which meant it wasn't Meisha.

The home phone rang again and she lurched off the couch, groaning when her back protested the sudden movement. Holding her back, she walked into the dining area and to the phone on the wall in the kitchen.

"Hello?"

The sound of a crowd and blaring music was the only answer. "Hello!" she cried.

"Hey, Lucy?"

"Yeah. Who is this?"

"Joey down at Sunset."

The bartender? Strange. "What's up?"

"I got a guy here says he needs a ride."

"A ride!" She laughed. "Who the hell is he?"

"Hold on a second… Buddy? What's your name?" There was a thump and a rustle. "Good Lord, he's real drunk, Lucy. Says his name is Reese and he knows your, ah…" Billy cleared his throat.

Lucy rested her head against the wall. "My boobs?"

"Something like that."

"Did he drive there?" Lucy asked, leaning back slightly to see the digital clock on the microwave. Midnight.

"Nope. Chris down at the garage dropped him off. Wait…he, uh, he says he'll pay you. Fifty bucks."

She laughed. Well, if Reese was that kind of fool she could chauffeur his drunk butt back up to Jeremiah's.

"Tell him a hundred and I'll be there in twenty minutes."

She hung up and stared at her chipped nails against the black of the phone. A year ago she'd been invited to the Academy Awards because her necklaces were being included in presenters' gift baskets.

Now she was a gardener and a chauffeur.

Life sure is funny.

TWENTY MINUTES LATER, she parked in front of the Sunset and went inside to pick up her passenger.

"Hey, Joey," she said, walking in.

Joey looked up from the pint of beer he was pouring and jerked his head toward the dark corner where the bar met the wall. There, his face resting peacefully on his hands, slept Reese.

"This something new you're doing?" Joey slid the beer over toward a man at the other end of the bar and walked toward Reese. "A taxi service?"

"I guess so." She sighed, thinking it was a joke.

"Well, it's about time someone did. You could make a fortune."

Lucy blinked up at Joey. "I thought you were kidding."

"Hell, no. We got a problem with drunk drivers around here. If there was someone I could call to take folks home I'd be doing it five times a night."

She put up her hands. "I am not in the taxi business," she said.

"Hey." Reese grinned up at her. "My carriage has arrived."

Joey turned his attention from Reese back to Lucy. "Sure as hell looks like you're in business to me," Joey said, arching his eyebrow at her as he walked to the other end of the bar.

"Come on, Reese, let's get you back to Jeremiah's."

She arranged him in the passenger seat of the car, putting his hat in his lap so it didn't get crushed against the roof. For good measure she rolled down her window.

"If you're going to puke, you do it out the window."

His salute was messy. Everything about Reese was messy.

"This is a shitty car," he said as if just realizing where he was.

"Well, it's the one taking you home, so keep your opinions to yourself."

"You always were tough, Lucy Alatore."

"And you always were trouble, Reese. But I hear you won yourself a big purse in Fort Worth."

"Yep." He burped. "Lots of money. Thought Jeremiah could help me spend it."

"Not quite what you expected, huh?"

"He used to be so much fun. So…wild. A night out with Stone and you had no idea what was going to happen. One time after he won we woke up in a fishing boat off the coast of Mexico. I'd gotten this." He yanked his shirt up to reveal the legs of a woman tattooed on his stomach.

"She's a beaut." Luckily, Reese was too drunk to pick up the sarcasm.

"I thought he'd dropped out of contact because of the injury. I didn't know he was taking care of his sister's kids. Christ…what a nightmare for him."

Her head jerked sideways at Reese's words. Did Ben think that Jeremiah hated him because he'd said that? "Did he say that?"

"What?"

"That his life was a nightmare?"

"No, but God…look at it. Three kids? And that Ben… wow."

Wow kind of summed it up. But Reese's attitude made her angry, like he was ready to walk away, writing off the whole situation. But to a guy like Reese, with his life, it probably was a nightmare.

"And stuck *here?*" Reese shuddered.

"It's not so bad." Lucy's words were as much of a surprise to her as they were to him. "It's quiet. Pretty." That much was true. These were aspects of this town she'd never appreciated growing up, with her eye always on the big city.

But the big city had been one big disappointment.

"I suppose that's true. But God…there's nothing to do here."

Nothing except work. If she had any creative spark left at all, she'd be getting so much work done right now. But that was a moot point.

"Are you angry about your car?" she asked.

"No. I mean, a little. But it's just a car. It'll get fixed." Reese shook his head, the sadness wafting off him smelled like smoke from a damp fire. "I wish I knew what to say to Jeremiah, but I came up here, took one look at what he was up against and started drinking. I don't know how he does it."

She took the pass up over the mountains. Out the passenger window Stone Hollow glowed in the darkness, the lights in the kitchen casting a golden glow. "Me, neither," she whispered.

Whatever help Jeremiah needed he'd made it obvious he wasn't going to take it from her.

"I'm leaving," Reese said. "My car's fixed on Monday, and I'm gone. I never should have come."

"You're a friend, Reese. I imagine Jeremiah needs friends."

"I don't know how to help, Lucy. I don't know how to be his friend like this. I'm for good times and drinking and picking up women. It sucks to feel like this."

She pulled to a stop at the front door, hoping that Jeremiah wouldn't come out. Reese dug his wallet out of his back pocket. "A hundred bucks?"

Gouging the cowboy didn't seem quite so enticing after talking to him so she shook her head. "Don't worry—"

"Here." He handed her a fresh hundred-dollar bill. Benjamin Franklin stared up at her as if he didn't recognize her, which seemed about right. It had been a while since they'd seen each other. "I have to go pick up my car on Monday morning. Can I hire you to drive me? Jeremiah would do it, but he's so damn busy."

"Ah, sure."

"Great. Thanks."

Then he was gone, and she was a hundred dollars richer.

This was ridiculous, she thought. *A taxi? What nonsense.*

But that was a hundred dollars in her pocket. Honest to God, the only money she had right now. And not every ride would be a hundred bucks. But let's say she charged twenty bucks.

How much would she make in a Friday night?

In a weekend?

She couldn't afford to be a snob about this. Couldn't afford to put her nose in the air over the chance to actually earn money, to create a cushion for her next move. It would be irresponsible to reject this opportunity. On her cell phone she hit the most recent number that called her.

"I'm in business," she told Joey when he answered. "Twenty bucks flat fee."

"That's steep for around here."

"Yeah, well." She pinched her nose. "A girl's got to make a living."

He said he'd be in touch and she hung up, tossing her cell phone onto the passenger seat.

She unrolled her window, laughing, letting the breeze dry the tears she didn't want to cry.

CHAPTER SIX

JEREMIAH HAD DEVELOPED a world-class sixth sense while sitting on top of hundreds of bulls determined to break his bones. In the circuit he'd been known not only for his courage, but also for his instinct. One rodeo writer said it was as if Jeremiah could read each bull's mind. In more than a thousand interviews over the years, when asked what his secret was, he'd almost always given the same answer—"I go with what my gut tells me. And my gut is rarely wrong."

But his gut, faced with the closed front door of the Rocky M home, was silent. Totally silent.

"Uncle J.?" Casey whispered up at him. "What are we doing here?"

"I'm not sure yet," he said truthfully. And Casey nodded as if he understood the implications of knocking on the Rocky M front door. Jeremiah could be making the biggest mistake in the world right now, all because his gut wouldn't tell him what to do.

"I'm hungry."

He stared down at Casey, who'd woken up this morning in bottomless-pit mode.

"You just ate breakfast." Sunday morning breakfast, too, with pancakes and eggs.

Casey shrugged. "My stomach is still hungry."

The kid was probably about to grow another foot or something by tomorrow night. Growth spurts with three boys in the house were dangerous. Especially if you were a peanut-butter-and-jelly sandwich.

Jeremiah scratched his head, just under the edge of his hat where the sweat collected and made him crazy. Maybe he should just bury this stupid idea. It would be easier to simply take Casey back home, make sure Ben and Aaron were cleaning up like they were supposed to, make sure Reese was packing and not drinking before his drive home tomorrow.

But if he left now he'd be heading home for more of the same and the same just wasn't working anymore.

"You don't have to do this alone," Dr. Gilman had said. "It's not a failure or betrayal to take help when it's offered. Not always being the bad guy with Ben might give both of you a break."

Fine, he thought, and pounded on the door. If his gut was silent he'd go with Dr. Gilman's.

Sandra Alatore opened the door, wiping her hands on a cloth thrown over her shoulder.

"Well, hello, Jeremiah," she said, with her sweet accented voice. It could have been twenty years ago for all she'd changed.

"Hi, Sandra, it's good to see you again. This old ranch looks much better with you in it."

"Listen to you." She laughed. "Still too charming for your own good. And who is this?"

Casey leaned back against Jeremiah's leg, suddenly shy. Jeremiah reached down to try and extract the kung fu grip the boy had on his jeans but Sandra leaned down and spoke right to him.

"My name is Sandra," she said.

When was the last time I did that? he wondered. All he did was bark orders at the top of the boys' heads.

"I'm Casey. I'm five."

"Five years old?" Sandra shook her head. "That's hard work, being five."

Casey nodded. "Especially at our house."

Sandra smiled, her black eyes twinkling up at Jeremiah.

"Is Lucy here?" Jeremiah asked. "I need to talk to her."

"She's in the backyard working on the garden. Come on in."

She stepped back and Jeremiah, with the Casey-size leg growth, followed her into the cool, dark house.

"I've got some banana bread I just made," she said, looking down at Casey. "I need someone to try it and make sure it's all right. Think you could do that for me?"

Casey glanced up at him, so hopeful that Jeremiah smiled, running his hand through the boy's curls. "Go on, buddy, but mind your manners."

Sandra led him off with a wink and Jeremiah walked through the living room to the back patio. Looking out, he supposed the mess of weeds was the garden but he didn't see any sign of Lucy.

From the knot of vines in the corner of the plot, there was some movement and a flash of red. It took him a second to realize it was Lucy, on her hands and knees wearing camouflage pants, Doc Marten boots and a brown tank top. The flash of red was the edge of her underwear, revealed by the slipping waist of her pants.

Lucy was gardening in a red thong.

Immediately it was about thirty degrees hotter on the back deck. And it felt dirty and illicit to be staring at her underwear, especially when she didn't know it, but he couldn't look away. Just a few nights ago he'd touched her skin and it had been soft and warm, alluring. What an idiot he'd been to turn her away that night. A woman like Lucy Alatore didn't give out second chances, she didn't need to. And he'd blown it.

Lucy was the hottest thing he'd seen in...hell, he didn't know how long. Maybe forever. And he could have stood on that porch watching her, thinking dirty teenage thoughts, for days.

"What are you looking at, son?"

Jeremiah jumped and spun at the sound of the old man's voice. Walter, propped up on a crutch, his foot in a cast, stood behind him. His face very knowing, and very disapproving.

"I'm, uh, just looking for Lucy."

Walter didn't say anything but he threw out a father vibe like Jeremiah hadn't experienced in twenty-plus years.

"It's good to see you, Walter. Sorry about your foot."

Walter didn't dignify his deflection with a response. He hopped slightly sideways to fall into a cushioned deck chair.

"That your boy in the kitchen?"

"Not mine. My sister's. Her youngest."

Walter, grizzened and craggy, just grunted. He lifted a shaking hand to wipe the sweat off his top lip, his forehead. The guy was always stoic—in every memory Jeremiah had of Walter, the man was expressionless. Not so now. Walter was clearly in pain.

"Do you need some help?" Jeremiah asked, stepping toward Walter only to stop when the old man started to laugh, wheezy and pained.

"I need a goddamned drink," Walter said, and then shook his head. "Go talk to Lucy or leave. But quit staring at her like she's cheap."

Heat crawled over Jeremiah's chest. It had been a long time since someone had talked to him that way and it didn't sit well; of course, it had also been a long time since he deserved to be talked to that way.

He tugged his hat down over his eyes and walked down the back steps to the garden. The steps squeaked and by the time he got to the bottom she was standing, that red thong hidden.

"Jeremiah," she said, her voice covered in ice. He wanted to tell her she had about a thousand smudges of dirt on her face and something green sticking out of her ponytail, all of which really ruined the imperial princess act. But since he was here to grovel, he figured that might not be the best way to start things. She tossed a handful of weeds toward the piles she had formed at the edges of the garden. He saw a lot of young vegetables in those piles and wondered if she just wasn't sure what a weed was or if she had an issue with carrots.

"What are you doing here?"

"I..." He rubbed his hand over his mouth and down his neck, wishing this wasn't so hard. Wishing it didn't feel like he was betraying his sister and Larry by bringing in outsiders to help. He wished it didn't feel like admitting to failure by...well, admitting to failure. "I'd like to take you up on your offer. If it still stands."

She hitched her loose pants up higher on her hips. "Which offer?"

That kiss was suddenly between them, as vivid as the dirt on her face, and he wondered if maybe that wasn't another complication. It was one thing trying to get help for Ben but he wanted to sleep with that help. And maybe that was too many blurred lines.

"The Ben offer?" she asked, using her wrist to push some hair off her face.

He nodded and forced himself to say the words he

came here to say. "I need help. And if you are still offering, I...I would appreciate it."

"I don't know, Jeremiah. You were an ass to me."

Leave it to Lucy to be so blunt. For a moment he was floored by it. But he decided to meet her bluntness with his own. Honesty, Dr. Gilman had said, was always the right decision. "I know, and I'm sorry. I truly am. I've just been doing this by myself for so long.... I'm no good at admitting I'm wrong and I just took it out on you. I am sorry. My mom raised me better than that."

She cocked her head at him as if he were something in the distance she couldn't quite see, or make sense of. And then, suddenly, she smiled. "That was hard for you, wasn't it?"

He blew out a breath, laughing slightly. "You have no idea."

"Why'd you change your mind?"

He stared off at the blue horizon. If he couldn't get Ben in to see Dr. Gilman, he needed to find another way to get some help and here she was.

"When Annie first died, people always asked me what they could do to help. And I had no idea how to answer. No idea. Either I didn't believe they were sincere, or I saw strings attached to every casserole women brought over, or I didn't...want anyone to see what a mess I was making of everything. I just told everyone I could handle it. I...pushed a lot of good people away. And then people stopped asking. Now, it has come to my attention that if someone offers to help, I should take it. And you're the only one who has offered to help in a long time. Apparently," he said, trying to make a joke, but it was so damn sad it came out like a lame calf, "I need a few more friends in my life."

He was utterly vulnerable. Utterly naked.

Help me, he thought. *I don't know what else to do.*

For a moment it seemed like she was going to say no and the defeat, something he was so unused to before taking on his sister's life, was crushing.

But then she smiled—saucy and real. The confident Lucy returned and, with her, his balance in the world.

"So? What do you propose? About Ben."

Relief made him a little giddy and he laughed. "Honestly, I have no idea."

"He's really got you in a knot."

"He's so angry, Lucy. You saw him, he's nine years old and he drove a sports car into a house! He could have killed himself. And I feel like every time I open my mouth I make things worse."

"He says you hate him."

It felt like his bones were breaking under the load on his back and he slumped.

"Come on, Jeremiah," she whispered. Her hand curled around his arm, squeezing for comfort, and he wanted— so bad—to pull her into his arms. To find even more comfort. To find a second of peace.

"Here." She dropped his arm and crouched to grab two bottles of water—one half-empty—and a bowl of strawberries she must've just picked. She led him over to a small hill, where the land sloped down to a gully that in early spring was a stream. Now it was full of columbine and Indian paintbrush.

Collapsing onto the ground with a sigh, she stretched out her legs and popped a strawberry in her mouth.

"Ugh." She pulled a face he'd seen on Casey's mug a thousand times. The boys called it the "yuck face."

"These aren't ripe yet." She set aside the bowl and cracked open the half-empty bottle of water. She was as beautiful to him right now as she'd been that night in the moonlight with the clingy clothes and the sexy boots. He realized she was blinking up at him, her dark eyes missing nothing.

"My offer to help was about Ben," she said. "Not about you. Or that kiss. If I help Ben there's no more kissing."

It was for the best, he knew that. Would have said it himself if he thought she wouldn't take it the wrong way. But still, he was torn right down the middle by her sound reasoning and perception.

Because he really, really wanted to kiss her again.

"I think that's…that's a good idea." It would be easier if he could just turn off his body. Blind himself to her appeal, but he couldn't. So, it was just going to have to be something he ignored. Which was sort of like ignoring a pink elephant in a tutu.

"I can't believe I'm going to do this," she muttered, but then clapped her hands together, brushing off dirt as if everything was all decided. "What if Ben were to come here two days a week after school? I could keep him busy in the garden here and replanting the roses that he destroyed over at the little house."

"Gardening? The kid crashes a sports car and his punishment is gardening?"

"If it makes you feel better I won't give him any food or water while he's here."

"That does make me feel better. If you could put together some kind of ball and chain…?"

"Better yet, I'll make Walter watch him."

"Now that would be suitable punishment."

They grinned at each other, the sizzle and pop of their attraction undiminished despite having agreed to ignore it. In fact, it was probably worse. Forbidden fruit and all that.

"I think if I tell Mia and Jack, they'd have some stuff for him, too. We can keep him busy."

"I can make arrangements to have the bus drop him off here on Thursday and Friday. I'll pick him up after Aaron's hockey practice around five. Does that work?"

"Sounds good to me."

"But…when are you heading back to Los Angeles?"

She tucked her long caramel-colored legs up to her chest, wrapping her arms around them, as if she were a turtle heading back into her shell for safety.

"Mom wants to stick around until Jack hires a care-giver for Walter."

"But don't you have some kind of jewelry empire to run?"

He had made it a joke, but she didn't laugh. Instead, she groaned low in her throat and put her head down on her knees, a little ball of Lucy Alatore. He clenched his teeth against the strong desire to touch her back, to run his hands along the curl of her spine. Memorize the press of her bones against her skin.

"I blew it, Jeremiah. I totally blew it," she said into her knees.

"Blew what?"

"My business."

"The jewelry?"

"Yes, all of it. I…" She pulled up her head and stared out at the flowers that filled the gully and every instinct screamed at him to run. Absolutely clamored that he get the hell out of there because she was about to confide in him and he had enough, more than enough, to deal with. He shifted away as if to stand but she opened her mouth and he forcibly relaxed back into the ground. An unwilling listener. Prisoner to the moment.

"I had this huge order for those stupid horseshoe

necklaces. An order so big I thought...I thought I had made it. I thought I'd struck gold. So I charged the store my regular wholesale price but when it became obvious that my little three-person studio couldn't produce all the pieces, I subcontracted out the work, but I couldn't raise the price that I charged the boutique and I'd never factored in the cost of having someone else make my jewelry for me. Suddenly, instead of making money on every piece, I was losing money. It was costing me everything to fill the order, so I had to back out of the contract. And now I'm waiting to hear from the accountant how much of a fee I owe."

"But don't you have other orders?"

"None big enough. And most of them, when they found out I'd started manufacturing pieces instead of making them by hand, started to lose interest."

She lifted her chin as if to tell him it didn't matter, the loss of that interest, but he knew better. You couldn't hide a slap in the face.

"What about your employees?"

"I closed the studio. Set all my employees free and closed up shop."

"Over one order?"

She blinked out at the columbines before turning to face him, her eyes bright.

Oh, shit. He'd made her cry.

Stop, he wanted to beg, *please stop. No crying. Don't cry.* He never handled this stuff right.

She blinked and the tears were gone. Thank God. "It was a doozy, Jeremiah, trust me. I had to sell my supplies, all the stones and gold, just to make my final payroll."

He knew he was gaping at her, slack-jawed and stunned. "But your family—"

"Has no idea and I don't want them to."

"Your business is bust and you're not telling them?"

Her eyes narrowed and she dropped her knees. "Don't make me sorry I told you."

He held up hands. "Sorry. God, Lucy...that sucks."

Her laugh was slightly wild, frayed at the edges. "That sums it up to a T, Jeremiah."

The silence that unfolded around them was heavy with everything she'd said. He wasn't anyone's confidant—he was everyone's good time, their drinking buddy and flirt. He didn't know what to say to make her feel better. All that bravado dried up and blown away and now Lucy sat there, looking and feeling like a failure, and he didn't know what to say to make it better.

"I apologize for dumping that on you," she said, slightly formal as if she, too, was aware of how the atmosphere between them was suddenly riddled with storm clouds.

"It's all right. I'm dumping Ben on you." He thought about the stress she must be under. "Are you sure you want to do this? I mean, it sounds like you've got enough on your plate."

"I don't have anything on my plate." She laughed. "That's the problem. Trust me, Ben will be a welcome diversion."

"All right." He sighed and pushed himself up to his feet. She did the same and the foot of distance between them crackled with awkward awareness. "So... Thursday."

"Sounds good."

He felt like he should hug her but it seemed strangely forward and she held herself so stiffly. But when he held out his hand to shake hers, she lifted her arms as if to hug him, and then dropped one arm just as he lifted his to hug her.

They laughed awkwardly, like strangers after a one-night stand.

And then, she lifted her palm and smacked his hand. A high five. They sealed the deal like they were in junior high basketball.

God, he thought as he walked away. *Could that have been any worse?*

THAT COULD NOT HAVE BEEN any worse, Lucy thought. *If one of them had spontaneously burst into flames that could not have been any more uncomfortable or strained.*

A high five? Really?

She tried not to watch Jeremiah walk away, but she couldn't seem to stop herself. The wind blew his shirt against his skin, outlining the muscles fanning up from his lean hips out to wide shoulders, caressing the thick dip in the middle as if to tease her. One big *na na na boo boo, you can't have this.*

She'd taken care of that sweet attraction, the electric awareness, and replaced it with a graceless disdain.

And that, she told herself, feeling sick with her own shame, *is why you aren't telling anyone about closing down your company.* She already felt like a failure—she didn't need everyone in her life confirming it.

"What were you thinking?" she asked herself, bending over to pick up the water bottles. She scattered the strawberries in the columbine.

That moment of weakness on her part was inspired by his moment of weakness. When he admitted that he didn't know what he was doing with Ben and that he needed help, she turned to pudding. His vulnerability, that heart-wrenching honesty that he wore so painfully, so terribly uncomfortably, had unlocked her.

As if his grief had been a key to all of her secrets.

She kicked the mud and dirt off the soles of her Doc Martens, brushed off the shovel and clippers she'd found in the barn and headed back inside to tell her mom about Ben.

She could do this. The knowledge was a little seed in her gut. And she was going to protect that seed, feed it. Not just for her own sake. But for Jeremiah's. The guy needed a break as much as she did.

The cell phone in her pocket rang and she dug it out. Joey. Again. On a Sunday afternoon.

"I'm on my way," she said once she answered.

CHAPTER SEVEN

THE DARK WAS A WELCOME embrace to Sandra as she sat on the corner of the couch wrapped in her mother's thin red shawl that always made her think of fresh tomatillos and God. The fringe at the corners was worn, as Sandra had run the silk through her fingers like the beads on a rosary for over twenty years.

It was Tuesday night and she sat in the dark and tried—with all the power of her prayer and the grace of her faith—to control her hate. It was hard with the sweetness of her memories growing bitter on her tongue. And that bitterness was turning to an anger that churned in her belly.

Mother used to tell her, when Sandra was a girl and she came home from school with scrapes and black eyes and skinned knuckles, that the only way to get rid of her anger was to pray.

Mother had forced prayer upon her: daily mass, Catholic school, special meetings with the Father.

But sometimes the prayer didn't work. And sometimes a person needed a fight to vent that anger.

This house she had cared for with her own two hands—baptizing the floor and the stove, the kitchen and every meal made here for twenty-five years with her blood, sweat and tears—this house was strange to her now.

And Walter just broke her heart. She knew Walter

loved her, could feel it in the desperate way he looked at her, as if he were drowning and she was his only chance at survival. Walter's wife had been right to worry. Not that Sandra would have taken advantage of Walter's feelings, but who knew what a desperate man would do?

He was not a man for love. Not for her, anyway, maybe not for anyone. Well, except A.J. A.J. had loved Walter when the rest of the world threw their hands at the heavens on his behalf. A.J. had believed in Walter's goodness. A.J. believed in everyone's goodness.

I'm sorry, A.J., she thought, running the fringe between her fingers. *I'm sorry, but I don't think I can help him. I don't think I want to.*

She couldn't do all the fighting for a man who wouldn't fight for himself. He skulked around this house like a ghost, his eyes on the ground like a kicked dog.

For a minute there after Walter's accident she'd thought she could be useful again and her heart had rejoiced. Her spirit dry and dead after living so long in that city had swelled with purpose. It could be just like it was years ago.

But days had passed and there was no more purpose to her life here than there'd been in Los Angeles. Here, she was surrounded by ghosts. And Walter was either locked in his room or sitting on the back patio—refusing to even look at her. Kicking aside the food she left at his feet. Ignoring her efforts to help. To talk. She had no idea if he was drinking or if he'd stopped.

She had no idea what she was doing here. *When did I get so lost?*

The easy answer was that it happened after her husband died, but the truth was an answer of a different color. Somewhere in the beginning of her marriage, when she dedicated herself to keeping up the pretense of happiness—that's when she'd lost herself.

"Hey, Mom." Lucy came into the living room. "What are you doing here in the dark?"

"Thinking."

"Never good, Mom. Never good." Lucy curled up next to her on the couch, and Sandra put her arms around her youngest daughter, stroking back her hair, holding her like she was seven years old again.

"Where have you been?"

"Well, this morning I took Reese to pick up his car."

"It's fixed?"

"Fixed and he's gone. And then I was giving a couple of women from the west side retirement village a ride to get their hair done."

"What are you doing, Lucy?" Sandra asked, baffled by her daughter. Not that the feeling was new.

"My civic duty, Mom, at twenty dollars a pop. The question is, what are you thinking about here in the dark?"

"I'm thinking about how you and Mia used to fight." Lucy laughed and Sandra rocked her, glad that she had lied. Glad that lying came so easy to her. "Oh, like cats and dogs. You used to give your father ulcers."

"Not you, though."

"Nope. Girls need to know how to fight."

Lucy was so different than Mia. Mia was a blunt instrument, hammering away at what she wanted until she broke down every wall in her way. Lucy took a good look around and figured out how to get around the wall, or if that wasn't going to work, she found the weakness in the wall and applied the right pressure.

As children, once Lucy was old enough to know her

own power, Mia could never beat her in an argument.
Which was why Mia usually started using her fists.

By instinct Sandra had so much more in common
with her oldest. But by practice she'd learned to be wily,
like Lucy.

"You and Dad never fought," Lucy said.

No, she thought, the old wounds opening up, oozing
resentment. "Your dad wasn't much of a fighter." She'd
grown so used to pretending, to forcing that fond sweet
smile on her lips. So used to it she didn't even know
what the alternative was. Screaming?

That wasn't her.

"You okay, Mom?" Lucy asked, and Sandra stroked
her cheek.

"Thinking of your father. Do you miss him?"

Lucy nodded. "Won't I always?"

The bite of grief stole her breath for a moment. Grief
for A.J., for a marriage that wasn't always what it seemed
and was never what she'd imagined for herself.

From the bedrooms in the back of the house there
was a terrible crash. A thick thud.

Sandra shared one glance with her daughter and they
were on their feet running toward Walter's room. Sandra got there first and threw open the door only to find
Walter spitting into a bowl on top of his dresser.

The light blue shirt of his pajamas was wet with
sweat, a wide V down the back. His shoulders heaving
over the dresser.

"Walter?"

He slammed his hand down on the dresser. "Get the
hell out of here," he yelled, wiping his mouth.

"Can I help?"

"I said get the hell out of here!" he hollered, and
something in Sandra leaped at the sound. The tiger of

her temper woke and it was as if she'd filled out her own skin suddenly. It was as if she were more herself from one moment to the next.

"Hey!" Lucy cried over Sandra's shoulder. "Don't talk to her like that."

Walter turned, pale and wan. The buttons of his shirt open, revealing his chest. Still strong, despite the disease and his age. The hair there was silver, catching the moonlight like wire filament. His eyes spit fire and his muscles were still thick and he was suddenly far more man than ghost.

Sandra's skin prickled awake, reminding her she wasn't dead. Reminding her how long it had been since it had just been prayer accompanying her to bed at night.

Walter suddenly turned toward the bowl on top of his dresser, his shoulders heaving. His back rigid.

Realization dawned. He wasn't sick, he was getting rid of the alcohol in his system. Detox. "You haven't been drinking," she said.

"I want you to leave," he gasped, his hands shaking as he wiped his mouth. "And you said that's what would get it done. So leave me the hell alone."

"Hey! My mom's here to help!" Lucy cried, stepping into the room as if to do battle with the man, and Sandra put her hand up, stopping her daughter.

This is my fight, she thought, suddenly protective of the man in front of them.

"I don't want help!" he cried. "I want you out of here."

"Leave him alone," she said, backing out of the room, taking her daughter with her. Sandra shut the door and both she and Lucy just stared at the wood grain. The silver doorknob.

"I don't like him talking to you like that, Mom."

"He's going through detox, honey. He's sick."

"You think he's going to be better when it's over?"

"I don't know," she answered honestly.

"Let's hope that ad Jack placed starts bringing in some nurses," Lucy muttered, and then she leaned in to kiss Sandra's cheek. "I'm going to bed."

She watched her daughter disappear into the shadows of the hallway and turned back to look at the door. From the other side she heard Walter swearing, thumping around.

Not drinking.

She touched the grain wide and rough under her fingers. Suddenly, she felt like she had a fight on her hands. Her mother would tell her to pray, to find peace in God's words. A.J....well, A.J. wouldn't say anything, would he? He kept his opinions and his secrets to himself.

She unwrapped the shawl from around her shoulders, folding it up in her hands. She'd followed her mother's advice for a number of years. It got her out of trouble as a kid, led her to A.J., so handsome and so devout. And with so many secrets.

Prayer saw her through the loneliest years of her marriage. She'd found peace. She'd found affection and companionship and a love for her girls so profound she felt touched by God's grace.

But she wasn't going to pray this time around.

She was going to fight.

WEDNESDAY MORNING LUCY sat back in her seat and watched Mia engage in a losing battle. It was sort of fun. Mia didn't lose many battles and she was getting all hot under the collar.

"What if we offered you more money?" Mia asked Gina Burshot, a registered nurse with hospice care experience. None of which mattered because Gina had no interest in the job. Not since meeting Walter.

Gina slung her bag over her shoulder, putting her shoulders back. "Let me make this clear," she said. "There is nothing you could offer me that would make me want to care for that odious old man."

Lucy snorted and then quickly composed herself when Mia glared at her.

"Thanks, Gina, for coming in, and I'm sorry…again." Mia led Gina to the front door and then came back into the kitchen. She braced herself against the dining room chair and sighed. Heavily.

"What did he do?" Lucy was almost afraid to ask.

"Threw that bowl he's been throwing up in at her."

"Was it full?"

"Full enough."

Lucy groaned, and frankly, if she wasn't jailed by this situation she would have laughed. Walter was not going down without a fight.

"I'll go let Jack know what happened. Maybe he can talk to his father."

"Right." Like that would do any good. Lucy stood up from her chair. "Hey," she said as her sister started to leave. "Remember Ben's coming over Thursday."

"Yeah, about that…what exactly are you going to do with him?"

"You don't have to be so skeptical."

"Well, how many kids do you know?"

"None. But I was a kid."

"Yeah. A well-adjusted artist with two living parents. Ben's a nine-year-old car-thieving orphan."

Lucy stood, her back straight, her pride slightly inflamed by Mia's doubt. Largely because Lucy shared that doubt and had her own huge misgivings about this arrangement. But she believed very strongly in the ancient proverb: fake it till you make it.

"We had a connection. He just needs someone to listen to him," she said. "I can do that."

"Yes. Of course you can. I'm sorry."

"It's okay." Lucy grinned. "Trust me, I know it's weird. But Jeremiah needs some help and...well, I'm not doing anything at the moment."

"Not doing anything? You've been giving Thomas Matthews a ride home from the bars every night."

Lucy lifted her hand. "Everyone's opinion on my taxi service has been duly noted. Let's move on."

Mia stared at her and finally rolled her eyes. "Well, you're right about Jeremiah. He does need help." Mia patted down her back pocket and pulled out a pen. "Hey, I need to write Mom a note. Can I borrow your notebook?"

Lucy went still. "I, ah, I don't have it."

"What?" Mia looked at her as if Lucy had said she'd forgotten her hands. And in a way, she was right. Since she was sixteen Lucy had walked around with a little notebook in her back pocket or her purse, ready to sketch something when inspiration struck.

But it had been so long since inspiration had knocked on her door, she'd stopped carrying the notebook.

"What the hell is going on with you, Lucy?" Mia demanded. "Last I heard you were doing great, the jewelry business was doing great, and the next thing I know you're hiding out here."

"It's just a notebook—"

"Bullshit, Lucy. It's one thing if you want to lie to everyone, but it's another thing lying to me. I know something's wrong."

Lucy sat back in her chair and studied her hands. "Is

it so strange that I might want to do something else? Design, art, jewelry—it's all I've ever done. Can't I be tired of it?"

"Sure. If you really are."

Lucy laughed, bitter and dark. *Tired of it? Sure. Terrified and destroyed—those, too.* "Trust me, I really am."

"So…what? You're going to do something else. For good."

"Is that so hard to believe?"

"Yeah. It is. You're my sister the jewelry designer."

"Well, now I'm your sister the parole officer, taxi driver and gardener. At least for a little while."

"You're pulling up half the vegetables."

"I didn't say I was good at it," she snapped, and Mia held up her hands in surrender.

"You know I support you. We all do. We just want you to be happy."

Happy, she thought, feeling as if she were suddenly drowning. Suddenly without air or chance of air.

She wasn't even sure if she could be happy again. Failure had done that to her. Her own mistakes suffocated her.

"You know, I'm here if you ever feel like telling me the truth." Mia put her ball cap over her head and pulled her ponytail out the back. "See you later."

Lucy nodded and listened to her sister's footsteps walk out the mudroom. In the silence of the dining room she pulled her cell phone from her pocket and cradled it in her hands like a secret.

She pushed two buttons, leveled her heart rate, found the center of herself and pushed aside everything else.

"It's about damn time," Meisha said when she answered.

"That's not how accountants talk." She closed her eyes. "Tell me."

"Twenty thousand dollars. That's the penalty for backing out of the contract."

Twenty grand. "Is that all?" she gasped, trying to force her lungs to work. "I thought they'd want a kidney. My firstborn."

"Very funny," Meisha said. "But you have options. You can declare bankruptcy."

"And then what?"

"And then…you have no debt, but you also have no credit. You'll need a cosigner for any loan."

"What are my other options?" she asked, her eyes still closed.

"You can sell your condo. The market is shit, but… you might get enough to clear out the debt, or at least take out a good chunk of it."

"We'll sell the condo," she said, making the decision in a heartbeat. Declaring bankruptcy seemed like an awful big shadow over the rest of her life.

"Your mother—"

"I'll figure out what to tell my mom." Another lie. More lies. One after the other.

"Lucy—"

"She'd just worry. And I don't need her worry on top of mine. I'll call my real estate agent."

"All right. Keep me posted."

Lucy opened her eyes only to look right into Walter's watery baby blues. Watery baby blues full of reproach.

Her blood turned to sludge in her veins.

She stood, the chair screeching over the stone of the floor.

"You're selling your mother's home?" he asked.

"It's my condo."

"Where she lives."

"You don't judge me."

He looked at her for a long time, his face immutable. He was made of freaking stone and her failures were like knives in her skin the longer she looked at him.

"Don't say a word to her," she spat.

He shook his head and quietly left. Limping toward the back patio and the cushioned deck chair he sometimes sat in.

Once he was gone, she stood there and shook.

WEDNESDAY NIGHT, AFTER getting Casey his thirtieth drink of water and making sure he went pee before finally turning off his light, Jeremiah stopped in front of Ben's room.

The light was shining out from under the door, a thin sliver that wasn't much of a welcome. It was nine o'clock and he had school in the morning, and then his gardening punishment with Lucy and the boy needed his sleep.

Jeremiah hung his head, bracing himself to be the bad guy one more time today. After the dinner battle and the shower battle and the cleaning-up-his-room battle. Now, the going-to-bed battle.

"Hey, Ben," he whispered, knocking on the door as he pushed it open. Ben's room was bare, his dresser and bed the only things in it. Jeremiah remembered the walls had been covered in SpongeBob SquarePants pictures and dozens of hand-drawn superhero action shots. But at some point, Ben had taken everything down.

When was that? he wondered. *How do I keep missing these things?*

Ben lay in the pool of light from the lamp clipped onto his bed frame. He was reading and very studiously ignoring Jeremiah.

"It's pretty late, buddy."

Ben turned a page.

"You're going to Lucy's tomorrow after school, remember?"

Silence.

Jeremiah took a breath and turned to stare at the bare walls sloping down to the floor. A window dormer had been cut out and the night sky was full of stars. All of them as far away as the boy in the bed.

"You can talk to me," he whispered, his throat burning. "I know…maybe it doesn't feel that way all the time, but…you can talk to me about how you feel."

He heard the quiet rustle of another page turning and then, not that he expected much different, more silence.

"Turn off your light in five minutes," he said, stepping out of the room without looking at Ben.

Please, Lucy Alatore, please be the help we need.

THERE WAS A FIRE in Walter's room. *No,* he thought, sweaty and disoriented. His stomach roiling with every breath. The fire was under his skin. He looked down at his body, naked and glowing on the bed. Christ. Was this hell?

Had to be. He'd plumbed the breadth and depth of awful on earth, there'd been no horrible stone unturned in his life and this—the burning body—was new.

He'd died. Thank God. Thank God the torture of trying to stop drinking was over. He took a breath, another. Too shallow. Not enough air.

"Walter." He turned, trying to find that voice. Searching the shadows for the devil come to escort him to his just rewards.

There. By the window. Tall and thin, grim and unforgiving. His ex-wife.

"You," he breathed.

"I told you, you would burn," she sang. "This is what you get for coveting another man's wife."

"And what do you get?" he panted. "For what you did to that family. To our son."

"You. You were my punishment."

"Good." He laughed at the thought. They'd deserved each other for a time there, he and his ex-wife. They were each other's just rewards—he just felt so damn awful his son, Sandra and the girls got wrapped up in their war.

"You think you will win her like this?" Vicki hissed. "You think your son will forgive you for the way you turned your back? You think those girls are going to think better of you because you lie in your bed shaking and vomiting and sweating like some pig?"

"Go away," he breathed.

"Never." He could smell roses. "You aren't half the man A.J. was."

He sighed, the knowledge a stone in his gut, a weight in his heart. "I know."

"You'll never have more than me. You'll never get anything better than the mess you made—"

Anger fed the fire under his skin and he pulsed with fury. "Shut up. I'm done with you."

She laughed and he screamed, opened his mouth and spilled fire over her, until his lips cracked and his skin crackled. With a strength that surprised him, a speed he would never believed he possessed, he lunged up and toward her, grabbing her wrist. Real in the fever. Odd.

"Walter," she said, her hand cool against his bare chest. The fire under his skin hissed at the contact. Like rain on a campfire. "You're hurting me."

"Good," he said, holding on to that wrist. "You won't win."

"I won't?"

"No. I can fight. I will fight."

A cool hand touched his forehead. And the fire fled the area. He pressed the hand in his grip to his chest, over his heart and the fire darted away, scared of the power.

Suddenly exhausted he laid down. His eyes closing. He tried to hold on to that hand, to keep his grip on her, on everything, but it was impossible. He was being sucked down, down, down.

And just before sleep claimed him, he smelled roses again. And cumin.

Sandra.

THURSDAY AFTERNOON LUCY had it all planned out. She waited for Ben in the back garden. Her mom would answer the door, calm him down because he'd probably be nervous. Give him something to eat because he'd probably be hungry. And then she would lead him out to the garden where Lucy would put him to work staking the vegetable plants.

Over the past few days she'd developed this theory, and the more time she spent with it, the more she believed in it. She would just ask him about his mother. She would talk to him, open him up. And like popping a blister, all that grief would pour out and then…he could heal.

He was clearly dying for someone to just listen. She could be that person. Hell, she'd be great at being that person.

So caught up in her daydream and potential plans of going to school to become a child psychologist, she didn't hear her mother coming down the rickety steps to the garden until she cleared her throat right behind her. Lucy jumped a mile, pulling out a strawberry plant as she did.

"Crap," she muttered, and tossed the plant to the side of the aisle. Mom stood beside Ben, who had his eyes narrowed and his arms crossed over his chest. He was throwing around a glower to rival his uncle's.

"Here he is," Sandra said, her eyes wide, sending Lucy the secret message that perhaps the plan was not starting with success. Mom wore a beautiful silver cuff around her wrist and it took Lucy a second to recognize it as something she'd made for her mother last year. She so rarely wore it. *Not bad,* she thought, as if the work were someone else's.

"Have you had something to eat?" Lucy asked.

"I'm not hungry," Ben muttered, dropping his arms to reveal the video game graphic on the front of his T-shirt.

Sandra shrugged and mouthed "good luck" before walking back up the staircase.

"You ready to work?"

"Gardening?" He sneered. His dark hair flopped over his eyes, making him older and younger at the same time. All the sweetness of his youth, going sour at the edges. The poor kid.

"You'd rather move rocks? Make license plates?"

He stared at her, her attempt at humor flying right past him.

"You're going to help me stake the vegetable plants."

"That's stupid."

She blinked at him, stunned by this sudden aggression. "I thought you wanted to be here!"

He pursed his lips and shrugged like some put-upon child pop star and she wanted to tell him he looked ridiculous. But instead, she took a deep breath.

"I think gardening is better than what your uncle had in mind."

Ben muttered something under his breath that would no doubt get him in huge trouble with his uncle so Lucy choose to ignore it, largely because she had no idea how to handle a nine-year-old swearing under his breath at her.

It hadn't even been ten minutes and this whole thing was already slipping out of her hands.

"Here," she said. "Let me show you what I want you to do."

She bent down to pick up the trellis things and the round green wire things she'd found in the back shed that she remembered from when she was a kid.

"These plants are peas and they're—"

"Those aren't peas."

She looked up at him and then down at the plants. "What are you talking about?"

"They're not peas."

"How do you know?"

Ben licked his lips, the facade crumbling a little. "My mom... We used to have a garden. Those are going to be flowers."

"Flowers." Which meant she'd probably pulled out most of the peas. Great. Total fail. "Well, good thing I have such an expert with me." She smiled, big and bright, and Ben's face boarded right back up. Eyes narrowed, lips drawn in a downward curve.

Remember, she told herself, *this is about getting him to talk. Not about punishing him.* "Was it your mom's garden?"

He blinked and she held her breath, waiting for the up swell in music, the small leak that would become a geyser of pain.

"I'm not doing this shit," he muttered, and sat down on the ground.

"Ben…" She sighed.

"Tell my uncle, I don't care."

Right. Tell Jeremiah that Ben wouldn't do the first thing she asked him to do? Not a chance.

"Look, I'm not a bad guy—"

He shrugged and she stiffened, offended by that shrug. As if that shrug spoke a whole new demeaning language all its own.

"You're the one that ruined that car!" she cried, and somehow, in some way, she knew she was handing him all the power, but what the hell was she supposed to do? Bodily lift him up and force him to work? Wasn't that illegal?

"Fine," she said. "But you're sitting there. The whole time. And you're coming back tomorrow."

He shook his head at her. "You're crazy."

"Yeah, well, you're not the picture of mental health, kid."

He scowled at her and she started to push the trellises into the earth around the flowers, winding the vines up and over the structures.

"That's a pumpkin," Ben muttered.

"Good," she snapped, and kept on working.

CHAPTER EIGHT

"YOU DON'T HAVE TO COME with me," Jeremiah muttered to Casey as the boy hopped up the steps toward the Rocky M's front door.

"What if Sandra has banana bread again?" Casey asked.

There was no arguing with a five-year-old's stomach. He'd learned that the hard way. But Jeremiah still wished the kid would just wait in the car with Aaron so he could pick up Ben and conduct his behavior interview with Lucy in relative privacy.

He put his hand up to knock on the heavy front door but before he made contact the door swung open and Ben poured out of the house like it was on fire.

"Hey," he cried as the kid stomped past. "What happened?"

"It was great. Can't wait to go back," Ben said, and then kept on toward the car. Jeremiah shared a stunned look with Casey, who only shrugged as if to say, *What are you going to do?*

A five-year-old with all the wisdom of the ages.

"Hey, Jeremiah," Lucy said, leaning against the door like a teenage girl waiting for her date to pick her up, and he felt something smooth and sweet slip into his bloodstream. That old desire to flirt, to lean back and charm this woman's secrets from her hands, to share a few of his with her—the harmless ones. The fun ones.

It was a powerful drug. Back in the early days of his rodeo career, he got ribbed all the time for nearly missing his call times because he'd be chatting up the girl at the snack bar.

But that was a million years ago and he stifled that smooth, sweet inclination.

"Hey, Lucy, how did it go today?" He put one foot on the first step of the porch and tipped his hat back. Casey copied him, his little boot on the step next to his.

"Good." She nodded. "Just fine."

He'd been expecting a little more. "Was he polite?"

"No." She laughed but when he turned toward the truck, she stopped him. "Stop. I…didn't expect him to be polite. But he was fine."

"What did he do?"

"Sulked mostly."

"Did he do what you asked him to do?"

She winced.

"I knew this was a bad idea. We can forget it. Just—"

"No, Jeremiah." She touched his arm, the contact burning through his shirt and his disappointment. "Let's not give up. Not yet."

"Did he…did he say anything? At all?"

In the movies the kid would open up to the pretty stranger, pour out some of his grief. Maybe develop a crush that would pull him out of the pit of despair he seemed to live in. Jeremiah had no reason to believe anymore that life was anything like a movie, but he could still hope.

"No, Jeremiah," she murmured, her eyes liquid with sympathy, "he didn't say anything. But it was the first day."

Behind Lucy, Sandra appeared, flushed and smiling.

"Well, hello, boys," she said, and Jeremiah tipped his hat, stupidly pleased when Casey did the same.

"Howdy, Sandra," Jeremiah said.

Casey took the three steps up to the door. "Excuse me, Sandra?" he asked, and she smiled down at him. *Here comes the banana bread,* thought Jeremiah, not un-tickled that his nephew seemed to have Jeremiah's way with women. There should be something of him in these boys he was raising.

"What are you having for dinner?" Casey asked.

"Brisket, corn on the cob, beans and a salad."

"That sounds real good. We're having peanut-butter-and-jelly sandwiches." Casey poured the orphan routine on thick.

"Casey," Jeremiah groaned. "That's not true."

Well, not totally. There was something in the freezer he could pull out.

"That's no way to feed a growing boy like you." Sandra winked at Jeremiah over Casey's head. "Would you like to stay for dinner?"

"Yes!" Casey cried just as Jeremiah said, "No."

Casey whirled and frowned at him as if he'd lost his mind. "Brisket, Uncle J. Bris-ket."

"Three growing boys," Jeremiah said to Sandra and the gape-faced Lucy. "They're like locusts, honestly, they'd eat the cupboards if you let them...."

"Excellent," Sandra said. "We've got a fridge full of leftovers no one is eating around here. Go tell your brothers that they need to come in and shuck some corn."

Casey jumped off the porch with a wild whoop and ran off to the truck to share the news. They were going to eat well tonight. But Jeremiah didn't like feeling like an interloper, didn't like spreading the burden of feeding three bottomless pits onto an unsuspecting Sandra.

"Wow," Lucy said, looking at Jeremiah with twinkling eyes. "The kid is a smooth talker. I wonder where he gets that from."

"You don't have to do this," Jeremiah said, ignoring Lucy. "He made us seem much worse off than we are."

"I'm sure he did," Sandra said. "But we would still love to have you. This house could use three growing boys in it for a night."

"What about Walter?" Lucy asked.

"What about him?" Sandra asked, her face falling into stern lines. She twisted the wide silver cuff on her wrist, as if turning a key in a lock.

"Well." Lucy laughed. "I'm pretty sure he won't like having three growing boys here."

"Then he can stay in his room," Sandra snapped in a voice Jeremiah had never heard from the woman before. Sandra left and Lucy stared after her mother with a wrinkle set deep between her eyes.

He wanted to kiss that wrinkle. Slide his hands into the satin of her hair where it touched her shoulders, her neck. He wanted to warm himself against her skin, warm those places inside that had been cold for so long he no longer felt them. Her fire blazed in her eyes and the stubborn, knowing set of her shoulders.

The truck door slammed and the three boys ran past him with varying speed. Ben, sullen and dragging his feet, brought up the rear. In a flash Jeremiah saw how tonight might end. How Ben with his disdain could hurt Sandra and the thought made him furious. Sick to his stomach.

"Ben—" he snapped, as if the boy had already done something, and Ben flinched away from him.

Goddamn it, he thought, *always wrong. Always so damn wrong.*

"Come on in, Ben. Mom's going to put you to work," Lucy said, ushering the boy inside, but not before he sent one poisonous look at Jeremiah over his shoulder.

Finally, standing alone outside the house where the sounds of the boys spilled out the front door, he realized, to his great shame, the person who might ruin it all was him.

As soon as Ben and Lucy cleared the hallway Ben shrugged her arm off.

"Ben." She sighed.

"What?"

Holy shit, did the kid ever give it a rest? "My mom is going to work very hard to feed you," she said. "And it will be good food, too. If you're rude to her or make her feel bad, you won't ever get fed by her again."

He looked at her a long time, trying, she could see, to hold on to his anger, but in the end his stomach won out and he just nodded. "Good, now go see how you can help." Ben walked off into the kitchen and then Jeremiah stepped into the hallway, just behind her. The skin along her neck and the backs of her arms shivered at his proximity. She was too aware, all too aware, of the dangerous cowboy.

What would be so wrong? a little voice in the back of her head whispered. What would be so wrong with a little comfort? Some release from the pressure that was building in her chest. What would be wrong with a little fun?

God. Fun. It seemed like such a foreign concept and she knew, despite the burden that rode Jeremiah so hard, he would be fun. In bed, he would be a carnival of delights.

And she wasn't one for casual sex, didn't really know

how to do it, but perhaps now was her moment to try. Maybe not every relationship had to be some dramatic melding of souls. Maybe she could have one that was just about the occasional melding of bodies.

She had no idea how to do that, but she had the feeling Jeremiah was well versed.

What are you thinking? You made a deal—no more kissing. Luckily, she had plenty of practice breaking deals.

"You want a drink?" she asked. "We've got some beer."

"That would be great."

The boys were shucking a giant bag of corn down by the garden and, after grabbing their beers, Lucy led Jeremiah out to the back porch so they could keep an eye on them.

Sandra was in the kitchen, pulling plastic containers out of the fridge with gleeful abandon.

"Thanks again," Jeremiah said, gesturing with his beer toward the knot of boys sitting on the ground, corn silk floating around them. "For Ben."

"No problem."

The silence pounded and shook between them and Lucy wondered if it would be better if they just stripped naked and did the deed on the splintered porch boards, or worse. Worse probably.

Jeremiah took exquisite care in tearing a strip off the beer label. She watched his wide blunt fingers with a weird fixated breathlessness. "I'm…I'm too hard on him. I don't even give him a chance anymore."

"I can understand the inclination," she said, leaning back in her chair. "He makes it hard."

"He used to be so sweet," Jeremiah said with a quick grin that sent pinpricks right through her heart. "Funny, like really goofy." He laughed a little. "He used to do this thing for Casey when he was a baby—a whole comedy routine. Ben would hit himself in the head and pretend to stagger around and then fall down and Casey would howl. I mean, he'd pee he was laughing so hard. Ben would do it over and over again."

Lucy smiled because Jeremiah was smiling, his face splitting into craggy lines by his bright white teeth. So different from that charming grin he used in other moments.

"But…" Jeremiah shook his head. "That kid is gone."

"Not gone." She touched his hand and, yep, as expected, a spark traveled from the dark, hair-roughened skin of his arm right to the core of her, where she went wet in a wild rush.

She jerked her hand away and he glanced over at her.

"Sorry," he muttered, waving his hand as if clearing the air. "I'm preoccupied. How are things going for you in Los Angeles?"

"Oh." She shot him a skeptical look. "You don't want to talk about that."

"I do."

"Jeremiah." She laughed. "The other day in the garden you wanted to run away so bad I could see it."

His smile was lopsided, rueful and utterly self-aware. A heartbroken cowboy who was self-aware? Good Lord, he was a country song brought to life. "I'm…I'm not good with the deep stuff," he said. "I'm totally shallow."

"Come on," she cried.

"It's true. I'm the king of small talk. Of one-night stands. Try to talk to me about your feelings, or anything deeper than the color of your underwear, and I panic."

"So, I told you about my business and you panicked?"

He opened his eyes wide. "I thought you were going to cry, Lucy. I freaked right out. I broke out in a rash."

"Well, then, all the more reason not to tell you about Los Angeles."

"True," he murmured, but watched her sideways, both of them slipping into waters so fast moving, so treacherous, they must be sick in the head. "But maybe you can change me."

She howled with laughter, even as something in her chest spasmed. "How many women have gotten their hearts broken believing that?"

"Probably too many," he said, sobering slightly.

She punched him in the shoulder, not enjoying the sudden downturn in mood. "Cads aren't repentant. Goes against type."

Again that grin. Again the electrical storm between them. "So? What should I be?"

Everything I want right now, she thought, *everything I need. Fun. Easy. Uncomplicated. A blind release from the pressure keeping me up nights.*

The words didn't come. It didn't feel as if anything was easy between them. Ben. Los Angeles. All of it complication upon complications.

But she still wanted him.

"You know." He leaned forward, just slightly. Not enough to be pushy, but enough that the equation between them changed and her better sense was drowned out by the sudden clamoring demands of her body. "I might be wrong, but I'm sensing that perhaps you're interested in breaking a certain rule you've given us."

"It wasn't just me," she whispered, looking at his lips, the pinkness of them. The lushness of them. How did she not notice those lips before? Gorgeous. She wanted to investigate them further. "You agreed that anything between us would be a mistake."

"Well." He sighed, the smell of his breath intoxicating. "Maybe we just need different rules."

"Like what?" Oh, Lord, was that her voice? She sounded as if she'd been running uphill.

His finger touched her hand, the knuckle of her thumb, and her nipples got hard in a wild cataract of feeling. "Like…we keep things casual."

"Casual?" She didn't know how to tell him that she wasn't very good at casual. She was trying, but it was hard for a woman who'd lived with a calling for most of her life. Who'd never had any other job but the one she'd just utterly failed.

"Yeah. Fun."

"Fun?"

He tilted his head as if to get a better look at her. "Am I reading you wrong, here, Lucy? I'll admit I'm out of practice.…"

"No, you're not reading me wrong."

She touched his hand, the roughness of his skin, the hair that prickled and teased her palms. So many textures, so many things to discover on him. He could be a project. Her imagination roared as she pictured his body. The perfect sculpture of it. The shadows and light of his skin. The flex of muscle, the tension of sinew.

"Lucy." She looked up into those endless blue eyes, rimmed in black, filled with fire. A kiss. Yes. She did love to kiss.

His lips fell across hers like sunlight. Light and warm and sweet and she melted into the moment, into him. He breathed out, she breathed in and the earth stopped rotating, as if someone had just pressed pause on the rest of the world.

"Hey, Uncle J." Aaron, the oldest boy, charged onto the deck from the steps like a wild animal and she and Jeremiah leaped apart. Her beer fell from numb fingers, rolling across the floor, spilling a trail of beer. "Sorry," Aaron muttered, darting forward to grab the bottle and hand it to her—half-empty and sticky.

"It's all right." She laughed, nervous and awkward, her heart hammering in her chest.

"I forgot to tell you, but our next game moved to Beauregard."

"Beauregard?" Jeremiah said. "That's two hours away, buddy. I can't take you that far on a Tuesday. Did you ask Mrs. Penning if you could ride with her?"

Aaron looked so crestfallen, so worried, that it was obvious there was no room with Mrs. Penning.

"Oh, man, Aaron," Jeremiah said, clearly pained. "I just...I just can't—"

"I can," Lucy blurted before she even thought about what she was doing. Aaron beamed, Jeremiah looked thunderous.

"What are you talking about?" Jeremiah demanded.

"I'm starting a taxi service. I can take him, but...you know...it'll cost you."

"We'll pay!" Aaron said.

"Now, hold on a second, Aaron. A taxi? Is this a joke?"

"What can I say, I see a need and try to fill it. My entrepreneurial spirit cannot be squashed."

"Lucy," he whispered, "You are an artist, a famous designer—"

Her body shook away from the words, not wanting to hear them out of someone else's mouth. She stood. "Fifty dollars should cover it," she said, unable to stare at Jeremiah's questioning face.

"Fifty dollars, Uncle J.—"

"That will cover gas and maybe a cup of coffee," Jeremiah said. "Your entrepreneurial spirit needs a business education."

She stared at him, wounded by his cavalier tone, the way he made a joke of what had happened to her, and then as if he realized what he'd said, he sobered. "I'm sorry, Lucy. I didn't mean... It was just a joke. A bad joke."

"So, can we do it, Uncle J.?" Aaron demanded.

Jeremiah, probably motivated more by guilt than anything else, nodded and Aaron whooped.

"Why don't we go inside and you can give me the details." She stood.

"Thanks, Lucy," Aaron said, all but falling over his too-big feet in an effort to open the screen door for her. "That's so awesome."

"Lucy?"

She turned back to Jeremiah.

"We're not done."

They weren't. Not by a long shot.

She grinned and winked—*fake it till you make it.* "I know."

THERE WAS A GODDAMNED party going on in his house. Walter could hear the voices of kids outside his window in the back garden. He was still deciding if he liked that sound. Normally, no. But this afternoon he'd woken up after twelve straight hours of sleep and he felt...different. Not necessarily better in every way, but in his head... he was better.

Walter limped down the hallway, his stomach queasy, his muscles weak. He'd lost some weight in the grueling torture of the past week. And he hoped to God he was through the worst of it, the last of the poison exiting his system last night, creating from the demons in his head that vision of his ex-wife.

Now, of course, standing in the shadows just outside the kitchen, he had a terrible fear that it hadn't been his ex-wife at all. The scent of roses and cumin clung to only one woman he knew.

It had been Sandra in his room and he'd sworn at her and who knows what else.

Had she told him he'd never be half the man A.J. was? It's not as if it would be news to him, but the words had extra punch from her mouth.

He was embarrassed and angry that she would have seen him like that. God, he'd been in his underwear. Naked in his dream, but he woke up in boxer shorts, so he prayed that had been the case while she'd been there.

But the real issue was that she would have ignored what he'd demanded of her—to leave him alone—and forced herself into his hell.

The rubber stopper at the end of his crutch made a nice thud on the floor as he stepped into the dining room. At the sound, Sandra poked her head up over the counter that split the dining area from the kitchen. Her cagey eyes unreadable.

"Sandra."

She stood all the way up, her hair slightly skewed, thin flyaway silver strands wreathing her skull like a halo.

"You look better." Her eyes traveled over him, missing nothing—his overlong hair, the scruff on his neck. He was obscenely glad he'd showered. Put on clean clothes. "You look very good."

Out of the blue he felt like smiling. He squashed the instinct.

"Were you in my room last night?" he asked, demanded really, his tone totally unchecked.

"I was." Again, he felt like smiling at that stubborn set of her jaw. No apologies from her. *Oh, Sandra,* he thought, *if we were only different people.*

"I asked you to stay away."

"I know, Walter, but you were so sick. You were—" She licked her lips. "In need."

He chewed on his tongue, the words he needed to say not coming with any grace. "I'm sorry." His voice was rough, too quiet, and he cleared his throat and tried again. "I'm sorry if I said something—"

"You screamed." She rubbed her wrist, and he noticed a wide silver bracelet there. "That's all. You thought I was Vicki."

He remembered grabbing his ex-wife in that dream, holding her wrist, pressing the thin bones together. As fast as he could he crossed the room, leaving the cane against the counter, and he reached for her hand.

She jerked away, her eyes knowing.

"It's nothing," she said.

Oh, he'd hurt her. He wanted to take himself out back and peel the skin off his back.

He just stared at her, his eyes locked on hers. Those black depths opening up and showing him her heart. Her too-big heart. She shouldn't be here, caring for him. But her heart would not allow her to be anywhere else. *Foolish,* he thought, *to be so kind. It would only get her hurt.*

"Please," he breathed, and slowly she lowered her arm. Carefully, with shaking fingers, he shifted the wildly beautiful bracelet that could only be one of Lucy's creations. Touching only the metal and never her skin, he twisted the jewelry over her wrist until the inch between the wide ends of the cuff revealed purple bruises.

A moan broke in his throat.

Before he knew what he was going to do he lifted her wrist and pressed his dry, cracked lips to that soft skin.

She pulled her hand away, holding it to her chest, as if he'd somehow hurt her all over again.

He wore his body like a too-big suit, feeling small inside. Where it counted. "I'm sorry," he told her. He was too wrecked to even feel embarrassed.

"It's…it's okay."

"You were right last night. I'm not half the man A.J. was."

Her eyes were wide. Coal-black. "I…I didn't say that, Walter."

He blinked. "Doesn't make it any less true."

From the living room he heard the sliding glass door open and Lucy arrived. A tall blond boy behind her.

She stopped in her tracks when she saw Walter.

"You're up."

He nodded, feeling suddenly like a zoo animal.

"Walter, not sure if you remember Aaron Bilkhead…" She shifted, holding an arm out to the kid.

"Of course I remember. The kid's a neighbor."

The boy smiled and stepped forward to shake his hand. "Nice to see you again, sir."

Walter smiled at his manners. Annie wouldn't raise her sons to be anything but respectful.

"You staying for dinner?" he asked, though the rough shape of his voice made it sound like an accusation.

Aaron glanced sideways at Lucy, who glowered at Walter. "I suppose I am," Aaron finally said. "If…if that's all right with you?"

"Be nice to have a full table," he said, and nearly smiled at Lucy's slack-jawed expression. It was good to surprise the girl. He grinned at her as he hobbled past her to the living room and the porch beyond.

The sun was shining and he wanted to feel it on his face.

JEREMIAH SAT ON THE BACK porch and thought about basketball. Laundry. Anything to cool the heat in his blood after that kiss with Lucy. But it wasn't working.

Filthy, dirty hockey equipment, he thought, but in his mind he only saw Lucy winking at him. And his body responded to the image like a young boy's.

Behind him, the sliding glass door slid open.

"Lucy—"

"Nope."

Jeremiah spun in his chair and then stood at the sight of the old man coming out onto the deck.

"Walter."

"That's my chair." He pointed with his cane at the seat Jeremiah had just vacated.

"Here," he said, jerking it sideways, closer to Walter, who then collapsed into it. Walter looked thinner, the skin on his cheeks and neck hung a little from his bones. He was pale and shaky, but his blue eyes were clear. Searing.

"You want a beer?" Jeremiah asked, lifting his empty bottle, hoping he'd say yes and Jeremiah could hide out in the kitchen. Check out the leftover situation, do some cherry-picking, anything but awkward small talk with Walter.

Walter stared at the bottle for a moment as if Jeremiah was holding up the proof of something Walter didn't quite want to believe. "More than you know. But no, thanks."

So much for hiding out in the kitchen. Jeremiah

braced himself against the railing and stared down at Ben and Casey, shucking corn in the grass. Casey was taking corn silk and hanging it over his ears like a patchy blond wig. "Look, Ben," he said, his little-boy voice carrying up to Jeremiah. "I'm a girl." Casey fluttered his eyes and pursed his lips like some kind of cartoon girl.

Jeremiah smiled. Such a goofball, that kid.

"You're a dork," Ben said, without looking up, tearing at the corn silk like he wanted to hurt it.

"Met your boy in there." Walter jerked his thumb back to the house. "The blond one. Very polite."

"My sister's boy," he said, looking over his shoulder at Walter. "Her oldest."

Walter's eyes focused in on him and it wasn't casual. Those eyes, they were dead serious. Jeremiah had the fleeting impression that he'd spent a lot of years underestimating this man.

"Your sister died, right?"

Jeremiah nodded, his throat thick, wondering what the hell was happening. The old man was a drunk but he'd been at the funeral. "Last winter."

Walter carefully put his feet out in front of him, tilted his head up to the sun as if he'd been in a cave. He closed his eyes.

"At some point you're probably going to have to get used to the idea that they're yours."

CHAPTER NINE

A FRESH START, LUCY THOUGHT on Friday afternoon as she stared into the dust plume kicked up by the bus traveling from town to the ranch. That's what she and Ben needed. She'd been naive to think that they'd pick some vegetables and everything would be all right. Life wasn't a movie, she knew that.

But she was determined to try again. If not for the kid, if not for her self-esteem, then for Jeremiah. Because the guy needed a break. And because she wasn't about to tell him that she couldn't handle Ben. That she'd failed. Again.

She waited out by the end of the drive where the bus would drop him off. The wind had picked up, swirling dust into her eyes despite her sunglasses.

There had been a lot of details about ranch life in Northern California she'd forgotten. The dust wasn't one of them.

The bus arrived with a squeal of brakes and the creak of the doors opening.

Lucy's heart hammered into her throat.

What makes you think you can do this? she thought, panicked and full of doubt. *What do you know about any of this?*

But there he was, stepping out of the bus, his face blank, his eyes angry.

"Hey, Ben," she said.

He stared at some spot over her shoulder.

"It's normal, when someone says hello to you, to say hello back. Or nod. Or grunt. Whatever."

"Whatever."

"Oh, ho! He jokes."

There was no smile, but that cold blue anger in his eyes was a degree warmer.

Progress, she thought, like a kid who'd somehow managed to blow a giant bubble and was afraid to pop it. She turned toward the ranch and, after a moment, she heard Ben's feet follow.

"How was school?"

"Boring."

"All of it or just some of it?"

He was quiet and her little bubble of satisfaction was in danger of being popped. "Some of it," he said. "Math was boring."

"Ugh. Tell me about it."

"Division."

"The worst."

"We had art today."

Oh, the satisfaction bubble was soaring to new heights. She suddenly imagined healing his wounds with sketch books and charcoal pens.

"That's good?"

He grunted and she wasn't entirely sure if that was a yes or no, or if it mattered. He was responding. Maybe that career in child psychology wasn't a total loss.

"I'm an artist," she said.

"Uncle J. said you stopped."

She waved her hand as if that little matter was inconsequential. "Once an artist, always an artist. What do you like about art?"

He started talking about the papier-mâché sculpture

he was working on. "I'm not sure what it's going to be," he said, "but when I'm working on it, no one bothers me."

"That's true." She nodded, all too familiar with the loneliness of art. "You like to be alone?"

"I don't like talking."

Well, she thought, *at least he knows it.*

They came up to the barn and Lucy ducked inside to grab the gardening things, and when she came back out Ben's eyes were frigid.

"I'm not gardening."

She blinked, stunned by the sudden change in him. "What do you mean?"

"I mean, I'm not gardening. And I'm not watching you do it."

"Ben—"

"I'm. Not. Doing. It."

"Ben. Is it because of your mom?"

That chill in his eyes grew angry. Mean.

"Shut up about my mom."

The bucket made a heavy thunk against the ground. "You should talk about your feelings, Ben."

He stepped away, all that anger and meanness flared like a lit match. "I'm not talking to you about anything."

"I know you must miss her—"

His eyes went dead and she felt it all slipping away. Again. But worse because she'd felt closer to him. A sudden painful empathy for Jeremiah welled up in her, a terrible understanding of how hard it must be to try and love this boy.

"If you don't want to be in the garden, then we'll work somewhere else." He wasn't responding and she got desperate. "I know I have some sketch books around here somewhere, we could sit—"

"This is bullshit."

The curse word was so ugly coming out of a nine-year-old's mouth.

"Ben," she said, trying to be implacable. Trying to have limits without losing her temper. "You can't talk to me that way."

"Why?" he snarled. "You're just some woman Uncle J. is having sex with. Aaron told us he caught you two kissing—"

"Ben!"

"Screw you," he yelled, and ran into the shadowed barn.

For a long terrible moment she was rooted to the spot. Her stomach in her heels, that big bubble in sticky pink ruins all over her face.

What? Just? Happened?

Obviously, she couldn't chase after him just yet. There'd be no point in that. Jeremiah had been right that day at his ranch—she had to just give Ben and herself a chance to cool down. And then she'd try again.

Carefully, as if walking away from a ticking bomb, she backed away from the barn and headed into the house, where she could watch the barn and see him if he tried to leave.

She could sit and try to come up with a new fresh start.

WALTER HAD TO FIND a different place to sit. The back patio was too close to the house. Too close to Sandra. She'd started leaving the sliding glass door open during the heat of the day and he could hear her in the house. Humming.

A special kind of hell for sure.

And after breakfast Mia had ambushed him with another one of her babysitter candidates.

"You don't want this job," he'd told the woman's stunned round face. "I'll make your life hell."

He didn't have to tell her twice. She was up and gone in five minutes.

Mia had lit into him, which he'd sort of liked. He rarely saw her anymore. Having Mia lay into him reminded him of the good old days. If his ankle would have let him, he'd have jumped into the truck and… He stopped at the thought. And what? Gone to Al's downtown? His bar days were over.

Face it, he thought, stepping across the hard ruts in the parking area, using his crutch more than he'd like. *You have nowhere to go. Nowhere to go and nothing to do.*

Walter stepped into the barn feeling like a green cowboy looking for his first job. This barn had been his home but he barely recognized it sober. Of course, he barely recognized it at all because Mia and Jack had updated everything. Fixed the stall doors. There was a cell phone sitting in a charger on top of a filing cabinet that had never been there before. A cell phone. In a barn.

What is the world coming to?

But the hard-backed chair that was always in the office was still there and he grabbed it, placing it securely in the sun just outside the open door. From the deep right pocket in his shirt he pulled out his penknife. A gift from his father when he turned ten, the bone handle worn and warm. An old friend.

Now, he just needed something to work on. Whittling when his hands shook like this might be about the dumbest thing ever. But he had this hope that it would help. Help his hands. Help his head.

Without drinking to fill the hours, he was bored. List-less. All too aware of the mess he'd made of everything.

With some effort he turned himself around, heading back through the wide center aisle to the back where they had stacked wood for winter fires. There was some white birch that was about the right size and he picked it up, pulling off the long splinters that snagged on the cuffs of his shirt.

From behind him he heard the rustle of hay, the scuff of a boot, and awkwardly he turned, hoping to see his son. But instead, in the stall opposite, he saw a kid's tennis shoe and the frayed hem of a pair of blue jeans. "What the hell?" he muttered, and shuffled his way over to the doorway.

It was the kid. The troublemaker, Ben, sitting in the clean hay.

"What?" Ben barked when he looked up and saw Walter standing there. The tone of voice was uncalled for and Walter nearly told him to get the hell out of his barn. But the boy had been crying. Those defiant eyes were rimmed in red.

He thought of Annie Stone Bilkhead, and understood the kind of hole a mother like that would leave behind in her sons.

Ben scrambled to his feet. "Am I in trouble?"

"Probably," Walter murmured.

"I wasn't doing anything."

Walter nodded. He remembered the night, a year or two after his wedding to Vicki, when he realized what his marriage was going to be like. The long lonely years that stretched out in front of him, bleak. Joyless. He'd come out here and started drinking. In the same spot the kid stood.

"You all right?" Walter asked.

The boy seemed like he was going to laugh, and for a moment it seemed like the kid's emotions were going to overflow their banks. But then he cooled himself down. "Sure," he finally said.

Walter nodded and arranged his body to turn back around. He had his wood. The chair and his knife were waiting for him.

"You gonna make me leave?" the boy asked.

"Only if you want," he said, and sat down on his chair, leaving the boy to his demons, if that was what he wanted.

Moments later Walter heard Jack's voice coming in through the back of the barn. "Okay, Mia," he was saying. "Yes, I'll deal with him. No, I can't promise that. You know my dad."

Walter ran his thumb over the smooth wood revealed by his knife. If only he could do that to his life. Whittle away the mess, leave what was useful. Clean. New.

That, he thought with a bitter laugh, *would make for a mighty thin stick.*

Jack appeared at his elbow.

My son, he thought. Jack had come back to this ranch a few months ago a broken man, a scientist. Now he was a rancher, a husband, and looked every inch the job. Walter had heard Mia talking about how Jack was getting calls from all across the state asking questions about irrigation systems and water tables.

I'm proud of you, he thought, but for whatever reason couldn't say it.

"Hey." Jack pushed his hat back on his head. "You can't keep chasing off the women who come to interview."

"I'm not chasing—"

"You threw a bowl of vomit at one woman."

Not much to say about that, so he kept his mouth shut.

"You swore at that woman today."

"A woman who can't handle some rough language has no business on a ranch."

"Dad—"

"It's true and you know it."

"No." Jack stepped forward. "What I know is that you are making Mia's life miserable, Dad. Miserable."

"Can't see how I'm doing that, I barely even see her anymore." Jack opened his mouth but Walter stopped him. His ankle hurt. His face hurt and he had something he needed to say.

"I don't want a nurse."

Jack sighed, heavily. "I don't think you get a choice on that anymore—"

"I'm sober."

Jack blinked. Blinked again.

"A week now."

"Wow…ah…wow."

Walter couldn't help but smile at his son's astonishment, which had the strange effect of making Jack smile for a minute before he tucked it away, out of sight.

"How you feeling?" Jack asked.

"Like shit. But…better."

"You ever done anything like this before?"

Walter shook his head, embarrassed for all sorts of reasons that he couldn't really put words to.

"I take my pills like I should," he said. "I've stopped drinking. My ankle is healing. I don't want a nurse."

"Sandra—"

Sandra. The touch of her body, the smell of her skin— for a moment the thoughts were a terrible sweet torture. But then he shoved them away where they belonged.

"—is leaving." Walter said it with as much authority as he could muster, as if just by saying so he had the ability to make it happen.

"Then we're going to need someone around here, Dad. Even more. Someone to cook and—"

"Cook, fine. But I don't want a nurse. A goddamned babysitter." He was beginning to yell, frustration making the back of his throat burn for a drink. *Christ,* he thought, it was hard being sober when he was just falling asleep in the sun. Dealing with people was worse. Painfully worse.

"Dad, we're hiring someone. It's just the way it is." Jack shrugged as if his hands were tied and Walter knew he'd done that. Tied his boy's hands. Drinking had ruined so much.

Resigned, but bitter, he turned in his seat, careful of his ankle.

"Dad?"

Walter paused without looking up. Too much effort getting his broken body to fall in line.

"I'm proud of you. About the drinking."

Well, thought Walter, *that was something, wasn't it?* He listened to Jack's footsteps and blinked back the burn behind his eyes.

The sun crawled across his feet, yellow and bright, until it filled his lap and Walter picked up his knife again.

"They're trying to get you a babysitter?" a voice asked, and Walter turned to see Ben standing in the shadows outside of the stall he'd been hiding in. He'd forgotten about the kid.

"Seems like it."

"You do something wrong?"

Walter laughed and pressed his thumb to the point

of the wood. Sharp but it didn't break the skin. "I don't seem to do much right these days."

"Me, neither," the kid said.

In a burst of angry and desperate animation, Walter stood. "I'm hungry. You want to get something to eat?"

The boy shook his head. "I'm gonna stay here."

Walter was going to argue—it seemed maybe the kid spent too much time alone. But maybe he'd been told what to do a few too many times, too.

"Suit yourself," he said, and left the boy to his demons, taking his own with him.

CHAPTER TEN

"Is HE RESPONDING TO HIS time with Lucy?" Dr. Gilman asked at their Saturday appointment.

"Well, he hasn't stolen a car this week," Jeremiah joked.

"What's he doing there, with her?"

"Gardening. Which makes sense. He used to do that with his mom all the time. She always said he was more farmer than rancher."

"And that connection to his mother seems to be working?"

"He's more...I don't know...quiet and intense at times, but it's better than the constant fireworks. All and all, things are looking up."

"And the only change in your life is Lucy?"

"Just Lucy." He tried, honest to God, he tried to keep the smile out of his voice, off his face, but he couldn't.

"You like her," Dr. Gilman asked. She had pink flowers in a little cup beside her chair. Her daughter had picked them for her, that's what Dr. Gilman had said, and for some reason Jeremiah couldn't stop staring at them. Almost all the petals were off one and the other was bent.

"Sure." He shrugged, trying to be nonchalant when he felt oddly like jumping on a couch like Tom Cruise.

Dr. Gilman smiled slightly and wrote something

down in her notebook, her long feather earrings brushing her cheeks.

"Come on," he groaned. "What are you writing?"

"Nothing."

"You're lying, I know you're writing down 'the patient seems to be interested in the neighbor.'"

"Would that be wrong?"

He stopped. *No. No. It wouldn't be wrong. Exactly.*

"It wouldn't be right, though, would it?"

Her brow furrowed and she crossed her legs as she leaned over her knee. Like he was utterly fascinating. It used to put him off, the way she reacted to him, as if he were so important, or so interesting. Now he liked it. Lord knows he was rarely interesting or important these days.

"Why?" she asked.

"Because of the boys." He couldn't quite believe she needed to ask that question. Wasn't it obvious?

"You think it's going to bother the boys if their uncle has a relationship with a woman. Don't you think it would be odder if you didn't?"

"I don't want any more upheaval. What if we date and it doesn't work out?"

She sighed. "How long has it been since you've been on a date?"

Eight months, three weeks and a couple of days. He wasn't much of a dater but that was the last time he'd had sex so that's what he was going to count.

"You're entitled to a life, you know," Dr. Gilman said.

"Tell that to the boys."

"You tell that to the boys." She put down her notebook. "Get out of here."

"What?" He glanced up at the clock. "We have twenty more minutes."

"Right, but you know what you need more than me, right now? A beer. At a bar. With other adults. Perhaps you could call Lucy."

"But the boys—"

"Are safe at home with their grandparents."

"You trying to skip out on our appointment?"

"No. I'm trying to get you to see that your life isn't over. It's just different."

She stood and reluctantly, slightly belligerently, he stood, too. "I better not get charged for this," he grumbled, grabbing his hat from the rack.

"I'll see to it myself," she said, and slowly walked him to the door. Crazily, he wanted to ask her how. How was he supposed to go to a bar? Alone? What was he supposed to say? The King of Small Talk had a case of the nerves.

"It'll come to you," she said, as if she could read his mind. "It's like riding a bike." She patted his shoulder, all but pushing him out the door.

An hour later he stepped into the Sunset Bar, took one look at all the backs and hats and the people in conversation and realized this was no longer his scene.

He used to pride himself on the fact that there wasn't a bar in the world he couldn't call home. And now the first bar he ever drank in was totally foreign to him.

I should go, he thought. Head on home and maybe spend some time with Ben and Cynthia. See why no one ever picked flowers for him. He had one foot back out the door, when the bartender spotted him over some guy's hat.

"Jeremiah!" Joey cried, lifting a hand. "We haven't seen you around here in a long time."

Two men turned toward him and with a huge sigh of relief he recognized both of them.

"Hey there, Joey," he said, walking into the bar and picking a stool next to the men he knew.

"What can I get you?" Joey asked.

"A Bud."

"How you been keeping?" Joey asked, popping the top off a bottle and sliding it across the wood toward him. Jeremiah caught it like the beer-catching pro he used to be.

"Busy," Jeremiah answered, "you know."

"Three kids will do that to you," the quiet man next to him said.

"Phil, good to see you," Jeremiah said. Phil ran the feed shop, and twice a week they talked about weather. It wasn't much of a relationship, but right now Jeremiah clung to it like a lifeboat. Shaking hands like they were old friends.

"Our youngest just started sleeping through the night," Phil said, "and Mary's talking about having another one...."

Jeremiah shuddered but the man on the other side of Phil smiled, splitting his wild Grizzly Adam's beard.

"Dr. Puese," Jeremiah said, leaning forward to shake the big-animal vet's hand. "What's got you out at a bar on a Saturday night?"

"Susan's got book club. I learned it's best to skedaddle or I get an earful about things I got no business hearing about. Those girls don't talk about books." He arched a bushy eyebrow before taking a sip from his bottle. "Worse than a locker room, I swear."

Jeremiah laughed and eased back on his stool. His shoulders adopting the international beer-drinking posture. His elbows finding that sweet spot at the edge of the bar, where the wood had been worn into divots by a hundred other elbows.

"Aren't you going to say hello to me, Jeremiah Stone?" At the far end of the bar, the person reading the newspaper lowered the paper. And sitting there, like a teenage dream in a clingy black shirt with red lipstick and glittering eyes, was Lucy Alatore.

And suddenly this night was looking a whole lot better.

JEREMIAH SPUN TOWARD HER, his back to the men he sat beside.

"Well, well, well," he said.

She tried to breathe normally, but it was as if her skin got tighter just by his attention.

Everything just seemed sharper with him around. As if there was an edge of excitement to the mundane. As if there was a chance that this could be the most thrilling night of her life.

She'd always sensed this about him, but tonight it was turned way up. No wonder Reese came up here to spend his money; Lucy would do the same thing if she had any money.

Such was the power of Jeremiah Stone.

His eyes touched Lucy's face, the lipstick she'd put on because she thought she looked so tired and worn without it. The black shirt that her mother said was going to give men the wrong impression, and from the look in Jeremiah's eye as he traced the neckline with his gaze, she'd have to give the point to her mother.

Jeremiah was getting an impression all right, but Lucy couldn't say if it was wrong.

"What's a nice girl like you doing in a place like this?" he asked, and she laughed, because he'd meant her to, because he was so charming that such a cheesy line got new life coming from his mouth.

"Waiting for you to get so drunk you pay me money to drive you home." She lifted the cup of coffee she'd been nursing all night to her lips and took a sip. Terrible. Really, really awful coffee. If this taxi thing was going to work out, Joey was going to have to invest in some decent coffee. Maybe clean the machine out for the first time this decade.

"You're still doing this?"

"A woman's got to work." She tried to sound as if she believed in this taxi thing. But she knew it was ridiculous. She knew it was a bizarre downward turn for her. It was one thing to run Patty and the girls to the Snip and Curl for their hair appointments, but hanging out here waiting for drunk cowboys was a new low.

But she could not sit at that ranch tonight, doing nothing. Counting the money she owed people, praying the condo sold well enough to clear her out of half her debt.

Watching her mother knit.

It was insane. And this…this ridiculous taxi business was her only alternative.

"You're going to drive drunk cowboys home wearing that?"

"You sound like my mother." She leaned back, confident in not only what she'd worn, but in the fact that she could handle a drunk cowboy. She'd been doing it for a number of years. Drunk men were sort of a specialty of hers. A product of Walter.

"Well, your mother is a smart woman." He stood up from his seat, all smooth charm gone as he towered over her. "You want to drive people around, fine—you can drive my boys all you like. I'll pay you. But this…" He jerked his thumb behind him at the crowd of men and women behind him. "This is asking for trouble."

"You know, Jeremiah," she said, her temper pricked by his high-handedness. "I am a grown woman."

"Yeah, a beautiful, sexy grown woman who shouldn't be alone in a car with half the men in here, even when they're sober."

The beautiful sexy thing she'd seen in his eyes when he looked at her, in his lips when they'd kissed. But it was sort of shocking to hear him say it. An electric current charged through her, waking her body up in a painful rush.

"You sure you want to talk about this?" she deflected. "I'd hate for it to get too deep and you break into hives."

"If I do just tell me what color your underwear is."

It was the devil, the devil in her, the devil in his eyes, the devil that didn't understand what she was doing wasting her time with a taxi service. The devil made her lean forward, close enough to smell him, spicy and manly and clean. "What underwear?" she whispered.

His laughter boomed through the bar, turning everyone's head. "You are a wicked, wicked woman, Lucy Alatore."

She leaned back, satisfied and giddy with the power of the attraction between them. It was dangerous, she knew that, but...well, it was fun.

"So, this taxi business?"

"You won't let go of this, will you?"

His grin was pure sex. Knowledgeable, wild sex. This was going to be fun.

"I'm working on some commitment issues."

"Really? Me, too."

"I knew we were alike."

"I think I have the opposite commitment issue as you." She folded the paper with a sharp crack.

"What exactly are you saying?" he asked, pretending to be wounded.

"I've done one job and one job only my entire life. It's been jewelry and design since I was a teenager—over twenty years, Jeremiah."

"You say that like it's a bad thing, most people would love to have a calling. Hell, if I could still ride I'd be in the rodeo."

"But I failed at that calling. Or it failed me, I don't know. I just know it's time for me to do something different."

"What does that have to do with commitment? Or us?"

She leaned forward, resting her chin in her hand, looking him square in his beautiful eyes. "How many woman have you slept with?"

"No way." He shook his head. "I will never tell you."

"Because you're embarrassed?"

"No. I mean, it's not that many. Everyone thinks because a man knows how to talk to a woman he's slept with half the population."

"And you haven't?"

"I haven't."

"I've slept with three men."

He gaped at her. Shook his head as if he'd been punched in the ear. "Now, I've had a lot of sex with those men, but it's only been three. I'm thirty-six years old."

"You want to cat around a little? Sow some wild oats? Because if you're taking applications—"

"Cat around? Who says that?"

He shrugged. "Desperate men."

She stared at him, close enough to see the flecks of black in his brilliant blue eyes. Close enough to smell him, to taste him if she was bold enough to lean forward to press her lips to his. And she was plenty bold, but she wasn't ready for that. She wanted more of this delicious possibility that seemed to surround Jeremiah Stone. She wanted more of the buildup, the ecstatic expectation. "When have you ever been desperate, Jeremiah?"

He touched her arm, just the tips of his fingers against the fragile skin at her wrist, and the night detonated around her; lust and excitement laced the air she breathed, filtered through her clothes to touch her skin with sparks.

"I have never been as desperate as I am right now."

Enough, she thought, and leaned forward to kiss him.

Lucy was situated right beside the hallway leading back to the bathrooms and one of the last standing pay phones in the world. A cowboy stepped out of the hallway into the bar, adjusting his zipper and belt buckle, shattering their little bubble of intimacy.

Jeremiah dropped her wrist just as the cowboy weaved toward them and Lucy had the suspicion she was looking at her first customer for the night.

"Hey." Drunk Cowboy smiled lewdly. "You that woman giving guys a ride home?"

The way he said it was slightly skeevy, a little too close to ugly innuendo, but before she could say anything, Jeremiah was up and off his stool.

"Walk on by." Jeremiah stepped close to the man in a way that was only aggressive.

"Just asking the woman a question about her business practices." The guy laughed and she quickly leaned between the two men, smiling at the drunk cowboy.

"If Joey says you've had too much to drink to drive home, I can give you a ride. My rates double, though, if you're an asshole."

Drunk Cowboy was offended. "Are you calling me an asshole?"

"Not at all. But my friend might, so I'd keep going, just to be safe."

Drunk Cowboy scowled at her and at Jeremiah, who bristled. The former rodeo champ saddled with his dead sister's three children was a bad kind of powder keg and he didn't need this kind of drama.

The man walked by and Jeremiah gaped at her. "You're kidding with this, right?"

"I'm not talking about this with you." She sat back down and picked up her coffee, ignoring the look he was giving her.

Finally he returned to his stool and finished his beer in one long swallow. Catching Joey's eye he lifted his hand for another.

"Is it your intention to get drunk so I have to drive you home?" she asked.

"No, but it's a good idea, if it keeps you away from guys like him."

"It's not, and you know it. You'd have to pay me to take you back to your truck tomorrow morning and miss half a morning of work."

Joey slid him another beer and he took a quick sip.

"What are you even doing here, Jeremiah? Where are the boys?" she asked, peeved with him. All that quiet heat between them earlier was raging into a different fire and she found herself itching for a fight.

"With their grandparents." He stared up at the ceiling, stretching his long neck so much that she saw the white skin under the edge of his shirt.

"You all right?" she asked.

His laugh was bitter and dark, like the bad coffee in her cup.

"I do not want to talk about whether or not I am all right. I don't want to talk. I am so done with talking about myself."

Okay, she thought, leaning away. There was a dangerous sparkle around him, something manic in his eyes.

"You want to get out of here?" he asked, and her stomach twisted, torn between desire and better sense.

"And do what?"

His eyes sparkled. "Minigolf. What do you think?"

She laughed, low in her chest, more turned on just sitting here than she'd been in years. Just the prospect of walking out that door with him, the half-formed imaginings of what they would do to each other, made her fingers shake. Her breathing speed up.

Part of her wanted to play a game with him, drag this out. The anticipation was so delicious. And part of her was scared. Scared silly to leave with him. To embark on some affair when she was such a mess. When she liked him so much.

"You want to leave?"

"That is just the beginning of what I want." He tilted his head, watching her, studying her, his eyes hot with appreciation. "I'm tired of being in my own head, Lucy. Worrying constantly if I'm doing the right thing. And I think…maybe you're tired of that, too."

It was as if he'd read her mind.

"I want to feel something."

This was her time to back out, to put the right kind of distance between them, but then he leaned in, his breath smelling like beer and gum.

"I dare you," he whispered.

In the blink of an eye she was on fire for him. The wildness surrounding him—the excitement that crackled in his eyes. It was contagious, that excitement, and she wanted more.

She felt alive. For the first time in a very long time, she felt utterly alive.

Attraction and intent sizzled and burned in the air around them. The bar, the twenty people milling around, all of it vanished and it was just them. In the whole wide world it was just them.

Normally she didn't think about how long it had been since she'd had sex. Because sex in her relationships was only part of the equation. When lust attacked she could handle it on her own, but the burn in her body was specific to this man.

She wanted him. Needed him. And only Jeremiah Stone would do.

And he was looking at her like he felt the same way.

"Joey," she said without looking away from Jeremiah, "don't call me. I'm busy."

She reached back, grabbed her purse and followed him out the door into the night.

CHAPTER ELEVEN

THE CHILL IN THE EVENING air did nothing to cool her down—if anything she stepped closer to Jeremiah, longing for his skin against hers, his heat through the thin fabric of his shirt.

She had no idea where they were going—a car, probably. A bed, hopefully.

But once they were in the shadows on the far side of the bar, he turned and jerked her into his arms, rough and wild, and she met him halfway, leaning back, her hips against his, her arms around his neck.

She found his lips in the darkness and the night exploded.

Kiss after kiss, a hundred of them, a thousand spilling into one another. She opened her mouth, let in his tongue and he groaned, pulling her against him until she could feel the hard ridge of his erection beneath his zipper.

Yes, she thought, *yes, and more please, more.*

He sucked on her tongue and she gasped, pulling herself into him with her arms, unable to get close enough. She could crawl into his skin and it wouldn't be enough.

Porn star words were coming to her lips; she wanted to ask him to do things to her they had no business doing against a building.

As if he realized that, too, he broke away, his face tight in the shadows, his lips wet. Her breath shuddered in her body and she honestly didn't know what to say or do. She slid her fingers up under his shirt, feeling the situation gaining a dizzying momentum.

"You're so beautiful. So alive," he breathed, pushing her hair back off her cheek, his thumb touching the corner of her mouth and she licked it as it went by. He groaned and brought his thumb back to her lips, tracing the edges with rough calluses.

Frustrated, and so very turned on, she put her teeth to his skin, raking them across his thumb, and he smiled, wicked and dirty.

"That's how I feel, too. Come on."

He grabbed her hand, putting distance between them, but then stopped. "My house is too crowded," he said. "Yours is, too."

Some of the glitter drained off him, real life returning drip by drip to destroy the excitement, the life in his face.

"Oh, man," he muttered, his shoulders slumping.

She had no idea why she was doing this, except that she knew her excitement was tied to his, and if his died, hers would and she wasn't ready for that. She wanted to see where this kind of desire led.

And she wanted to see him animated. Not worn down. Jeremiah as he used to be, as he could be again, with her.

She tugged his hand, pulling him into the shadows behind the bar, glad the garbage Dumpster was on the other side, until she felt the roughness of the brick against her back. They bumped into something in the dark and he fell against her, kicking whatever was at their feet aside.

It was nothing but darkness back here, bushes along one side—honeysuckle by the smell of things.

"Someone could come out here," he said, arching himself, bit by bit, against her. Hips, chest, lips. They were a combination lock, and he knew how it worked.

"They could."

"They could see us." Both of his hands pushed up against the bricks by her head, blocking her in. Securing her. It was just them and the heat and the lust and the fire between them. A delight of their own making.

"I suppose."

His tempting grin was back. "Why, Ms. Alatore, I had no idea you were so naughty."

I'm not, she thought. *It's you. It's us. I've never done anything like this. I've never felt even a tenth of what you're making me feel and we still have our clothes on.*

He brushed his face against her neck, the rough scrape of his stubble sending sensation racing over and under her skin. His breath kissed her skin, her cheeks, the points of her ears.

Oh, she was melting inside, melting against him. He pushed a knee between her legs as if to keep her up and she thanked him by pressing her hot core against the hard muscle of his leg. Riding it, her own thigh pressed high against his erection, and he leaned his head against the wall beside hers. Groaning low in his throat.

Reckless, wild with adrenaline and lust, she put her hand against the hard muscles of his stomach and slipped her palm down the waist of his pants until her fingers touched the top of his erection. The soft spongy head, the little drops of liquid he couldn't control.

His hand helped hers unbutton his jeans and she sighed with delight as she had full access to Jeremiah. She cupped him, reached beneath his erection to find all of him, and he growled, clenching her hair in his hands as he kissed her.

Wild, he kissed her with none of the finesse she'd expected from a man like Jeremiah. No teasing. No seduction. It was rabid need and barely controlled. It was Jeremiah as she never, ever thought she'd experience him. Utterly undone and at her mercy. His hips arched into her hands and she stroked him, harder, faster, not sure of where this was going, but not wanting to stop.

"Lucy," he breathed, biting her lips, sucking on the skin of her neck. "Oh, God, baby, it's so good. So. Good."

She didn't realize but she was bucking her hips against his knee, pushing herself toward her own orgasm even as she pushed him toward his. She felt powerful and feminine and desired in the extreme.

"Baby." He put his hands over hers, stopping her, though he couldn't seem to stop himself from pushing himself through their fingers. He hissed, arching his head back and she licked his throat.

His laughter was dark and pained and he stepped back, and she followed but he put a hand at her hip. Between her legs fire raged and she felt as if she'd had a thousand too many drinks.

"I don't have any condoms."

It took a second for the words to make sense.

"Do you?" he asked. She would have laughed at his hopeful expression if she'd been able to; instead, she shook her head.

He swore, resting his forehead against hers. "Probably for the better. I don't want the first time I have sex with you to be outside a bar."

"That's very sweet, Jeremiah, but I'm dying."

His lip quirked. "Dying?"

"You have no idea."

He glanced down at the shadows between his legs where she knew his erection was probably pounding in time with his heartbeat. Much like what was happening between her legs.

Slowly, one by one, her fingers found him, curled

over the hard muscle and skin, until he was back in her palm, stepping toward her willingly.

"There are other things we can do," she whispered. She took his hand and put it against her breast.

Jeremiah was a smart man and she didn't have to give him any more hints. His big broad hand, those long calloused fingers, cupped her breast, found the hard point of her nipple and rolled it slowly until the tension hurt. Deliciously.

"Is this what you want?" he breathed.

"More."

Both hands slipped up under her shirt. Rough, his hands yanked at the lace and silk of her bra; something tore and she loved it. *Yes. Yes, and yes.* A barely in control cowboy, this was what she wanted. What she'd needed and never known.

His fingers pulled at her nipples; his eyes watched her face, gauging just how much pain she liked with her pleasure until he found the combination that made her wild.

She used her thumb to gather what moisture leaked from the top of his erection and spread it down the shaft. And then again. Again. Faster.

"That's what you want?" he asked through clenched teeth, his hands fumbling at the button at the top of her jeans. In a heartbeat, his hand was down her pants, twisting, shifting until…

"Oh, God. Yes!" she cried as his finger, one and then another, speared into the slick heat of her. His thumb found the hard ridge that made her see stars. Her hand squeezed his erection until he laughed, pained.

"You," he said, lifting her hand away from his body. "You first."

He worked her. Owned her.

She cried out, her head tilted back. "You have to be quiet," he breathed in her ear, even that sensation sending her someplace new.

"I can't… Oh, Jeremiah." She put her hands against his shoulders, using him as leverage as she arched herself against his hands, her hips a piston in the night.

He slapped a hand over her mouth.

"Someone will hear."

She cried out against his fingers, used her teeth against his palm, and in the darkness she found the light of his eyes. Blue fire that burned away everything but what he made her feel.

She didn't look away. Couldn't. His hand over her mouth, his fingers inside her, and she came, eyes wide open.

What the hell was that? Jeremiah wondered, feeling as if he'd been given a million dollars. The key to the city, a king's crown. Lucy Alatore was the most passionate, most exciting woman he'd ever had the privilege of touching. Ever.

And he was oddly humbled in the back alley behind this bar.

Oddly reverent.

He lifted his hand from her mouth and kissed her lips in apology. Kissed the red marks on her cheeks his fingers had left. Reluctant to leave the hot, wet pocket he'd found, he slowly slipped his fingers from her. Cataloging every silken inch of her. She shook and trembled, her body jerking in wild aftershocks as his fingers slipped over sensitive skin and then, just because he wanted to, he went back one more time.

"No. Jeremiah," she breathed. "No more."

"Sorry." He buttoned her pants and reached for his,

but her hands got there first and at the first touch of her fingers he jerked.

"Baby, I'm…" He felt like a teenager. Young and untried and so close to losing control it was embarrassing. If he just had a second, a minute even, he'd get himself under control so at the first touch of her hand he wouldn't come all over her like a fifteen-year-old.

But she wasn't going to give him a minute. Her hands, busy and hot, slipped into the open V of his pants.

"Hard," she breathed, licking his neck. "So hard."

Yes. Yes. He resisted, easing away, but she stopped him.

"Let me," she breathed, stroking him hard and then harder. Slow and then faster.

His grip on her shoulder was too hard, he knew that, and he was biting his tongue so hard he could taste blood. He was going to embarrass himself, but there was no walking away from this.

He jerked, putting his hand over hers to push her away, but she linked her hand with his, and the sensation was too much. He jerked. And again, spilling himself over their fingers.

All he could hear for several long moments was the pounding of his heart in his ears. His brain was short-circuiting, his wires crossed.

Did I just…all over her…behind a bar?

She shifted, her hands leaving his body, and all sorts of reason and sense rushed in with the cool air.

"Um…" Her fingers were a mess, so was he and he felt like such a child. Such a green boy. Eight months since he'd touched a woman and this is what comes of him. For a man who used to pride himself on being able to say no when the moment required, he certainly had been unable tonight.

He blamed Lucy. Irresistible Lucy.

"Here." He pulled his handkerchief from his pocket; something was stuck in there with it and it fell to the ground. He ignored it and wiped her hands. "Sorry."

"Sorry?"

He didn't look up at her, unsure of what he would see. Diligently he just kept cleaning them both up.

"That was—"

"A mistake?" He felt thin. Like all of the cracks in his foundation were creeping up and over his body, revealing all his weakness.

"Do you think it was a mistake?" She touched his face, lifting his chin so he had to meet her eyes. Her liquid, slightly wounded eyes.

It would be easy to say yes, to bundle all of this up as a one-off, a mistake never to be repeated, but he wanted a repeat. From what was happening in his pants he wanted a repeat immediately.

"No." He tucked his handkerchief back in his pocket. "But we could have been caught. Who does that, Lucy?"

"We do!" she erupted with light, a glee she'd clearly been suppressing. Her smile was womanly. Her black hair wild around her face, her eyes wide in the half-light.

Beautiful, he thought. *She's the most beautiful woman I've ever seen.*

"I've never done anything like that before. Ever." She made it sound like they'd egged a house, broke into the high school: something innocent and naughty at the same time.

The bark of his laughter startled a bird in the bushes past the stone wall they leaned against.

"Honestly, Jeremiah Stone." She leaned up and kissed his cheek, a spark against his skin. "That was perfect."

"Perfect? Perfect would have been a king-size bed. A couple of condoms—"

"Oh, I have no doubt but that you would rock a king-size bed. And I hope to find out all your tricks. But this…" She sighed, her head falling back.

"Just what you needed?" he joked, still uncomfortable, still shaken.

She stood up from against the wall, putting her hands on his cheeks, looking deep into his eyes in a way he found utterly intrusive but was unable to stop.

"Don't pretend like you didn't need that, too. Something wild. Something a little dirty? Fun?"

I just need to be touched. The thought came out of nowhere, and shook him down to his boots. He kissed her lips, and stepped away, needing a little distance from the satiated woman in his arms. The thing that had fallen from his pocket crunched under his boot heel. A half-eaten bag of crackers.

Casey's after-school snack.

Reality hammered down around him like a cold driving rain.

This is not for you, Stone, he told himself. *Do not get attached to the fun this woman brings to your life. Those boys, that's your life now.*

"It's getting late," he said, "the boys—"

She blinked, the radiance fading as he forced real life upon their wickedness.

"Sure. I, ah… Have you seen my purse?"

He picked it up from the ground behind them and handed it to her. "You're not…you're not going back in there, are you?"

"No." She took a deep breath and swung the purse up over her shoulder. "I know the taxi idea is ridiculous, Jeremiah. I know it's not me, or what I do, but I don't do the thing that made me me anymore and I…well…I guess I'm floundering."

"You're allowed to flounder, Lucy."

She smiled into his face, cupping his cheek in her soft hand. "So are you, Jeremiah."

"Well—" he took a deep breath "—I'd like to flounder with you again sometime."

She laughed and the bird in the bushes finally gave up his roost, flying up into the night. "Me, too, Jeremiah, me, too."

They walked, not quite hand in hand, but with their arms touching as if their skin was magnetized, and maybe it was, he thought.

"I'll pick up Aaron on Tuesday," she said.

"I thought you weren't doing the taxi thing."

Her fingers touched his face, glanced off his cheek, his lips. "It's a favor," she said. "For a friend."

She got in the car and drove away and he watched until the red of her taillights disappeared into the distance.

Friend. He tasted the word, rolled it around on his tongue. It's why he'd come to the bar tonight, why Dr. Gilman had sent him out of her office.

But she didn't feel like any friend he'd ever had before. And it wasn't because of what they'd done behind this bar. It was because in this new landscape he lived in now, he'd never had a friend. Maybe when life was hard, friendships came with some extra complexities. All his drinking buddies from the old life, they had faded away after the accident and he barely mourned them.

What could they possibly have in common?

Reese, the most stubborn of them, was still calling, but not with the same frequency after his visit up here.

Friend.

He didn't know how to feel about it, so in the end he just left it alone, watching her car vanish until the heat she'd called to his skin, to his heart, turned cool, and then finally when he was numb again he got in his car and headed home.

CHAPTER TWELVE

TUESDAY AFTERNOON, THE SECOND the car door closed behind Aaron he talked. He talked nonstop. About hockey. About school. Kids she'd never heard of. It was as if the boy's cork had been stuck and she managed to get it free, just by putting him in her car.

The only word in edgewise she managed to get in was when she noticed a sign for McDonald's and asked him if he wanted something to eat.

"I've got a sandwich," he said. He pulled out a smooshed peanut-butter-and-jelly from his school bag and offered her some of it.

So charming, these Stone boys. She smiled and waved it off. "I'm fine."

It took him a few minutes to eat and the silence that filled the car was slightly awkward. A little too aware.

"Is Ben actually working at your house?" he asked, scrunching up the sandwich's plastic bag and shoving it in his book bag.

"Why do you ask?"

"Because I don't think he is."

"He's not exactly cooperative."

Aaron laughed through his nose. "He's making Uncle J. crazy."

She put her elbow out her opened window, holding back the hair that wanted to fly in her face. "That is true."

"Do you think he'll leave?"

"Who? Ben?"

Aaron shook his head. "Uncle Jeremiah."

She gaped at him for a moment. "Why…why would you say that?"

Aaron shrugged and looked away and Lucy felt her stomach bottom out. These boys and their pain was so endlessly surprising. So shocking.

"He doesn't like it with us. He misses the rodeo. He… he misses his old life."

She could say no, he doesn't, but they both knew it was a lie. "Just because he misses his old life doesn't mean he doesn't like it with you guys."

Aaron shot her a look that was far too old. "Ben is going to make him leave. I know it."

"He's your uncle—"

"So?"

"So, you're family."

"That doesn't mean he'll stay."

"He loves you."

Aaron's lips twisted as if he were chewing on the inside of his cheek, and she knew, she could see it, that he didn't believe that for a moment. Not one moment did this boy believe his uncle loved him.

Oh, Jeremiah, what are you doing with these boys?

"So tell me about this team you're playing today. Are they good?"

"Best team in the league."

"So, you're gonna kill 'em, right?"

He grinned sideways at her and launched into his team's entire defensive strategy. Twenty minutes went by. A half hour. She thought about planting a salsa garden like she'd read about, all the ingredients needed to make the dip. So practical.

She realized he was silent. Blinking at her as if he expected a response.

"You really like hockey, huh?" she asked.

He looked down at his thumb, rubbing at a worn spot on the shoulder strap of his backpack. "My dad taught me."

His voice was gruff and he turned and looked out the window, hiding his face and grief.

She took the next exit off the highway and the community center was just to their left. She pulled into the parking lot and turned off the car.

"Here we are," she said, and checked her watch. "Right on time."

"Thanks," Aaron said, his earnestness making her blush, making her painfully aware that she was doing for money what other women would do for free.

"I'll be done in two hours," he said. "If you...you know where to meet me?"

"Are you kidding me?" she asked. She grabbed her purse. "This is my first hockey game, mister. I didn't drive all this way not to see it."

"You're going to watch?"

"Duh."

He beamed at her. Radiant in his pleasure.

"Awesome," he crowed, and barreled out of the car, into the sunlight.

Why was Aaron so much easier than Ben? she wondered. Maybe instead of trying to get Ben to work all she needed to do was lock him in a car and drive around until he broke.

She smiled as she climbed out of the car, walking across cracked pavement to a tiny, slightly run-down ice arena that she'd never even heard of before.

The ground dipped beneath her and she had one of

those moments—slightly out of body—of not recognizing herself in this landscape. Dressed in her own clothes, her own skin, she felt like a stranger to herself.

Dropping a boy off at a hockey game, making him happy by going in to watch, talking about his grief. She was miles, literally hundreds of them, away from the life she thought she'd have. The life she thought she'd wanted more than anything.

And she wasn't entirely sure that was a bad thing.

JEREMIAH TRIED REALLY HARD not to seem like some kind of hovering parent, but in the end he just gave up and sat on the porch, waiting for Lucy and Aaron to come back from Beauregard.

The game was a big deal—Aaron's team was up against their rival, and he felt really shitty that he couldn't be there. He liked being at the games, Ben and Casey sitting beside him while they watched Aaron carve up the ice. It was one of the few times he felt like they were really a family.

Perhaps it was time to change some things around the ranch. Hire a full-time housekeeper—he'd been reluctant up until now, largely because Cynthia was helping out and he didn't want another woman in the house making the boys upset. But he was missing too much of the important stuff, worrying about garbage and laundry.

But laced with his nerves and excitement to hear about Aaron's game was the fact that Lucy was going to be here. He hadn't seen her since Saturday night, but he'd been thinking about her nearly every other minute since then with a nearly fatiguing mixture of shame and excitement.

Honestly, it was like he was sixteen and he had the hots for the senior cheerleader. He'd put away his anxiety about growing too attached to her. She was leaving—it wasn't even a question. If he could just keep that in mind, then they could have all the fun and trouble they wanted.

Finally headlights speared through the bruised twilight and he stood, the rocking chair banging into the backs of his knees.

"They're back!" he yelled through the open screen door.

"Does that mean we can eat?" Casey asked.

The car stopped in front of the house and he stepped down off the porch just as the passenger door was thrown open.

"Well?" Jeremiah asked.

Aaron's face said it all. He gleamed in victory. "We won, four to three in overtime."

"Thatta boy!" he cried, pulling Aaron into his arms for a quick hard hug.

"He was great," Lucy said, and he turned, meeting her eyes over the roof of her car.

"You watched?" he asked, stunned at the thought.

"Of course!" She smiled at Aaron, who blushed. "It was a great game. Aaron was the star."

"Really?"

"Scored the winning goal," Aaron said, trying to be cool about it.

Oh, kid, Jeremiah thought, *you kill me. You really do.*

"Well," Jeremiah said, beaming at Aaron, messing up his hair. "This calls for a celebration."

"I thought Casey ate all Grandma's cake—"

"No. I was thinking pizza. In town."

From inside the house Casey whooped and Aaron pulled his hockey bag from where it had been crammed in the Civic's trunk.

"Sound good?" Jeremiah asked.

"Sounds great! You coming?" Aaron asked Lucy, his eyes alight.

"Ahhhh…" She glanced over at Jeremiah as if she, too, was aware of how every decision somehow changed the scales in their life.

It's just fun, Stone. Just some simple fun.

"Please," Jeremiah said. "It would be great to have you."

She drummed her fingers against the roof of the car, her bracelets and rings making a tinkling music. "Okay."

"Cool," Aaron crowed, and walked off, leaving him in the twilight with Lucy.

"I haven't been to the arcade in twenty years," she said.

"It's where I take all my dates."

Her eyebrows popped. "Is this a date?"

"Hell, yes. Meat lover's pizza and three half-size chaperones? This is top-shelf dating, Lucy. You better prepare yourself for some serious romance."

"Oh, I'm prepared." She tucked one leg back into the car, still watching him over the hood with her glittering eyes. "I'll meet you there."

When Lucy considered having a fun affair with Jeremiah Stone the Pizza World and Arcade had not been a part of her vision. She sat at a table, waiting for Jeremiah and the boys, surrounded by neon lights and the bleeps and buzzers of video games.

Pizza World had not changed one iota since her youth. Maybe the games had been updated, but the booths, the red candles, the pictures of the town's early days—still the same. For some reason, that made her inexplicably happy. The whole world changed faster than she could get ahold of, but right here, it was the same. There was comfort in that. Comfort in knowing who she was here. Instead of trying to change to fit the world she lived in, she didn't have to do anything to fit in here.

She just was.

It had been five long years since she just was. Since she wasn't compelled to be more, to more people. The lights flickered and beeped around her and she thought of a wide, thick-collar necklace. Amber stones set in gold. The colors of California dust. She jerked, the Coke in her hand sloshing over her fingers. Before she even realized what she was doing she reached for her purse and the notebook she kept there, but then she remembered— there was no notebook.

That belonged to a different life.

She was so thrown by the inspiration, the creative thought, that she didn't notice Jeremiah standing in front of her.

"Hey," he said, "you all right?"

"Fine." It took her a moment but finally she shook her head and smiled up at him. "Where are the boys?"

"I gave them each a roll of quarters and they scattered to the winds." His long lean body draped over the chair across from her. So elegant and controlled, graceful even. His body was sculpted by work and life and he wore his power so easily. Her fingers twitched, her body purred.

He was gorgeous.

The teenage girl who'd brought her the Coke came back, blushing and tucking her hair behind her ears.

"Hey there," Jeremiah said, grinning at the girl. "We're gonna need a pitcher of Coke and two pizzas. Large." He glanced sideways at Lucy. "You don't want anything crazy on your pizza, do you?"

"Crazy? Like what?"

"Like vegetables?"

"Tomatoes are madness, aren't they?"

"The Stone men don't want vegetables touching their meat." She snorted, but he wasn't kidding. He had said it with a straight face.

"Go for it. It's your party."

"Meat Lover's," he told the server. "Extra sausage, extra ground beef."

"Oh, my Lord." She sighed, heavily appalled. "Add a side salad," she told the server. "Ranch dressing on the side."

The server nodded and walked away, joining her comrades behind the register who all whispered behind their hands while staring at Jeremiah.

"I remember being here when I was twelve years old and even then the servers stared at you from the counter. Nothing has changed."

"If you clap your hands they'll scatter like birds," he said, turning toward her, his back to his audience.

"You think?"

He lifted his hands, clapped once and the girls split in four different directions. She howled with laughter.

"You should see what they do to Aaron. They practically stalk him."

"I can imagine."

"The first time we came here and I saw how the girls looked at him I freaked out, turned back home and gave him the talk."

"The talk?"

"Straight up birds and bees."

"How did that go?"

"It wasn't as bad as I thought it would be. Maybe because I'm his uncle and not his mom or dad, I don't know. But he asked questions and I tried to be as honest as I could. Gave him a handful of condoms—"

"He's eleven!"

"I know, but apparently kids are doing it in kindergarten these days!"

"Come on—"

"I'm barely exaggerating. He doesn't look eleven and eleven-year-old girls don't look eleven. And it's not like I think he's going to have sex tomorrow. I just...I just want him to be safe." Jeremiah ran his hands through his hair, the black curls looping around his fingers like rings.

"You're a good man," she whispered.

Don't, she tried telling herself. *Do not fall for this man and his doubt and worry and heartbreaker's grin.*

But she worried that in so many ways it was too late. It would be so easy to fall for him; she worried it was already done. She'd fallen and didn't even realize it.

"Because I gave an eleven-year-old condoms?"

"You care for those boys."

He carefully organized the cutlery into a tidy square in front of him, not looking at her. "Then why won't Ben talk to me?"

"Maybe he doesn't know how you feel."

He leaned back and stared at her as if she'd suggested he take off his clothes and dance on the pinball game. "They know. Of course they know. I'm there, aren't I?"

She'd touched a nerve. A terrible nerve. But she couldn't back down. Her investment in this family was too great. "Maybe they need to hear you say it."

He was blank-faced and it was obvious that the thought had never occurred to him. So well-intentioned but so lost, she couldn't resist him. She reached over for his hand, rubbing her thumb over his knuckles until he twisted his hand around and clutched her fingers. His

fingers slid between hers and she felt the ripple and tremble across her skin, like a stone thrown into still waters.
She was disturbed, restless at his touch.

"My parents—" He cleared his throat. "My parents
were really private people. Annie, too. Ben comes by
it honestly, all this silent brooding. Words…important
words don't come easy for us."

Carefully, not wanting to startle him, or stop him
talking, but unable to resist, she reached up and touched
the hair falling over his forehead. The silky curl twined
around her fingers into a ring.

"You know, Annie didn't even tell me she was sick
until it was too late." His pain was obvious, needles buried deep under his skin that were painful to pull out. "It's
not like I could have done anything, but…you know, I
could have been there. Supported her and the kids. But
that's the way she was. It's the way we all are."

"Maybe the boys need something different?"

"What if I don't know how to do that?" he asked.

"Then maybe you need to learn."

He sighed deeply, as if sucking down all these
thoughts, burying them back where they'd come from.
Obliterating them as if they'd never been.

Don't, she thought, *you need to deal with this stuff.*

But then he smiled and the moment was over.

"Thanks for coming out," he said. "The boys appreciate it."

"Yeah, I can tell." She laughed, pointing to the empty
seats.

"Well…I appreciate it."

His knee pressed hers under the table and they were
curved toward each other, two parts of a circle connected at knees and hands. The other night rushed back
in sensory bites, the rough warmth of his hands on her

stomach, the sound of his zipper in the quiet, his voice groaning "Baby" in her ear.

Her heartbeat pounded between her legs.

"My question," Jeremiah asked, cocking his head, studying her, "is for a woman who has only dated three men, what were you doing flashing your breasts at Reese McKenna?"

She laughed, not breaking contact.

"It was the state championship, Jeremiah. I had to do my part."

"How…how is it a woman like you is single?" He said it as if he were truly mystified and she preened under his compliment. She was quite a catch if she did say so herself.

"I'm driven. Or was." She pulled her hands away. "Once it got to a certain point, no matter how hard I fell in love, it always felt like I had to make a choice. My career—my work—or marriage. I couldn't be fully committed to both of them." The flirtatious gleam in his eyes had vanished and her stomach dropped. "Too deep for you, Stone? You hyperventilating?"

"No, no…I was thinking I know exactly what you mean. With the boys. I could have a relationship, or I could be there for the boys. I can't have both. I can't be pulled in two directions."

Funny, but when he said it she saw the ways in which that wasn't totally true. How the right person, the right relationship, wouldn't make him feel like he had to make a choice. The right relationship would feel like support. A team.

She'd never seen it that way in her own life. And it felt as if someone had turned on a light in a room she'd never realized was pitch-black. Before she could make any kind of response, Ben came up to the table. "I need more quarters."

"Hello to you, too," Jeremiah said.

Ben glanced sideways at her. "Hey." He turned back to Jeremiah. "Can I have more quarters?"

"I told you when we came in that roll was all you got."

"That sucks."

"Ben." Jeremiah didn't yell but his tone was stony. Implacable. She wondered what Jeremiah would do if he knew how Ben had been swearing at her the other day.

"Sorry," Ben muttered, and slid down in the seat opposite her. His eyes on the edge of the table. Utterly and totally disengaged.

What will bring you back? she wondered.

"I didn't get a chance to ask how things went last Friday," Jeremiah said, stretching his arm out across the backs of the seats, his fingertips inches from Ben, as if he wanted to touch him but knew what the reception would be.

You should tell Jeremiah, she thought. *Tell him the truth.* That it was awful. That Ben wasn't doing anything she'd asked. That she was failing, even at this. That things weren't better, not like he thought. Not like he wanted.

But Jeremiah was looking at her, the creases between his eyes gone, the heavy weight of responsibility off his shoulders. He was relieved things seemed to be going well between her and Ben. She couldn't burst that for him, not yet.

But after the things he'd told her, what happened between them, lying to him felt...utterly wrong. They could be the bad guy together, maybe. Share this load.

Telling him was the right thing to do.

Inwardly, she braced herself. "Jeremiah—"

"Fine." Ben lifted his eyes and looked right at Lucy, as if daring her to contradict him. Daring her to tell the truth. "We worked in the garden and stuff."

What is this kid doing? she wondered, trying to find his angle.

"Yeah?" Jeremiah asked, looking pleased.

The silence stretched and she found herself too intrigued and maybe too cowardly to set things right.

"Yeah," Lucy agreed, and Ben grinned at her. "Things are going fine."

CHAPTER THIRTEEN

THROUGH THE KITCHEN WINDOW on Thursday morning, Sandra watched Mia and Carla, the latest applicant for housekeeper and nurse, approach Walter where he sat in the sun near the barn doors.

If you asked Sandra—and no one ever did—after Walter chased away the last two, they were scraping the bottom of the barrel. Carla looked mean. Looked like the kind of woman who overcooked meat and didn't like kids. Might pinch her mother when she moved too slow.

Maybe that's the kind of person Walter needs, she thought. Someone who wouldn't care what he thought of them. Would only care about him as long as she was paid. Would let him sit out there and whittle all damn day. Turning big sticks into little sticks.

The interview was brief. Mia said something, smiling in that big way of hers that meant she was trying real hard to be pleasant when pleasant didn't taste good.

Walter didn't look up, but seemed to be saying something. Mia hung her head, defeat in every line of her body, and after a second Carla made a vulgar gesture, turned around and walked to her car.

Mia was saying something to Walter, who only shrugged, like some kind of spoiled, surly teenager. Mia threw up her hands and left, getting into her truck and driving away, kicking up dust. Walter looked up, watching Mia drive away, and then as if he knew she was watching him, he looked at the house. Right at her.

Like a schoolgirl caught peeping, she whirled and ducked out of the way. *Ridiculous,* she thought, her hand on her hammering heart. *You are ridiculous.*

Since the touch of his lips on her wrist, she'd been rattled around him. As if a layer of skin had been removed and every glance, every breeze, made her all too aware of her nerve endings.

Sixty-two years old and she felt like a girl.

She used to feel this way about A.J. before they got married. Every touch of his hand as he passed her the hymnal at church would send her into ecstatic contemplations. Fevered daydreams.

Before it all went cold.

Stupid, she told herself. It was a kiss. On her wrist. From a man she didn't much like. Had she totally lost her mind? But it wasn't just the kiss. Not totally. "I will fight," he'd said in that detox-induced nightmare. And her spirit, wayward and sleeping since childhood, liked that.

I will fight.

And he was making good on that promise. He wasn't going to be cared for and tended like a child. He made his own breakfast these days and forced her out of the kitchen when it was time to do the dinner dishes.

"You've done enough," he'd said quietly last night, loading the dishwasher.

All these housekeepers coming to apply, he was chewing up and spitting out. And it was rude, but he was not going to be pushed around and she respected that. Liked that. Was...proud of him.

And what are you doing? she asked herself. *Hiding like a girl scared of her shadow? What happened to your fight?* Earlier this morning, she'd been thinking about A.J., lying in bed counting her lonely moments like a rosary.

With the kind of belligerence born of being thwarted and embarrassed, she threw some ham and cheese between two pieces of wheat bread and slapped it on a plate.

It's not like she knew what she was angry about. Or what she wanted to fight for; she just knew she was angry. And that was enough to send her outside and across the parking area to stand in front of him, scattering stones with the heels of her boots.

He glanced up at her and his knife slipped.

"Damn," he muttered, and lifted his thumb to his mouth.

"Did you cut yourself?" She put the sandwich down on the ground and reached for him but he shook his head.

"I'm fine. Just a knick." He smiled around his thumb as if to convince her.

Her heart thudded hard in her chest at that sweet smile of his and she dropped her hands.

"Didn't mean to spook you," she said.

"Don't worry none." He glanced at her from the corner of his eyes, furtive and searching all at the same time.

She liked it.

All of those men at her church in L.A.—widowers and divorced men, asking her out for coffee or ice cream after prayer group—handsome men, devout and reliable, some of them were even rich. But they left her cold. Unmoved.

Why this man? she wondered.

"I brought you a sandwich." She pointed to the sad sandwich beside his foot.

"It's 9:00 a.m," he pointed out, and she actually willed herself not to blush.

"Thought you might be hungry."

He pulled his thumb from his mouth and she saw the thin trickle of blood from the pad of his thumb. "You don't have to do that."

"You need a bandage."

"I'm fine, Sandra. I've had worse cuts in my life."

The silence stalled and sputtered around them. "What happened with Carla?"

"She left."

Sandra laughed before she could help herself. "Any idea why?"

"I told her to."

Sandra nodded as if that made sense. As if that were the wisest course of action. "They're running out of people willing to come out here and meet you."

"Good."

"You mean to make it hard on them?"

"I mean to not have a babysitter." He went back to his wood, the knife in his hand, despite the fact that he was bleeding. Despite the fact that his hands trembled half the damn day, despite the fact that she was standing right in front of him. Itching. Absolutely itching for a fight.

"It's so simple for you, isn't it? Damn what everyone else wants or needs." She was nearly yelling and Walter gave her one astonished look before glancing back down at the wood in his hands.

The impulse to rip that wood out of his hands startled her. *I'm so damn tired of being ignored by the men in my life.*

"I don't want to fight you, Sandra."

"Then what do you want?"

His eyes glittered, hot and then cold, and she couldn't breathe. Couldn't even begin to talk.

Yes, she thought, *this is it. The beginning of something. Anything.*

"Thank you." He attacked the wood as if it had attacked him. "For the sandwich, for taking care of this ranch like you have all these years. We are in your debt. I…am in your debt. But please…" His eyes held worlds of sadness. "Leave me alone."

You said you were going to fight, but you avoid me. You love me and you can't even look at me. I don't know how to do this. How to feel this way and not be ashamed.

But I am not going to leave you alone.

"No."

"I hurt you, Sandra. Put hands on you."

"You thought I was Vicki."

"Doesn't matter. A.J. would skin me alive."

A.J. A.J. It always came back to A.J. For her, for everyone around her, and she couldn't stand it anymore. She couldn't keep up the act anymore. Years of being the dutiful wife and she was sick to death of it.

Enough, the tiger of her temper roared, *enough.*

"A.J. didn't love me."

Walter nearly dropped the knife. "What…what are you talking about? Sandra, you were married for thirty years. He worshipped you."

She laughed, unable to stop it. "Worshipped? What a funny word to use."

"Sandra. You're confused, you're—"

"Do. Not. Tell me what I am," she said. "He didn't love me. Not…not like a husband should."

"He was a hard man, quiet."

"It was more than that, Walter."

"What…what are you talking about?" He stared at her, a lost kid confused.

Oh, what was she doing? Why was she going to inflict this secret on Walter?

Because I am stuck behind it.

Lost behind it.

Tired of carrying it.

She couldn't admit she wanted this man, this damaged but determined man. She certainly couldn't fight for him when the whole world believed she and A.J. had been happy.

"What are you saying, Sandra?"

She'd never said it. Not out loud. Didn't actually have proof other than years of observing a man who was constantly repenting something. And suddenly looking at Walter she couldn't do it.

She turned to flee back to the house, but Walter stood, grabbed her hand. She gasped at the touch, the heat of his skin against hers. The size of his hand, the strength. She closed her eyes in surrender to it. In longing for it.

"Sandra—"

"He loved me as a friend," she said.

"Was it an affair?"

She shook her head. "I…think he was gay."

Walter dropped her hand, his face red. "Nonsense."

"He was my husband, Walter. He had secrets."

He stepped back. And back again. "You're wrong."

"I spent years praying that was the case, but…I don't think I am. I think there was someone before we were married. He hated himself for it. I think—secretly—he hated me for it."

Walter stared up at her and, in an instant, all that anger was gone. And she was left cold and guilty. So cold.

"I shouldn't have told you," she murmured, and

walked away, ashamed that she wanted him to stop her and then more ashamed when he didn't.

LUCY MET BEN AT THE BUS stop again on Thursday afternoon. Gray storm clouds clung to the mountains, sending thick feelers over the peaks. The whole world looked dark and fierce. Exactly like she felt.

"What are you doing?" she asked once the bus was gone. She crossed her arms over her chest determined not to be undermined by a kid.

He's a kid. You're an adult. Act like it.

"It's Thursday, I'm coming to your house."

"Yeah, but why did you tell Jeremiah that everything was going fine. Why did you lie?"

"Why did you?"

"Ohhhh, no." She took a step back. "What are you after?"

He shrugged. "I like it here."

"Sleeping in the barn?"

"I'm not sleeping."

She had visions of matches and dry hay, the ranch on fire. "What do you do?" she asked in a hard voice.

"Talk to Walter."

If he had said "talk to the chickens" she wouldn't have been any more surprised. "Walter?"

"The old guy. Yeah."

"What…" She didn't even know how to compute this. "What do you talk about?"

Ben shrugged, lifting his backpack over his shoulder. "Stuff."

"That's…crazy."

Ben didn't like that and he turned, stomping toward the ranch.

"Ben, I'm sorry."

"Whatever. I thought this would be good for you. You get to be the hero with my uncle and you don't even have to deal with the screwed-up kid—"

"You're not screwed up," she said after him.

"That's all you've been calling me since we met."

She gasped, stopped in her tracks. *Oh, no. Was that... was that true?* "Ben...I'm sorry."

"Whatever." He sneered over his shoulder and just kept on walking toward the barn.

She'd hurt him. When she'd meant to help.

Walter wasn't at his seat and she watched Ben disappear into the shadows at the back of the barn. Ben wasn't going to talk to her. It wasn't a matter of letting him cool down, she'd crossed a line with him. Crossed it nearly the first time she opened her mouth.

With her heart like lead in her chest, she realized that she had to go ask Walter—of all people—to look after Ben.

She'd blown all her fresh starts.

WALTER PACED THE HALLWAY, the thump and slide of his crutch loud in the silence. He knew Sandra could hear him in her room, but she wasn't coming out. In front of her door he lifted his hand to knock but found himself unable to do it.

Good Lord, he wanted a drink. He wanted a whole damn bottle. He wanted to drown himself in whiskey.

A.J. Gay?

What a secret. And the real ache—the real pain—was that it didn't matter if it was true or not; Sandra believed it was and she lived her life with that doubt.

Beautiful Sandra pretending for all those years that her marriage was perfect. And his friend. His best friend, A.J., living a lie.

Gathering his ragged courage he knocked on the door and waited. She didn't open it, but he could feel her on the other side.

"I'm sorry," he said to the wood. "I...didn't do that right. If...you... Ah, Christ, Sandra." He thunked his head against the door. "If you want to talk...or whatever...I'm here. I'm...yeah. Here. For you. If you want that."

Why would she? he thought. *You desperate old drunk.*

He waited one more second, the silence pounding and pulsing in his head.

"Walter?" Lucy's voice flooded the hallway and he turned as quickly as he could with his gimpy foot and headed toward the kitchen. Not wanting to be caught outside Sandra's door.

They met in the foyer. There was something in the air for the Alatore women today. Lucy looked as shattered as Sandra.

Did Lucy know about her dad? Did anyone? Had Sandra carried that all alone?

"You okay?" he asked, and she stopped in her fancy boots, her feather earrings lifting in the breeze she'd created.

"No, Walter. I cannot believe I'm about to say this—" She shook her head like she just couldn't believe what was happening. "I need you."

"Me?"

The big breath she sucked down shook at the bottom and he realized she was far more upset than she appeared. "It's Ben."

"He in the barn again?" He leaned sideways to look out the glass surrounding the front door.

"He says...he says you talk to him?"

"Well, I'd hardly call it talking."

"Then what do you call it?"

"I didn't kick him out of the barn. He told me he gets in trouble and I could relate. That's about it."

"Whatever it is you're doing—" she was getting shrill, accusatory "—it's certainly better than whatever I'm doing. I'm totally failing...." She stopped herself, swallowing her wild emotions, and Walter, without the cushion of being drunk, felt scraped raw just being near her. He wasn't sure what to say, what she needed him to say.

It was Sandra all over again.

For a wild moment he thought about saying nothing and walking away. Surely there had to be a bottle around this house somewhere? That's what he would have done two weeks ago. And hell, maybe two weeks from now he'd do the same thing, but right now he was stuck.

Lucy hung her head. "I need your help, Walter," she whispered.

It had been a very long time since he'd been needed for anything and for a moment it was uncomfortable. Resentment reared its head.

Sober and needed. Never thought he'd see the day. Again.

But then purpose shored him up, stayed his childish tongue. Once upon a time he'd been a man people could count on. A man other men pointed to and said, "Walter McKibbon can get the job done."

He'd been proud of that. And how long had it been since he'd been proud of himself?

More days than he could count.

"It's all right, Lucy. I can handle it."

Her unhappiness with the situation was no vote of confidence. Obviously reluctant, she nodded. "Thank you."

Walter headed out to the barn and he didn't let himself

doubt. He didn't even give himself a chance to wonder if his instinct was right or not. He'd been stuck in mud for so damn long, doubting himself, that if he gave himself a second he'd get stuck again.

Work was what was needed. Some good honest labor. He found the bucket in the tack room and filled it up with two parts water, one part vinegar. He threw in some sponges and rags. Water sloshing down his leg, he carried them over to his chair.

Back in the whitewashed tack room he pulled his saddle and bridle out from behind Jack and Mia's gear. Mildew and mold had turned the brittle leather white. There were two other saddles behind the tack that got used more often—his ex-wife's—and the small one he'd used with Jack when he was little.

They were white and brittle, too.

What the hell, he thought, and tried to pull them out. He strained, dropping his cane, stumbling slightly with the awkward weight. He swore, loud enough that anyone in the barn could hear.

"Do you need help?" a voice asked, and Walter turned to find Ben.

That worked at least, he thought.

"I would, son. Thank you."

The nine-year-old wasn't all that strong, but at least his ankle worked. It took them a few turns to get all the stuff but soon they had all the old gear spread out in the grass in front of his chair.

"What are you going to do?" the boy asked.

"Grab a cloth," Walter said as he sat and pointed to the ripped T-shirts hanging over the edge of the bucket.

The boy hesitated and Walter squinted up at him, the muted end-of-day sun resting just over Ben's head, creating a halo. Unlikely, but he wasn't the one to judge.

Walter bent back over his work, pushing the cloth into the mixture until it saturated, and then working it over the brittle leather, trying to get rid of the mildew.

"It stinks," Ben said.

"Vinegar."

"What's it do?"

"Gets rid of the mold."

"Why is it moldy?"

"I haven't used it in a while."

"You're sick, right?"

Jesus Christ, what the hell is this? Was he asking about the Parkinson's or the drinking?

"I guess."

"You gonna die?"

Walter paused, his heart taking a hard, heavy chug in his throat. He'd been killing himself with drink. Not taking his medicine. It was all part of his plan to ease right on out of this life.

He thought about Sandra, the bruise on her wrist, the fire in her eyes. Why did she tell him about A.J.? Him? What did she want? What could she possibly be looking to him for? A month ago he'd been a dead man walking and now…now he didn't know what he was.

But maybe he'd earned himself a few years to figure it out.

"Everyone dies. But hopefully I've got some time."

"My mom died."

Walter nodded, not daring to look up at the boy. He was too old for this. Too uneasy in his sobriety. Too lost in his feelings for Sandra. He couldn't add Ben's grief to his already full plate.

Full plate? He nearly laughed at himself. There was nothing on his plate. Not one damn thing. Scaring away nurses? Ignoring Sandra? Trying every damn minute of every damn day not to drink?

He needed distraction. He glanced sideways at the boy and saw a kid so twisted with grief he didn't know where to go.

He'd been there. Spent years in that place. Turned to a bottle to make it better.

"I'm real sorry about your mom. And your dad."

"I barely remember him."

Walter nodded like he understood, but he didn't. No one could. Silence stretched and pulled so hard Walter shifted just to break the soundless scream in the air around him.

Ben collapsed cross-legged next to him and reached for a cloth. "Everyone wants to talk about my feelings."

He said *feelings* the way Walter would say *feelings,* like it was a bad word.

"I don't." Walter wanted that clear.

Halfheartedly, the kid rubbed at the brass tack on Jack's small saddle.

"You won't get any mildew off like that. You gotta get in there."

The kid put some elbow grease into it and Walter nodded in approval.

"But no one wants to talk about my mom." The kid attacked the leather, his hand a blur. His face red.

He wants to cry, Walter thought.

"What if I forget her, too?" the boy whispered.

Oh. Oh, Lord. Please let me do this right. Please.

"Your mom is a hard woman to forget."

"Then why doesn't anyone want to remember her?"

Because it hurts to remember. It's why he drank. But there was no explaining that to a nine-year-old.

"You know that creek that separates our spreads?"

Walter asked, putting the T-shirt back in the bucket and squeezing it out.

"Yeah."

"You know how it rises when it rains?"

"Mom always told us to stay away from it after the rains. She said it was dangerous."

He laughed. "Well, I figure she would know. I had to save her and a nearly drowned calf one year. She couldn't have been much older than you."

"What…" The boy stopped rubbing the saddle, his hands fists in his lap. "What happened?"

"There'd been a big storm the night before. Scattered all our new calves to hell and back and she was chasing one down and they both got too close to the creek."

"She fell in?"

He looked up at the boy. "Your mom? Hell, no, boy. Annie Stone jumped in after that calf. Got caught in a tree limb that had fallen across the water and I found her about an hour later, screaming her head off."

A muscle twitched in the boy's face—a smile maybe.

"Where was the calf?"

"On the side of the creek waiting for her. Two of the saddest animals I've ever seen."

Again, that little muscle twitched in the corner of his mouth. And then slowly, Ben reached into the bucket and rinsed out his cloth. He bent back to his work, but calmly. The frantic emotion gone.

"Work on the white stuff on the bottom," Walter said, passing the saddle to the boy and picking up the bridle.

"You know any more stories about my mom?"

Oh, man, so many of them were lost to the booze and the years. But there were a few pieces he still remembered.

"She had a dog—"

"Pirate. She told us a lot about Pirate."

"Did she tell you Pirate nearly killed my dog Duchess?"

Ben's eyes opened wide, and that smile was real, no longer a twitch, and Walter felt something warm and strange in his chest. Like the sun coming up after a long cold night. "Keep working, now," he chastised, and the boy got back to scrubbing. "And I'll tell you what I remember about your momma and that Pirate."

JEREMIAH DROPPED OFF THE BOYS at school, like he did every morning, no matter what was going on. It was something Annie had always done and he'd worked really hard to make sure he could do it, too. The boys took the bus home in the afternoon, but he drove them, every morning, twenty minutes into town.

Today he raced back to the ranch to interview a new housekeeper. They had a little cottage out back. Hopefully he could convince someone to come and live on the land. He didn't know how the boys would react, but he couldn't do this alone anymore.

Halfway over the pass he dug out his cell phone and called Lucy.

"Hey, cowboy," she answered, and blood pooled below his waist.

"Hey, yourself. I've got to cancel Ben coming over to your place today."

"Why?' she asked, quickly. "Did he say something?"

"Ben? Say something? No. He has a thing to attend after school. Could we maybe do it Monday?"

"Monday? Sure—"

There was something odd in her tone. "Is that a problem? Are you...?" He swallowed, forcing himself to address something he wanted to ignore. "I know you guys aren't staying indefinitely. Are you…you making plans to leave?"

"No. No plans. Walter's stopped drinking, but he insults every person who comes over to apply for the housekeeper job."

"Well, that's good." He winced. "I mean, not that Walter is difficult. But that you're staying."

She laughed and he wondered what kind of magic this woman had to make him feel so childish.

Enough, he thought. He was Jeremiah freaking Stone and she might not know it yet, but there was a king-size bed in their future.

"I was wondering if maybe you'd like to go out tomorrow night," he said, getting to the real reason he called.

She laughed and he heard the jangle of jewelry against her phone. He imagined those silver feather earrings she wore. He liked them, liked how they gleamed against her skin.

"Let me check my calendar," she joked. "Nothing, totally free."

"I'll pick you up at six."

"Sounds good."

They hung up and with his chest getting tighter with every breath he called Dr. Gilman and canceled his appointment for Saturday. It was one appointment, he told himself to ease the strange guilt that was suffocating him. And she was the one who told him to go out and have some fun. Hell, she'd probably approve.

It didn't change the fact that it felt like he was doing something wrong.

CHAPTER FOURTEEN

LUCY STARED DOWN AT the drawing she'd made on the paper towel. A wide silver cuff with delicate cutouts of roses and pistols, and skulls.

Weird, she thought, twisting it around. Not at all like her usual work. Usually she worked in delicate wire, pieces that looked as if they floated against a woman's skin.

This was heavy. The pistols and skulls were dark.

"Hey," Mia said, stepping into the bathroom behind Lucy. "My jewelry-designing sister is designing again."

Lucy fought the urge to crumple up the towel. "A little, I guess." She didn't know what this meant for her. But that was the nature of her days right now. She barely knew herself.

This thing with Ben.

Lying to her family. To Jeremiah.

Fooling around outside bars. Casually dating a man she feared she didn't feel at all casual about.

Who am I?

"That's a cool bracelet," Mia said, pulling the paper towel closer to her. "I would wear that."

"Where?" Lucy laughed. "The high pastures?"

"Jack takes me out. In fact, that's why I'm here." Lucy met her sister's eyes in the mirror. It could have been a snapshot from their childhood. The two of them getting ready for something in the same bathroom. Lucy fussing over her makeup and hair. Mia putting her hair in a ponytail, making fun of Lucy for all her girlie primping.

But marriage had changed Mia and primping was something she did now. Not very well, or often, but she was learning. And Lucy was delighted to be a part of the process.

"You want to borrow some clothes?"

"Did you bring a dress?"

"Just a yellow sundress." Lucy started walking toward her room and closet of clothes. "The rest are in storage—"

"Storage?"

Lucy closed her eyes. Shit. All she needed now was her sister asking questions about the condo. "I put some stuff in storage before I came. Let's see what I've got—" She bulldozed her way through any questions Mia might have had, not giving her a chance to talk.

She pulled out the yellow sundress and Mia made a face. Lucy gave it a quick glance, though. *Jeremiah would like this. With cowboy boots, Jeremiah would really like it.*

"This is pretty hot," she said, pulling out a thin white top, clingy in all the right places. "You've got the right chest for it, that's for sure."

Mia lay across Lucy's bed, ignoring the clothes.

"Have you noticed Mom acting strange lately?" Mia asked.

"Yeah, pretty much since the moment we got here."

"No. I mean…she hasn't come out of her room all day today."

"Is she sick?"

"I asked earlier and she said she was just tired."

"She's dealing with Walter—" She felt a little sick

speaking ill of a guy who'd helped her out on Thursday, but one good deed could not erase years of mistakes.

"But she's not. He's not letting anyone help him. Especially her."

Lucy paused, an animal-print chemise in her hands. "Maybe she's depressed. Missing Dad."

Mia shook her head. "Usually when she's sad she wants us around. I knocked on her door tonight and she snapped at me to leave her alone."

Lucy collapsed on the foot of her bed. "We should have left weeks ago."

"Do you think she liked it better in the city?"

Lucy shook her head. "Honestly, no."

"I didn't think so. I don't know, Lucy, I feel like it's something else. She's mad about something."

"Mom? Mad?"

Mia shrugged. "Stranger things are happening around here. Walter's still not drinking. And now you're designing jewelry again."

Lucy grinned at Mia. "What you need to do is have a kid. Give her some babies to hold."

Instead of protesting Mia blushed.

"No…" Lucy gasped.

"No, I'm not. But…we're trying."

Lucy howled and hugged Mia. "What a ridiculous thing to call lots and lots of unprotected sex. But I'm thrilled for you."

Mia squeezed her and then snatched the white tank top and the filmy camisole. "This should help."

"Go get him, sis."

Mia headed for the door and stopped. "Why…why are you all dressed up? You doing something tonight?"

"I—" Lucy stood and pulled down the hem on the thin red sweater she wore with her jet necklace. Beneath she wore her favorite black bra. She called it her Betty Boop outfit.

"Have a date."

"With who?"

"Jeremiah—"

"Stone?"

Lucy nodded, her smile fading fast the more solemn Mia's face got.

"What's wrong?"

"Nothing…I just… You're, like, a relationship person, Lucy. And I don't know whatever crisis you're having with your design and your business. But I'd hate to think of you using Jeremiah as a substitute—"

"How can you say that?" Lucy asked, but wondered if Jeremiah thought the same thing. "I'm a grown woman, Mia. I know my mind. My life." *My heart. And my heart is slipping into familiar territory.*

"Really? Because you're not acting like it. Look, I love you both, and I don't want to see anyone hurt."

"We agreed it would be casual."

"Yeah—" Mia lifted her eyebrow "—that sweater looks real…casual." And she was out the door. Lucy turned to face the mirror over her dresser and considered the V-neck of her sweater. After a moment she pulled it down a little farther.

She'd hate Jeremiah to get the wrong idea.

JEREMIAH COULD NOT STOP talking. He was listening to himself ramble on about restaurant choices and he honestly wanted to punch himself in the mouth.

"The Roundup has a pretty good steak if you don't mind listening to the band they've got there. Or if you want down by the highway, I think there's, like, an Applebee's. They've got salads and stuff. You like vegetables. Right?"

He glanced over only to see her propped up against the passenger's side door, laughing at him. "I do, Jeremiah. I do like vegetables."

Was he sweating? He was. It trickled down his hairline, got caught in the band of his hat. Frustrated, embarrassed, he pushed it off his head.

"You got any better ideas?" he asked.

"Yes." She dug into her back pocket. "I got you something."

And she pulled out a long strip of silver.

Condoms.

A bunch of them.

"Dinner later?" he asked.

"Dinner later."

And he pulled a U-turn and headed out toward the highway and the hotel reservation he'd already made.

Fifteen minutes later he stood at the front desk very conscious of the fact that they didn't have any luggage.

Classy, Stone, he told himself, *very classy.*

He wondered if Lucy felt awkward as they walked down the carpeted hallway, silent and not touching. Maybe this was more of that slightly dirty stuff she wanted, something wild. Something to relieve the stress of her life.

Be grateful, he told himself when the thought rankled. *It's not like you have anything else to offer her.* He wasn't even sure if he could offer her something dirty and dangerous. More like quick and sweaty.

We should have had dinner, he thought, *this would be a whole lot easier with a couple of drinks under my belt.*

"Here we go," he said, and slipped the key in the door.

The light flashed red and he did it again. No luck; he swore and tried harder.

"Calm down, cowboy," she murmured, and took the key card out of his hand. She swiped it, the light flashed green and the door popped open under the flick of her wrist.

She slipped past him, grinning over her shoulder as she walked into the dark, slightly sterile hotel room. The red of her sweater, her eyes and smile—they glowed in the room. A beacon in the shadows.

He followed—the room could have been on fire, or filled with bees, and he would have followed. He would have followed her anywhere.

The door shut behind him and she lifted her hand to the tiny buttons at the bottom of her thin sweater. Slowly the material parted to reveal the tops of her tight jeans, the sweet curve of her tummy, her belly button, the bottom of her ribs. And then finally the sweater slipped off her shoulders, revealing her breasts, lovingly cradled by black lace.

"You going to help me out here?" she asked, her fingers dropping to the button on her jeans.

"You are doing great all by yourself." His mouth was a dust storm.

"Maybe…I'm shy." Her hair fell over her eye as she pretended to play the maiden.

Good Lord, she is hot. The act, the game, all of it— she made the air sizzle, his body burn.

He pulled his T-shirt up over his head and threw it backward over his shoulder, eyes on her fingers as they toyed with the zipper of her pants. He bent over and pulled off his boots, barely noticing that his socks didn't match.

Slowly she pushed down her pants, easing them over hips revealing black lace and satin.

"Turn around," he said, and for a moment the game waivered. She didn't give up control easily, he realized. She liked to choose what and how she revealed herself.

But then she turned, bending over as she pulled down her pants the rest of the way. Beautiful, sexy. She grinned at him over her shoulder and that was it. All he could stand.

He stepped up behind her. She wanted dark. Dirty. She wanted wicked.

He could give her all of that.

Slipping his hand around her waist he pulled her up tight against him. In lock step, he crossed the room to the desk and spread her hands out there.

She chuckled low and deep in her throat, pushing back against his erection. "I thought you wanted a bed."

"We got all night."

He shoved down his jeans with one hand while his other hand slid over the satin skin of her tummy into the lace edge of her underwear. She gasped, groaned, arched against him.

"Too fast?" he asked, and she shook her head, her black hair drifting across her shoulders.

"Hurry."

He didn't need another invitation and pulled the condoms she'd brought out of his back pocket. While she pushed her underwear down to her ankles, he used his teeth to rip open the condom. He fumbled slightly, panting, dying.

And then…yes…oh, yes…he was inside her. All the way.

Inside, her muscles clutched and she whimpered and he pushed as high and as hard as he could into her.

She pushed back and he couldn't have said who was inside who.

And then…she laughed. Dark and dirty. The laugh crept over his skin like fingers.

The moment was suddenly transcendent, he was inside his skin and at the same time watching himself. Loving all of it. This moment, the two of them, made sense in a way he'd never expected. In a way he'd never had.

Sex was sex for Jeremiah, even with women that he really liked, but somehow, with Lucy, sex was different. Sex was an extension of who they were, of what brought them together. The sadness and heartache and desire all snowballed inside of him.

No, he thought, his panic buttons screaming. *Too much. Ease off. Make a joke.*

He desperately wanted to find the shallow pools he was used to, but Lucy wouldn't let him.

She groaned and cried, pushing herself on her tiptoes so that, impossibly, he sank even deeper into her, finding a friction that lit up the night. All of him, that's what she wanted, what she expected.

Can I do that? I've…I've never done that.

"Jeremiah." She sighed. "Please. Stay with me?"

Enough of his own head games. Enough of his own fear. He wasn't going to waste a second of his time with Lucy because without a doubt she would be gone soon. And he'd be right back where he started.

Alone and lonely. Probably lonelier for having had her, but that was a problem for a different day.

He slipped a hand up under hair to her neck and tipped over farther across the desk.

"Jeremiah," she gasped slapping her hands against the wood.

He grinned in the half dark and set about being as wicked and dirty as he could.

"I'm with you. Right here with you."

LUCY DOZED SLIGHTLY, her head buried in Jeremiah's armpit. Their skin was stuck together with sweat and when she could move again, and decided to, it would hurt peeling herself away from him.

In more ways than one, she thought in a rare moment of total honesty with herself. All of her excuses and pretences, her rationales and justifications, they'd abandoned her in the past few hours. Run out of her life by Jeremiah and his endless, bottomless, control.

"You won that round," she muttered. Her body stretched and pulled, boneless. He'd been…amazing. She was no slouch in the sex department, but he… She was going to make him a love-god T-shirt.

His laughter shook her head. "I'd say it was a tie." His fingers lazily walked up and down her spine, coercing goose bumps all over her skin, but she didn't tell him to stop. Just like she didn't move.

I don't want this to end, she thought, sighing deeper into her doze.

Suddenly, from the utter blankness of her thoughts sprang the idea for a ring. Wide, wider than most, masculine almost. Hammered gold. And another one, a thin braid. Silver? No, she recast it in gold. White gold. And wider, Celtic in flavor. Or Viking… Oh, cool.

"Wedding bands," she murmured.

"What?" howled Jeremiah, jerking away from her.

Their skin split apart and both of them winced. "Did you say…?" He stared at her, horrified, and honestly, she couldn't blame him. But she also couldn't explain it, not until she sketched the ideas down before she lost them entirely.

Naked, she bounced out of bed and toward the desk. The pen was on the floor, the little notepad shoved up under the phone.

While sketching the hammered gold ring, two more ideas came to her. A wide white-gold band with a garnet in a thick circular setting. Medieval-looking.

As if it were someone else doing it she watched what appeared under her pen.

Five rings. Wedding bands for both the bride and the groom. One-of-a-kind pieces.

Meredith Van Loan, a boutique owner in Santa Monica, would love these. Too bad Meredith Van Loan wasn't speaking to her after that mass-produced horse-shoe necklace debacle.

"Lucy?"

She turned back to the bed and the cowboy sitting in pooled sheets. The moonlight filtering through the windows cast the muscles of his chest and arms in shadow, making him look as if he'd been dipped in silver.

She smiled at the thought. This was the way her brain used to work, everything was an extension of her work and her materials.

"You all right?" Jeremiah asked.

"I…I think I am. Or maybe I will be. I'm not sure yet."

"You've lost me, Lucy."

You found me, she thought but didn't say. Perhaps the argument could be made that all she'd really needed was a few weeks away from her work.

Away from that city I never loved and that never loved me. Perhaps the argument could be made that she only really needed to be home again. Back where inspiration struck the first time.

But looking at the increasingly nervous cowboy on the bed she knew, in that secret heart of hers, that this man had somehow seen her back to herself. Like walking her to her front door after an absence.

I don't love him, she thought. *But I will. Soon.*

She crossed the carpet to the foot of the bed and then, slowly, crawled up the messy sheets toward him. At her approach he grinned and leaned against the headboard, the muscles of his chest and stomach flexing and relaxing, standing in relief against his skin.

"You inspire me."

"Me?"

She put a hand on his shoulder and it took very little pressure to get him to shift and roll over on his stomach. His back was split by the long surgical scar along his spine. He could have died. Lost the use of his legs.

"My scar?" He shot her a dubious look over his shoulder. "Inspired you?"

"All of you," she said, and kissed his scar. *How do I bring you back to you?* she wondered. *How do I return you to your front door?*

"Lucy," he whispered, and rolled back over. He looked pained and she let the matter drop, kissing her way across his chest, the beautiful muscles covered in silken skin, sprinkled with curly hair.

She pushed the sheets away from his lap, revealing his erection, the long, dusky length of it. He hissed through his teeth and the air became oddly charged with all of the things she wanted to say to him.

How beautiful he was, and kind, and generous. How brave he was in the face of all he was up against, how courageous despite knowing he was failing in so many ways.

But he wouldn't want to hear it.

So, she curled herself against his legs and used her mouth in other ways.

Tenderly his fingers touched her face, as if learning her by touch as she sighed in pleasure.

"Come here," he whispered, pulling her away from him, lifting her with just that touch against her cheek, up against his body. His other hand sank into her hair and for a moment, long and suspended, they just looked at each other. Right at each other and then, because she couldn't contain herself, she smiled at him. She smiled and let him right into her heart.

CHAPTER FIFTEEN

SANDRA HEAVED, EVERY MUSCLE straining, her feet slipping on the rug, and she still wasn't strong enough to shift the mattress.

This is why women needed husbands. To lift things.

She'd spent twenty-four hours hiding in her room and she was done with that. What this room needed was to be cleaned. Top to bottom. The cobwebs and the ghosts and the regrets—all needed to be swept out.

"Good Lord, Sandra, what are you doing?" Walter's voice startled her and she dropped the mattress, which knocked over the bedside table with a loud crash.

I shouldn't have left that door open, she thought. She'd known he'd been prowling around her bedroom, could hear the shuffle and thump of his gait. Could feel him through the wood and stone—his concern. His... pity.

Walter rushed forward to set the table right and Sandra caught her breath, leaning against the footboard on her bed. She used to do this job no problem. Funny what a few extra years and a soft life in the city will take away from a woman.

Walter used his knee to push the mattress back onto the box spring as if it were made of air.

"Sorry," he murmured. "I didn't mean to startle you."

Leave, she thought, *please leave. Go. I should never*

*have said anything. I should have taken that secret to
my grave. Just like A.J.*

She turned to face him, ready to tell him to leave, but
instead clapped a hand over her mouth.

Pink as a little pig, he was.

"You can laugh," he grumbled. Wincing, he pressed
his fingers to his sunburned face. "It's funny as hell."

"That's what you get for spending so much time outside."

"No, that's what I get for having spent too much time
inside. What are you trying to do here?" He pointed to
the bed.

"Flip the mattress."

"You should have asked for help."

"I never needed help before. But I'll ask Lucy to help
me, you don't need to do this."

"I was...I was surprised to see your door open."

"There's only so long I can stay locked inside when
there's work to be done." She grabbed the sheets on the
floor at her feet and headed out of the room.

She wasn't proud of herself but she was running from
him, thinking he wouldn't keep up, but he did. *That cane
is an act,* she thought darkly.

"Sandra—"

He followed her all the way into the laundry room.
She wondered if he'd ever been back here.

"I've got a lot of work to do, Walter."

Without looking at what was in the washing machine
she started shoving the sheets in, cramming them inside.
She opened the door for the detergent and without mea-
suring she dumped in the powder.

His fingers touched her arm and she dropped the
soap, spilling it all over the floor.

"Good Lord, Walter, look—" Frantic tears were burning behind her eyes as she knelt to gather the granules in her hands, but he stopped her, his hands cupping her elbows and forcing her to stay upright.

"Forget what I said," she whispered. "Please."

"I can't."

"A.J. would never forgive me for this—"

"A.J. is dead, Sandra," he whispered. Carefully, as if she were a glass sculpture he was setting up on a table, he moved his hands away as if he were afraid she would wobble and crash.

But Sandra Alatore never wobbled, or at least she never did before the other day when she told Walter about A.J. And now she felt as if she were always off balance.

"I don't know if what you said is true and I don't really know if I care. It doesn't change how I felt about A.J. Doesn't change who he was for me."

Her eyes flew to his, surprised to hear him say that. She wished she could be that forgiving. That accepting.

"But I care about you and how…how that must have been for you."

"A.J. was a good man, a good father. I was blessed in many ways." She tried to get out of the laundry room but he shifted sideways and stopped her.

"Sandra, you don't have to pretend to me." A sad, sweet smile split his craggy and dark face. Lifting it somewhere toward handsome. "I know better than anyone what it's like to be in a bad marriage."

"It wasn't bad. It just—"

"It wasn't what you wanted."

Oh, sweet Lord, it was so hard to say the words. It was one thing to think them, but to let them leave her lips, it felt like nothing would be the same.

She nodded, a coward.

"Do the girls know?" he asked, and she shook her head.

"I don't want to change the way they think of their dad."

"That's…noble."

"It's necessary." His poor face was as red as a tail-light and she did not want to talk about this anymore. "Do you want some aloe? For your face?"

He winced. "Would it help?"

"Yes. Come, I have some in the kitchen."

She felt him at her back as she walked through the dim, silent house. Suddenly she was all too aware of how alone they were. The ranch was empty. Jack and Mia weren't even at the little cottage. It was just them for miles.

Stop, she chided herself, *you are thinking like a teenager.*

But it didn't stop her skin from burning where he touched her. It didn't stop her from asking questions she had no business asking.

Who is this man? Why do I feel this way for him?

The Walter that emerged from his room weeks ago was a different Walter than the man she'd endured for so long. He was older, yes, in many ways, his body more frail. But his eyes—for the first time, his eyes were young. Lit with a fire she'd never seen. Never even dreamed of seeing. And he was smiling. Not a lot, but some.

And a sunburn? Why was that so endearing on a man as tough and as hard as Walter? Why did that make her heart twist and her stomach hatch butterflies?

That kiss on her wrist a week ago. Why did that still ache? Why could she still feel the scrape of his beard against her skin? The dry press of his lips.

In the kitchen, she used her scissors to snip off a

piece of aloe from the plant on the windowsill and she turned to hand it to him but he stood on the other end of the kitchen counter.

"Here." She held the aloe out across the white counter but he just stared at her.

"I'm worried about you," he said.

She laughed. "Worried? About me?" Her voice cracked on the last word. People didn't worry about her. She worried about everyone else and she didn't know what to do with the weight of his concern.

"I would think your worry plate is about full," she said as she put the aloe down on the counter. After a moment, as if waiting for her touch to wear off, he lifted it up but then put it back down.

Wouldn't it be something to have the right to pick up the aloe and spread it across his face? To have such casual care between them. She'd never had that. A.J. hadn't been one for touching. He was a man who took care of himself.

"I'm going to make some tea—would you like some?" There was comfort in turning toward the stove and putting on the kettle. Familiar things. Familiar work. In a landscape that was growing increasingly unfamiliar.

He laughed low in his throat. "No, thank you."

"You want a drink?"

"Of course I want a drink. I'm always going to want a drink."

"But...don't you feel better not drinking?"

He put his hands down, pressing the pad of his thumb against the hard sharp point of the aloe plant.

Stop that, she wanted to say, *you'll hurt yourself.*

She swallowed, wondering if she was overstepping her bounds. Hell, she knew she was overstepping her bounds, but who they were and what they were to each other was in flux. "What about that AA meeting down at the Presbyterian church?"

"I'm not going to an AA meeting." That was the Walter she knew. Gruff and closed off.

"You should have someone to talk to."

He looked at her for a long moment and she felt as if the barriers she'd put between herself and the world were melting. Barriers she'd put up years ago to keep people from looking too closely at her marriage. To keep people from looking too closely at her.

"You could talk to me," she said.

"You know a lot about drinking?"

No, she thought, *but I know a lot about lying. A lot about regret. A lot about wanting something more.*

"I'm sorry." He sighed, rubbing his hand over his face and then wincing. She smiled at him. He was a bear with a hurt face. "I'm not...I'm not one for talking."

"Really?" she mocked.

He flashed one of his rare smiles at her and it felt like finding twenty dollars on the sidewalk—unexpected and lucky.

"There's a lot of shit I have to deal with, Sandra, years of things I've pushed away and ignored and let fester, and drinking made that easier. Made all the mistakes I made go away and now, sober, well, I suppose I need to deal with it."

"Jack." It wasn't a question. The cool distance between him and his son was obvious to everyone at the ranch.

Walter nodded, his lips thin. "We're better than we were, but...there's still work to do."

"There is always work to do. In every relationship."

"Says the woman whose children adore her."

She smiled at that. "They are good girls."

"They are."

His rusty praise warmed her and the moment unfolded around them, a flower in bloom. She looked up only to find his shrewd gaze waiting for her, full of hundreds of things he'd never said, but she knew, anyway.

He desires me, she thought. *Loves me.* Awareness crept in on cat's paws and it thrilled and worried her.

She wanted to touch him and from the way his eyes blazed with fear, like an animal being backed into a corner, he knew how she felt.

"What…what do you want from me?" he asked.

You, she thought. *To feel something besides doubt again. To feel…wanted.*

"When are you going home, Sandra?" he asked, and she jerked at the question as if poked by a knife. "Don't look at me like that, you said you would leave when I was sober. I'm sober. You need to go on home."

"You're sober, but you're not well, Walter."

"A sunburn isn't going to kill me."

"Your ankle…"

"Better every day." He pushed himself away from the counter. He didn't have his cane and he didn't look like a man who needed it.

She felt suddenly bereft, not just because he was leaving, but because she was so alone. And had been for so, so long. She'd raised her girls to be independent and they were, but where did that leave her? Where did she belong if she wasn't needed anywhere?

"Where's home?" she said aloud—she hadn't meant to, but now that she had she felt a certain righteousness in that question. "Where do I belong?"

When he looked at her, she felt the way he loved her. The way he'd always loved her. Vicki had seen it, she'd seen it. Only A.J., blinded by his faith and self-loathing, had missed it.

A.J., her nonhusband. The father of her children, the head of her family. But not her husband. Not really.

Alone, she thought, *alone for so long.*

She stepped around the counter and Walter took a deep breath. "What are you doing?" he asked, his voice thick, and her body awoke to its power. Her power. She was still beautiful. And he was a man. More of a man every day.

"You don't want me to leave," she whispered.

"Don't, Sandra. You can stay if you want, but don't do this—"

She stopped in front of him. His chest touched hers with every breath and he looked so terribly pained she reached up for his cheek, but he caught her hand, crushing her fingers in his grip.

"I'm sorry Lucy sold your condo," he said, and she froze—from the inside she went totally numb. Lucy sold the condo? "And you can stay here if you want, but don't do this to me. I beg you."

He squeezed her fingers once and then dropped them before turning and walking out.

Shaking, she sat down at the empty dining room table, while the kettle whistled a warning.

THANK YOU, LUCY ALATORE, Jeremiah thought as he walked into his house feeling like a new man. Whistling even. A swagger in his step.

The house was dark, quiet, and he suspected Ben was asleep. Casey had a sleepover and Aaron was at an overnight hockey tournament, under the eagle eye of Kathy Owens.

Maybe Cynthia had bunked down in Aaron's room,

since Jeremiah was home so late. He glanced at his watch and winced. Two hours later than usual, but not yet midnight. Lucy had more than understood when he told her he had to leave.

"I'd better get back, too," she'd said, shimmying into her skinny jeans. "My sister is worried about my intentions toward you."

"She thinks you're going to use me for sex?" he asked. "Because I really don't have a problem with that."

She'd hummed, but changed the subject, and after dropping her off at the Rocky M, he'd driven home wondering if Lucy was beginning to feel like things were more than just casual between them.

That wedding band thing had been weird.

His stomach growled and he was reminded that they'd never gotten to the dinner part of their date. He smiled at the thought and headed into the kitchen to make himself a sandwich and saw the floodlights on off the back porch, illuminating the entire backyard.

Strange, he thought, and then about jumped out of his skin when something knocked on the sliding glass door.

It was Cynthia, wrapped up in a quilt sitting out on the deck. He tugged open the door and stepped outside.

"What—?"

"Look."

The light flooded the far back of the lawn where the old garden had been. Nothing but weeds since Annie died, but not even that now. Someone had pulled up everything.

"Ben's been working out there all night," Cynthia whispered.

"Is he cleaning it up?" he asked, squinting into the shadows for a glimpse of the boy. But then he heard the lawn mower start. "What the hell is he doing?" He stepped for the stairs but Cynthia stopped him. Her wide sad eyes damp behind her glasses.

"He picked it clean and he's mowing it down," she said.

Annie's garden. Granted, he hadn't had time to take care of it, but she'd poured her heart and soul into that thing. Every spring she put the boys to work out there and all through the summer. Ben had been good at it, seemed to like it more than the other two. Annie had called him "green fingers."

"He's destroying it," he whispered.

"Dry-eyed," she said, and then took a deep breath. "I know you have him over there gardening with one of those Alatore girls—"

"Lucy." He swiveled to look at her. "I had to cancel Friday afternoon with her. But what's that got to do with this?"

She opened her eyes wide. "You don't think there's a connection?"

He rubbed a hand over his face, clinging with everything in him, with his fingernails and teeth, to the good mood he'd had while walking in here. "No." He sighed, though the connection was pretty damn obvious. "He's been working hard for her over there."

"Is that what Ben says?" she asked.

"Why, what did he say to you?"

"That he hangs out in the barn."

It felt like his stomach bottomed out. Like a punch to the side of his head. "No," he said, not wanting to believe it. Lucy wasn't lying to him. "Ben's lying."

Cynthia shrugged. "Could be. He has before."

Jeremiah collapsed back into one of the deck chairs, watching the far corner of his lawn where Ben was pushing a lawn mower over what was left of Annie's tomato plants.

"What am I supposed to do?" he asked.

Cynthia unwrapped herself from the quilt she'd surrounded herself in and threw a corner over his lap. Warmth he clung to, pulling it up over his suddenly cold chest. "Be here when he's ready to come in."

Jeremiah nodded, numb. Another twenty minutes passed and Ben put the lawn mower back in the far shed by the barn and trudged up through the shadows back to the porch.

Jeremiah stood, the blanket slipping off his lap.

"Ben," he said when the boy started up the stairs. In the white floodlights Jeremiah saw the scratches and blood on his arms, the dirt on his hands, the broken nails. Ben had been in his own fight tonight, but when he looked up at Jeremiah, his eyes were dry.

"What?"

"You…all right?"

Ben glanced back at the garden he'd laid to waste. "No one used that stupid garden anymore."

It wasn't stupid, he wanted to say. *It was one of the few things of your mom we had left and you just destroyed it—*

Cynthia's cool hand touched his arm.

"Go on in and shower, Ben," she said. "It's late."

Ben nodded and didn't once look back at Jeremiah.

LUCY WOKE UP WITH a long slow stretch, clinging to the fevered dream she'd been having of Jeremiah. Paper crinkled when she rolled over and she quickly sat up. More designs. Wedding bands. Leather and silver cuffs. Jewelry for men.

The designer she'd been was gone. Moved out. The

delicate girlish pieces, replaced by jewelry with weight. Literally and figuratively.

"Wake up, Lucy." Her mother's voice snapped her right out of her thoughts and she turned, paper in hands, to show her mom the work.

But Sandra was standing in an angry-mom pose at the end of her bed.

"What's wrong, Mom?"

"Why are you selling our condo?"

Lucy was never quick on her feet in the morning and despite all the lying she was doing currently in her life, she didn't have a lot of practice with it.

"What—?"

"Don't you dare lie to me, Lucy. I called the real estate agent, and she said she's been boxing our stuff up to stage it."

Oh, no. No. She didn't want to wake up to this mess, not after last night. Lucy tossed off the covers, deciding the best defense in this situation was a good offense.

"I'm just checking the market, Mom—"

"Our things!"

"In boxes. Safe in storage."

Sandra's eyes didn't let up. "This is not like you, Lucy. There are secrets you're keeping. Your business—"

"I sold it." As soon as the words came out of her mouth she wanted to suck them back in. Sandra's body went lax with shock.

"No, honey, you didn't—"

"I did." She tried to hug her mother, to make this all sound like a celebration, but Sandra stepped away.

"Did you get a good offer?"

Ah, twenty thousand dollars in debt or bankruptcy? Not quite. "Good enough to sell."

"Why didn't you tell me? Or Mia?"

"Because I knew you wouldn't understand."

"You're right, I don't understand. You've been making jewelry your whole life—"

"That's right, Mom, my whole life, and I can start a new business. Look—" She tried to distract her mom with her new designs but Sandra wasn't going to be deterred.

"But your employees? The studio? You were so successful. You loved Los Angeles."

She nearly snorted, but managed to stop herself. "Mom, I hated Los Angeles, almost as much as you did."

"Is that why you sold?"

"One of the reasons. Look, I'm sorry I didn't tell you but I didn't think anyone would care."

Sandra scowled at her for that. "When have I not cared about every single part of your life?"

"Maybe…maybe I just didn't want you to care. Maybe I just wanted it to be private."

Oh, that hurt her mother and her face turned to stone before she left the room, leaving a chill behind.

"Uncle J.?" Casey asked for about the twentieth time. "Are we going to go inside?"

"Yep." But Jeremiah didn't move. He had his arms crossed over the top of the steering wheel and just kept staring out the windshield at the Rocky M. It was Monday afternoon and they were early. He had some kind of half-baked notion that he might catch Lucy and Ben in whatever kind of elaborate lie they were working on.

Or, he thought, trying to look on the bright side, *maybe he'd catch them back in that garden working hard.*

All he had to do was ask Lucy if she was lying to him. Before Saturday night it would have been hard, but after Saturday night…he just felt like the biggest asshole even thinking she'd lied to him. That woman in the hotel room, and even that night at the arcade—that woman wouldn't lie to him. That woman had haunted him for two days. And for two days he'd let himself get consumed by the work of the ranch, the work of the boys, so he wouldn't have to think about the chance that Lucy had been lying to him.

But, of course, Ben could be lying about hanging out every day in the barn instead of working with Lucy on the garden. His gut was telling him that something just wasn't right about this situation.

So, he had to ask. He just had to man-up and ask.

"Let's go, Casey." He popped open the door and Casey scrambled out of his booster seat in the backseat of the cab.

"Is someone in trouble?"

"Why?" Jeremiah asked, opening the door so Casey could jump down.

"You got your trouble face on."

Jeremiah forced a smile and rubbed his nephew's hair. They took three steps toward the front door and it opened. Lucy stepped out, her hair in inky damp curls down her back. Her long, lithe body was dressed in a yellow sundress that hugged her breasts and flared at her waist, leaving miles of her legs bare. The finishing touch—cowboy boots. Honestly, she was his dream come true.

His heart hammered at the sight of her, his blood churning in veins suddenly too small.

She'd dressed that way for him. He knew it.

But she stopped when she saw him and for a moment, one moment, her panicked face revealed everything. Disappointment replaced desire.

"You're early." Her voice was a death knell. *Friends,* he thought, bitterness creeping into his heart like poison. *Friends don't lie.*

"Where is he?" he asked, and she took the steps down to him carefully, her face composing itself. Her quick brain was probably coming up with a hundred excuses and he couldn't stand it. When she stopped in front of him and opened her mouth, no doubt to feed him some lie, he held up his hand.

"Don't," he said. "I know he hasn't been working with you."

"How?"

"Does it matter?"

Her dark complexion had paled, but now blush crept into her cheeks.

"I guess not."

"You lied."

"It's not like that, Jeremiah."

"No? Is it like you're lying to your family about your business?"

"Don't—" She reached as if to hush him and he stepped back, pinning her in place with his eyes. Beside him, Casey clung to his leg, freaked out by the animosity between him and Lucy.

"Casey, go and wake your brother up in the barn. That's where he is, right?" he asked Lucy.

"He's there but he's not sleeping," she said.

"Well, he's certainly not gardening with you, is he?"

Casey ran off, leaving them alone.

"You lied, Lucy. Right to me. About Ben…you know what kind of trouble he's in—"

"I was going to tell you. I was, but I could see it was such a relief for you, not to have to be the bad guy again."

"Don't make this about me, Lucy. You lied. You."

"Fine. You're right. It started and I thought I would get him to open up and talk to me and it would all pour out, all of his feelings, and I could be the hero. But he just...he wouldn't do what I told him."

"Really? And you don't think I have some experience with that?"

The look she gave him was so naked and he realized why he was so angry right now. It wasn't about Ben. He was angry because he'd shown her more of himself, more of his despair and confusion, in one kiss than he'd revealed to anyone in over two years.

But she'd done the same to him and he turned it on her, a blade she'd inadvertently sharpened.

"Let me guess what this is really about—you didn't want to fail again."

She barely flinched. "Something like that."

He put his hands over his eyes, rubbing his forehead. He wanted to hold on to his anger, his righteousness, but...damn it, as much as he'd revealed to her, she'd done the same and he understood, when he didn't want to. He wanted to hold on to his anger a little longer.

"Hey, Jeremiah, you staying for dinner?" It was Sandra, standing next to a daughter who looked about as guilty as a woman in a bright yellow sundress could look.

"No, Sandra, but thanks."

"Are you sure? Mia and Jack are coming, too."

"Sounds like a party. But we've got to head home."

"Next time, then?"

Lucy hung her head for a moment and he felt bad for her, he really did; she was carrying so many damn lies right now it had to be making her sick.

"I don't think there's going to be a next time, Sandra. Ben's not going to be hanging around anymore."

"What?" Sandra looked shocked—at least she hadn't been in on the lie. "Why not?"

"Ask your daughter."

He turned at the sound of Casey's laughter and saw the highly unlikely trio of Casey, Ben and Walter walking across the parking area from the garage.

Ben had his hand under Walter's elbow like the boy was keeping him upright. And he was smiling. Not a lot. Not like he used to, but more than he had in months.

Jeremiah shot a quick look over his shoulder at Lucy.

"I told you, he hasn't been napping," she said. "I know it sounds crazy, but he's been working with Walter."

Walter? The thought did not inspire confidence.

"Hi, guys," Jeremiah said, walking toward the trio. At the sound of his voice, Ben's face dropped its smile and the scowl came back. "You need some help, Walter?" he asked.

"I'm all right." Walter stopped in front of Jeremiah and Jeremiah felt Sandra and Lucy come up to stand beside him.

"Ben," Jeremiah said, "you need to say goodbye."

Ben nodded. "See you later, Walter," he said to the old man, ignoring Lucy entirely.

Jeremiah shook his head. "You're not coming back."

"What?" Ben howled.

"The deal was you were supposed to work off the damage you caused to Reese's car with Lucy. You haven't done a single thing with Lucy, have you? You haven't been working in the garden like you told me you were—"

Ben turned bright red and Jeremiah braced himself for a screaming fit.

"He's been working with me," Walter said.

"That's great, Walter, but it doesn't change the fact that Ben has been lying to me."

"Sounds like Lucy's been lying to you, too," Sandra said, her voice ominous.

Oh, God, he did not want to get tangled up in this. He wanted to get his boys back home and figure out what to do next in the privacy of his own house. He'd been wrong to ask Lucy for help, that much was obvious. Annie would be furious with him right now, spreading their dirty laundry around to the neighbors.

"Come on, Ben. Casey. Let's go."

"Hold on a second," Walter said, holding out a hand. "If he can't stay and work for Lucy, can he stay and work for me?"

"What are you talking about?" Lucy asked.

Ben was staring at the old man like he didn't know what was going on, either.

Walter lifted his chin. "Everyone thinks I need a nurse, well…I want Ben to be my nurse."

CHAPTER SIXTEEN

THEY ALL SAT AROUND an empty table.

I should get some food, Sandra thought. But she didn't. No one was going to eat it. Everyone was too full of emotion to eat.

Jack had his head in his hands, his hat on the table beside him. "Dad, he's just a kid."

"He helped take care of his mother," Walter said, looking like a man who'd just managed to get out of a trap.

This is how badly he wants me to leave, she thought. *He would have a child in my place.*

"You did?" Jeremiah asked Ben. "You took care of your mom?"

Ben nodded. "Before she got so bad she had to go to the hospital. I just got her a lot of ice when she asked. Read her some books. It wasn't a big deal."

But it was, she could tell by Jeremiah's face that it was a very big deal.

"That's incredibly noble, Ben," Mia said. "It's amazing really, but Walter—"

"Is sitting right here," Walter said.

"Fine," Mia said, sitting up in her chair and looking right at Walter. "You've been sober...what? A week?"

"Two and half."

"And you've been taking your medicine how long?"

"Three months."

"You've terrorized every person we've brought in and I'm supposed to believe that you'll let this…child help you?"

"He is who I want."

"Nonsense," Sandra said, getting to her feet. "You just don't want me." Everyone turned to look at her and she didn't care.

"You are so desperate for me to leave that you are willing to use this boy." She stared at Walter. "Do you deny it?"

Walter nodded his head. "I do want you to leave."

"What the hell, Walter," Lucy snapped. "She's been nothing but good to you."

Walter wouldn't look at her eyes and Sandra felt the devil in her, the devil that used to make her punch kids in the playground for saying things about her fanatic mother. About her worn, ill-fitting hand-me-downs. The devil took control.

"If you want me to go, tell them the truth. Tell them why."

Walter shook his head.

"Dad," Jack whispered, "what is going on here?"

The silence in the room had screws and all of them felt the pain. Finally, Walter looked up. "Your mother was right," Walter said, looking his son in the face.

"About…about what?" Jack asked, looking quickly at Mia, who only shrugged.

Walter looked up at Sandra, and the shame on his face gave her pause. Made her wish she had better control of her devils. "I loved Sandra."

The entire room gasped and Sandra nearly smiled. So strange how, listening to him confess it made her so happy.

Jeremiah stood, his hands on the shoulders of the boys beside him. "We're going to go."

Walter stood, too, and looked at Ben and Jeremiah. "I know it's different. And I know why you don't exactly trust me. Or Ben. But—" Walter cleared his throat and the room was silent. Sandra held her breath. "But Ben's doing good work for me. And he's working hard."

"I…" Jeremiah shook his head. "I'm going to have to think about it."

"Do that," Walter said.

Ben and Casey followed Jeremiah out the door and then, surprisingly, Ben turned back around. "Thanks, Walter."

"You're welcome, Ben."

In the hallway Jeremiah's face registered shock as well as profound pain and Lucy gasped. Sandra saw that Lucy's hands were knotted in her lap.

When did it happen, Sandra wondered, *that Lucy started to feel so much for Jeremiah Stone?*

Once Jeremiah and the boys had left, Jack stood.

"Dad, what did you think would happen when you had Sandra come here? Did you… I mean, were you hoping—" Jack looked supremely pained and Sandra almost laughed, but the tension in the room suffocated it "—to be with her?"

Walter shook his head. "I just…I just wanted to make things right. Sandra belongs here. This was her home and I let Vicki take that away from her."

"But now you want her to leave?" Mia said.

"It was one thing when she didn't know…" Walter stopped, shook his head and then abruptly turned away. He snatched his cane from the side of the table and lurched out of the room, down the darker hallway.

"Dad—" Jack took a step after him but then stopped and turned wide eyes to Mia. "What do we do?"

Mia shrugged. "I have no clue," she said. "None."

Sandra could feel Lucy's eyes on her, shrewd and knowing, and she braced herself for the question to come. "Mom," Lucy finally asked, "do you...do you have feelings for Walter?"

"Would that be so wrong?"

Lucy's jaw dropped. "Ah, yeah."

"Why?"

"Because he's Walter, Mom."

"Lucy—" Jack sighed.

"He helped you with Ben, a favor for which you seem very ungrateful," Sandra chided, and Lucy shut her mouth. But Lucy couldn't keep quiet for long.

"Okay, he seems to be trying—"

"He is trying," Jack said, "pretty damn hard."

Lucy stared at Sandra, clearly reluctant to give Walter an inch despite his deserving it. "But what about Dad?"

"He's been gone five years," Sandra said, choosing once again not to tell her daughters the truth about her marriage. "I am lonely."

"For Walter?"

"For a friend," Sandra clarified. "And I think Walter could use one, too."

"Very noble, Mom," Lucy said.

Oh, thought Sandra, *you have no idea.* "If you're going to be snide, I'd rather not talk to you about this."

Lucy appealed to her sister. "Mia. Come on, you can't think this is a good idea."

Mia took a deep breath. "I do, actually. Walter... Walter's made a lot of mistakes and he's paid for every one of them. He was good to me when you all were gone. He...he is family."

Sandra smiled at Mia, proud of her baby.

"Jack?" Lucy asked, still searching for support.

"I'm worried about his drinking," Jack said. "And, Sandra, he's not very good with friendship—I'd hate to see you get hurt."

"You're talking about me as if I'm a child," Sandra said.

"But," Lucy said, still obviously unable to understand this, "what does this mean? You're staying? Like… indefinitely?"

Sandra lifted her chin, ready to get to the bottom of Lucy's web of lies and secrets. "It would seem I don't have a home to go to in Los Angeles."

"What are you talking about?" Mia asked.

Sandra arched an eyebrow. "Ask your sister."

Lucy stood up in her pale yellow dress, a ray of sunshine with a gloomy face. "I…I have something I need to tell you guys."

IT WASN'T EASY. IT WAS, in fact, exactly as hard as she imagined it would be. She told her family how she failed and she couldn't look at them, instead staring at her feet. The grout in between the stones on the floor. And with every truth she told, every lie she reversed, it felt like she was cutting off another body part.

When she was done, she finally looked at her sister. Her mother. And to her sick satisfaction, they were reacting exactly the way she thought they would. Mia was horrified, Mom was worried—which made Lucy feel guilty.

"Twenty thousand dollars?" Mia asked. "That's your debt?"

After Lucy nodded, Mia whistled.

"What about all the gold and gems from your studio?" Sandra asked. "That has to be worth some money."

"I sold it to make payroll before laying off my employees." Mom sat like a rag doll in her seat. "That's... that's why I was looking into selling the condo."

"You were going to sell the condo without telling Mom?" Mia asked. "Are you crazy?"

"A little," Lucy answered honestly. "But I just wanted to see what I could get. I wouldn't have sold it without talking about it with Mom."

"You sure about that?" Mia knew her so well, even in those moments like this, when she wasn't herself.

"Honestly? No. I'm sorry. I've been turned inside out. I didn't want anyone to worry. I didn't want anyone to be ashamed—"

"Ashamed!" Mia cried, and glanced sideways at Mom. "How in the world could we be ashamed of you?"

"Because I blew it? Because I was too stupid—"

Sandra stood and grabbed Lucy by the arms, jerking her into a crushing hug. "No one talks about my daughter that way," she whispered.

"But I was, Mom." She sighed. "I was just so stupid."

"Stop, please, Lucy. You weren't stupid. Everyone makes mistakes."

"Twenty-thousand-dollar ones?" she asked while her mother wiped the tears off Lucy's cheeks.

"Well." Sandra smiled. "You always were an over-achiever."

Lucy smiled and hot new tears seeped over her eyelashes. "Do we need to sell the condo?" Sandra asked.

"It's either that or I declare bankruptcy."

"Then we can sell. You were right. I never liked Los Angeles."

"So, you're…you're just going to stay here?" Lucy asked.

"It *is* my home," Sandra said proudly. "When Mia and Jack move into their house, I'll take over the cottage again."

"And take care of Walter?" Lucy said, not able to hide her disappointment.

"He's doing that on his own, it seems. But someday there might be children on this ranch again." Sandra looked at Mia and Jack. Jack's blush was about the sweetest thing Lucy had ever seen and very telling.

"I, ah, I need to go check on Dad," Jack said, and quickly skedaddled out of the room.

"The question," Sandra asked, "is what will you do? Where will you go?"

"I don't know."

"You're designing again," Mia pointed out. "You can start over."

"I burned a lot of bridges." She explained the attitude of the boutique owners who sent back her designs after learning she was mass-producing the horseshoe necklace. Meredith Van Loan had sent a snobby note saying, "We don't cater to the masses."

"Maybe they only look burned?" Mia asked.

"It doesn't matter," Lucy said. "I don't have any materials. Or equipment. I had to sell it all."

"Lucy," Sandra said, "I'm not without money."

"And I'm not going to take it, Mom. Besides, I don't even know if I really want to do this. I don't…know what I want to do just yet. I'm still figuring it out."

Mia nodded. "That's allowed, I suppose. But the taxi thing?"

"Over," Lucy insisted. "Over before it really started, except for taking Aaron to some hockey—" She stopped.

She imagined she wouldn't be taking Aaron anywhere anymore. Tears burned hotter behind her eyes. Quickly, she blinked them away, surprised at the pain.

"Well, you're staying here," Mia said, wrapping her arms around Sandra's waist and Lucy's shoulders. "As long as you need. This place has been empty too long."

"Thanks." Lucy sighed, grateful for the invitation.

"Come," Sandra whispered, kissing both her girls on their foreheads. "Let's have something to eat."

"I can't, Mom. Not just yet." She grabbed her keys off the counter.

"Where are you going?" Sandra asked.

"You're going to go chase after Jeremiah," Mia said, her feeling about the idea more than obvious.

"I have to try and talk to him. Explain why I lied."

Sandra looked between Mia and Lucy. "Is there…is there something between you and Jeremiah?"

"I like him, Mom, a lot. And if I let him cool off he'll convince himself he should never speak to me again. He's a mess like that."

"Maybe he's sensible like that," Mia said.

"Whose side are you on?"

"The side that causes less bloodshed."

If Jeremiah had his way he would never speak to her again. Never see her again. Certainly never meet her at the hotel by the highway. And the thought opened up a hole in her chest.

He'd left not even an hour ago and she missed him.

Missed the idea of him. The boys.

"I have to try."

"Wait, honey, at least until he settles the boys down. Give him a chance to deal with what's on his plate before you go rushing in to explain yourself."

Mom was right, it would be selfish to go charging over there right now. She could wait a few hours. A few very painful hours.

THE BOYS STOOD BEHIND Jeremiah. Without even looking at them he knew how they would be arranged.

Ben, of course, would be slouched against the wall, under the phone, his arms crossed over his chest. His nine-year-old glare getting sharper by the second. Jeremiah knew this because the skin between his shoulder blades itched.

In the doorway, Casey would be cozied up to Aaron, and as the stress in the kitchen got deeper and thicker Casey would contemplate putting his thumb in his mouth. But then he would remember the number of times Jeremiah had yelled at him to stop sucking his thumb like a baby, and instead he'd grab Aaron's hand.

Aaron would squeeze his brother's hand but stay silent, just like Jeremiah had told them to—barked at them, actually—the second they'd gotten into the truck to leave the Rocky M.

How much longer would that last? Jeremiah thought, picking up the book bags that covered the kitchen table and chucking them in the corner. *How much longer before Aaron starts yelling back to protect his brothers from their crazy uncle? The uncle who only pretends to know what he is doing. The uncle who yells too much, who never seems to say the right thing.*

Once the table was cleared, he spun.

"Sit." He pointed to the chairs. His temper and his confusion was a boiling-hot mess in his chest. As he watched the boys cross the room, he thanked the Good Lord that Ben didn't mouth off. He didn't know what he would do otherwise. He really didn't. His back was so far up against the wall he was lost in the paint.

Ben sat, Casey and Aaron followed.

"Why are you mad?" Casey whispered, looking guilty and worried and scared.

"I don't like being lied to."

"I didn't lie," Casey protested, and Jeremiah took a deep breath. Counted to ten.

"I know, Case, but…but we're having a family meeting."

Casey looked at Aaron, who shrugged.

"It's our first." Jeremiah took another deep breath and reached deep inside for his heretofore unseen internal Dr. Gilman. He'd been seeing the psychologist for months now—something had to have rubbed off.

"We need to talk," Jeremiah said. "Not yell. Not go stomping off when we get mad, we need to sit here—" He spread his hands across the faded and scarred wood of the old table. The table he grew up at, the table his sister inherited and was now his again—full circle. "And talk stuff out."

"Good," Aaron said, and Jeremiah fought the urge to throw his arms around the kid.

Jeremiah turned to Ben, who sneered. "Yeah, you mean me," he said. "I'm the one who has to talk."

"I just want to know why—" He thought about saying, "You lied to me," but the Dr. Gilman in his head vetoed that.

Too accusatory. You've gone that route before.

He thought about asking, "Why Walter and why not Lucy?"

Too close to your own hot buttons and not quite the problem, is it?

"Why do you want to work with Walter?"

Ben blinked at him, as if surprised, and the Dr. Gilman in his head nodded in approval. But Ben just shrugged.

"What kind of work do you do with him?"

"We're cleaning up all his moldy saddles and stuff."

It was Jeremiah's turn to be surprised. That was not fun work.

"And you like that?"

"Better than gardening."

Careful, he thought, *careful here.*

"You know, you could have just told Lucy you didn't want to garden."

"I did."

Jeremiah could just imagine how that went and he hung his head for a second looking for another way into the boy's head.

"Walter tells me stories about Mom."

Jeremiah's head jerked up.

"What stories?" Aaron asked, his eyes alight.

"Ones about Pirate—"

"Who is Pirate?" Casey asked.

"Mom's dog growing up," Aaron told him. "Mom said he used to chase the mailman so much that he would leave the mail down at the bottom of the drive."

"That's not all," Ben said. "Pirate nearly killed Duchess, Walter's old dog."

Jeremiah sat back in his chair, blown sideways by the boys' reactions to these stories. Aaron's eyes glittered and Ben—Ben was smiling.

You don't talk about her anymore, he thought. *You don't want to upset the boys so you just stopped talking about your sister. Their mom and dad. They died and then you put the memories away where the boys couldn't reach them.*

You thought it was the right thing.

"First of all," he said, sitting back. "Pirate was my dog! Your mom stole him."

He could see on their faces that they weren't sure what he was doing. They looked as if the ice under their feet wasn't totally solid.

"How'd she steal him?" Casey asked.

"She used to go to bed at night with dog treats under her pillow and Pirate would sleep on her bed because she fed him all night. He used to sleep like a person, too. You know how dogs usually sleep all curled up?"

Casey jumped away from the table to demonstrate, curling up like a doughnut, while Aaron and Ben watched. Their mouths curving slowly into smiles.

"Well, Pirate used to sleep stretched out, on his back with his paws in the air. He used to push her out of bed all the time."

"But she still let him sleep in her bed?" Aaron asked.

"Every night. She really loved that dog."

The boys smiled at one another over this piece of their mother he'd handed back to them.

"Did I ever tell you about your mom and dad's wedding?"

"No!" Aaron said, and Casey got up off the floor and crawled into Jeremiah's lap. It took Jeremiah a second to swallow back the barbed lump in his throat and he pressed his lips to Casey's curls, until the moment passed.

The boys all leaned forward, toward him as if he was fire and they were cold.

I'm sorry, he thought, *I should have told you these stories all along.*

"Your mom," he whispered, "wore white cowboy

boots under her wedding dress. And your dad nearly threw up at the altar."

He skipped the part about how he and Conner, their dad, had gotten drunk as skunks behind the church before the ceremony.

"Did Mom get mad?" Aaron asked.

"Furious."

"How'd she even know?" Ben asked. "If he didn't actually throw up?"

"Your dad burped. And it did not smell good."

Casey howled and Jeremiah laughed, remembering. Before he knew it, Aaron was laughing and so, remarkably, was Ben.

"I know that wedding album is around here somewhere." He set Casey down and wandered into the rarely used den, where all the photos were kept. The boys followed and it was a good night. Magical almost. The kind of night he never thought they'd have.

Jeremiah watched the boys, heads bent over Aaron's baby album, and he decided not to waste time feeling bad for having denied them this. Instead, he was going to go back over to Walter's tomorrow and tell him Ben would be working with him.

Because it made Ben happy and it was about time something did.

CHAPTER SEVENTEEN

LUCY DROVE SLOWLY over the pass, trying to formulate her argument. Trying to screw her courage to the sticking point, but her stomach was in knots.

All she could think about was how angry Jeremiah had been. How betrayed.

What did you think was going to happen? she asked herself. *This is the way you handle every problem in your life, you bury your head in the sand and hope it will go away. Hope something will magically change. But all that changes is that it blows up in your face.*

Honestly, she should be used to this by now.

The wind whipping through the window made Lucy more nervous, so she rolled it up and tried the radio but every song jangled and the DJs sounded like children.

What did they know about life? she thought, listening to them talk about it. *What did they know about anything?*

What did she?

This past year had been such a blur of worry and constantly swimming up from rock bottom. It had exhausted her and blinded her and made her doubt every part of herself. And now that the dust had settled in a way that she'd never expected, she had sudden clarity. She could see for miles in every direction.

And all she saw was Jeremiah. How he made her

feel and that was too rare to let go because of pride. On both their parts.

She'd forget about logic and focus on what she was good at. Feelings. And what she'd felt had been real, and if he didn't agree, there was no argument to make.

She parked and started up the porch steps. The house was dark, as one would expect at nearly ten o'clock at night. She hoped he was up. It was daunting to consider having to muster up the courage to try this again in the morning.

"Lucy." His voice nearly scared her right off the steps.

"Christ, Jeremiah," she gasped, her heart pounding under her hand.

She heard the quiet thrum of a rocking chair against the floor and then he was there—in front of her. Solemn and steady. His hands tucked into his pockets, his red T-shirt stretched taut against his chest.

"Lucy." He sighed. "It's been a pretty dramatic day already. Why are you here?"

"I…" Every word that came to her mouth felt selfish. *I wanted to make you forgive me, like me, kiss me. I want it to go back to the way it was.* "I wanted to make sure you were all right."

"I'm fine," he murmured.

"You don't sound fine."

"We talked about Annie and Conner for two hours. Looked at pictures. The kids loved it."

"And you?"

"Who doesn't love a trip down memory lane?" His smile was not convincing and the tension and pain was palpable around him, like heat waves off sun-baked asphalt. She reached for him and he stepped immediately backward.

Her hand hung there, rebuked.

"I think you should leave."

It's okay, she told herself when her skin shrank, her heart stuttered. *He's right to be angry. You just have to tell him how you feel.* "Is it because I lied?"

"No, actually. I get why you lied. I probably would have done the same thing in your position."

"Somehow that doesn't sound like forgiveness."

He stepped farther away, as if containing himself and pulling back everything he'd ever shared with her. "I can't be distracted right now. I can't be pulled in two directions."

"Jeremiah, you deserve a life—"

"I see a counsellor every Saturday." He didn't let her reply. "A shrink. With a couch and tissues…the works. And it's a secret. No one knows. Not the boys. Not their grandparents. Because she asks me about my feelings. And I tell her. Every damn week I spill my guts."

Lucy didn't understand what he wanted from her. Was she supposed to denigrate him for getting the help he so clearly needed? "That's…that's great, Jeremiah. You've had a rough two years. I'm glad you have someone to talk to."

"Yeah, well, I canceled last week. So I could have sex with you in that hotel. And I was going to do it again this Saturday. And for however many Saturdays you were going to be here. For as many Saturdays as I could get."

He made it sound so villainous. So evil.

"I didn't make you cancel those appointments."

"I know. It's me, Lucy. I can't…I can't have you and be what the boys need."

"Oh, my God, Jeremiah, if you'd told me we could have had our dates on another night—"

"That's not the point."

"Seems to me like you're making it the point."

He was silent for a moment, gathering his argument, and she could only stand there and wait; she had no position anymore to convince him. No weapons to sway him.

"I told you, I can't be distracted. I can't be torn when it comes to those boys and all you are is distraction."

She was breathless with pain. Eviscerated by his words. Her heart and guts spilling out onto the shadowed porch.

She forced enough air into her body so she could respond. "So that's it?"

He shrugged. "It has to be."

Lucy wanted to protest but she knew it was pointless. She saw it in the chill of his eyes. He was gone for her. A million miles away.

Without saying goodbye or looking back, she turned and walked away, back to her car.

Funny how when this thing started all she'd wanted was distraction. *Now what,* she wondered, feeling nauseated and rejected, numb and cold in those places he'd warmed—*could possibly distract me from this?*

THE NEXT AFTERNOON JEREMIAH picked up Ben from school. Casey, amazingly, had agreed to stay home with Adele, the new housekeeper. It probably had something to do with the chocolate chip cookies Adele was planning to make. The boy had a thing about cookie dough.

"I could have taken the bus home," Ben said.

"I wanted to talk to you."

Ben gave no response to that, but it seemed as if the temperature in the truck had gone down a few degrees. *Talk* was synonymous with *yelling.* With a grounding, or extra barn work. *Talk* was a bad word at the Stones' house.

Dr. Gilman would be ashamed.

"Where are we going?" Ben asked when they didn't turn left at the grocery store toward home. Instead, they went right.

"Rocky M."

"Am I in trouble again?"

Ben kicked the dashboard and Jeremiah forced himself to count to ten. *Pick your battles,* he thought, remembering some old words of wisdom from Cynthia.

"You wanted to help Walter," Jeremiah said.

"Yeah. But you said no."

"Well, now I'm saying yes."

Ben's face waivered somewhere between happy and skeptical. Distrustful.

"Why?"

"Because you want to, don't you?"

"Yeah."

"And it makes you happy?"

"Maybe."

Ben looked away, as if hiding his happiness, a secret he had to keep in fear of Jeremiah taking it away. Jeremiah wondered how many times he had done that. Taken away the things that made Ben happy so that all that was left was unhappiness.

"I want you to be happy, Ben."

"Yeah, right," he sneered.

"I do. I liked seeing you happy last night and if I had known that remembering things about your mom—that talking about her—would make you happy, then I would have done it more often. I'm sorry."

Jeremiah parked the car in silence, right in front of the Rocky M barn.

Walter was sitting in the shade just inside the barn door and glanced up. A miserable old man, sick, getting sicker every day.

What the hell am I thinking? Annie would skin me.

But Annie wasn't here and that was the problem.

"Do you believe me? That I want you to be happy?" Jeremiah asked, watching his nephew, knowing the question was so weighted that the boy would have to say yes or risk some kind of deep conversation about happiness or lack thereof.

Predictably, after a moment, Ben nodded.

"Good." Jeremiah popped open the truck door. "Now let's go see if Walter still wants a nine-year-old nurse."

JEREMIAH AND BEN GOT OUT of their truck but they didn't head toward the house. They turned toward him instead.

Uh-oh, was all Walter could think, but he kept rubbing the linseed oil on the old reins.

"Hello, Walter," Jeremiah said, pushing his hat up with his thumb, revealing dark curls matted with sweat. *Lord knows the man puts in an honest day's work between the boys and the ranch.*

"Jeremiah." Walter nodded. "Ben."

"So." Jeremiah cleared his throat. "About the, ah, the nurse thing?"

"I don't much like the word *nurse.*" Walter rubbed the reins with his thumb, harder than needed, but these days it was work hard or go back to drinking. And today the work was only barely saving him. His head burned for a drink.

"Okay." Jeremiah sighed. His patronizing tone made Walter take that imaginary swig. "What would you call it?"

Walter shrugged.

"'Helper,'" Ben supplied. "That's...that's what Mom called me. Her helper."

Walter noticed the way Jeremiah stared at Ben, as if

he were some kind of exotic animal that had sidled up and started talking. When Ben saw this, the hurt was right there on the kid's face.

When it came to the boy, Jeremiah was a blind man.

Walter nodded. "'Helper' works."

"All right. We can all agree on that."

"Not sure why you need to be sarcastic," Walter said. It was one thing when Mia was sarcastic, it was her mother tongue. She didn't know how to talk without it. But he didn't need it from Jeremiah. Not in front of the kid.

Jeremiah took his hat all the way off and looked up at the sky as if talking to God. Walter looked over at Ben and winked.

The boy smiled. Score: one point for Walter.

"You're right," Jeremiah said. "I apologize. I have considered what you said and if you think Ben can help you and you want that help…I think it could work."

"Glad to hear it."

"But I'd want a couple of assurances."

"Like what?"

"Like if your condition gets worse and you need real help, you tell me right away. No pride here, Walter. I won't have Ben feeling overwhelmed or scared."

Walter looked over at Ben and wanted to say he'd never scare the boy, but his pride was often a problem.

"I promise," Walter said.

"And every day I get a report on his behavior—"

"I'm not a teacher, Jeremiah. The boy will work. If he doesn't he won't be welcome back. Past that, I don't have much to tell you."

Jeremiah looked like he wanted to argue but Ben piped up. "I'll be good. I promise."

Jeremiah ran a hand over his face, mumbling something that sounded a lot like "I cannot believe I'm doing this." He dropped his hand. "All right. When would you like him to start?"

"Right now suits just fine. You could go pick up the other boys and bring 'em back for supper. Sandra likes that."

The front door slammed and Jeremiah and Ben both turned toward the house. It had to be Lucy—Walter didn't even have to look, he could see it on Jeremiah's face. The man was as gutted as a fish.

"I'll be back in two hours." Jeremiah took off for the car, nearly at a run. Lucy stood on the porch, her hand up to shade her eyes from the sun. She wore a green-and-white plaid shirt and looked so much like Sandra twenty years ago, Walter had to look away.

"There's a pile of reins in the tack room," Walter said to Ben. "Go and grab 'em, would ya?"

Ben nodded and vanished into the barn.

A nurse, he thought, chewing over the word and the idea, surprised when the taste was sweet. The boy felt more like a second chance.

And why, he wondered, with a dry mouth and sweaty hands, *does that make me so damn nervous?*

LUCY WATCHED JEREMIAH drive off and told herself she'd suffered worse rejections. But none had ripped her legs out from under her. After last night's restless sleep she'd woken up resolved to forget Jeremiah, since that seemed to be the only thing she could do. But the second she saw his truck out the window, she'd entertained, for about half a second, the idea that he had changed his mind. About her. And she'd charged out the door like a lunatic.

But it was Walter he'd been here to see and the disappointment was bitter.

His truck kicked up dust as he charged away from the ranch and when it settled there were Walter and Ben, sitting in the shade, a pile of leather between them. Bits of metal flashing in the sun.

She thought of her leather bracelet designs and realized that right under her nose might be the materials she needed. Carefully, unsure of being welcome, or truly what she was doing—only knowing she had to do something or lose her mind thinking about Jeremiah— she approached the two of them.

"Hey," she said.

Walter looked up and then did a rather comical double take. "Lucy?"

Ben just stared at her, the little turncoat. Really, she wondered, what did Walter have that she didn't? *Maybe I should find out,* Lucy thought. *Maybe I should find out why my own mother wants a "friendship" with this man.*

Maybe I should give him half a chance.

"What…" She gestured limply toward the pile of beaten-up leather reins and bridles. "What are you doing?"

"Cleaning," Walter said.

"Oh. Could I join you?"

She laughed at the face Walter made. Oh, so funny that face. Horrified, he was utterly horrified at the thought of spending time with her. She couldn't totally blame him, it's not like she'd been overly pleasant to the man.

"I guess not." She started to turn on her heel.

Surprisingly her support came from Ben. "You can stay," he said.

She turned back just in time to catch Walter glaring at the boy.

"What?" Ben asked. "There are a lot of reins here."

"Actually," she said, plunking herself down in front of the piles of leather, across from Ben. "I was wondering if I could look at the pieces you're getting rid of."

"The garbage?" Walter asked.

"You know what they say—one man's garbage is another woman's jackpot."

"Suit yourself." Walter used his cane to push a small pile of beat-up leather straps at her. She dug into it with gusto, sorting pieces she could salvage and pieces that were too far gone.

"So," she said, needing to occupy her brain as well as her hands if only to fill the empty space Jeremiah used to fill. "What are we talking about?"

Ben and Walter shared a look. Apparently there wasn't a whole lot of talking going on yet.

"Do you have any stories about my mom?" Ben blurted.

"Do I?" Lucy cried, taking her own cloth from the pile to clean the ruined leather. Distressed leather was cool but distressed leather that smelled like horse—not so cool. "Your mom used to babysit Mia and me when we were kids." She launched into the story about their epic and elaborate games of hide-and-seek in the barn.

"And then…" she cried, lost in the memories, "when we'd hear Walter coming in, we'd—"

She stopped, suddenly embarrassed. They'd been little shits to Walter when Mom and Dad weren't around.

"What?" Ben asked, wide-eyed, the leather forgotten in his lap.

"Nothing—" She winced.

"Go ahead," Walter said, not looking up from his oil and cloth and the strip of leather he was working on. "Tell him."

"We'd hide Walter's things. His glasses, his hat. We'd

bury them in the hay. We'd move his horse between stables. We were...we were mean."

"Mom?" Ben asked, shocked and delighted at the same time. "Mean?"

"It wasn't ever her idea," Lucy said. "It was always Mia and me."

An apology rose to her lips but she swallowed it down. Those little pranks had been righteous retribution for what Walter had let Vicki do to Jack when they were all kids. Lucy and Mia had hidden his things and felt like Robin Hood, righting wrongs.

"Do you think I didn't know?" Walter asked.

Lucy blinked. "Did you... I mean, you never said anything. Or stopped us."

"I could hear you giggling while I dug through hay for my hat. I knew what you were doing." He looked up and Lucy saw intense blue eyes, less runny and more startling these days. More piercing. "And why."

Lucy broke eye contact first, discomfited by the vulnerability in his eyes. Yesterday, Mia had said that Walter had paid for all his crimes and Lucy had dismissed the notion.

But maybe she was wrong.

WHEN JEREMIAH SAW Dr. Gilman that week, he felt compelled to confess why he'd canceled last Saturday's appointment.

"Would you like to reschedule our meetings to a different day?" she asked.

"No. Saturday's fine."

"But if you're going to be dating...?" She trailed off suggestively, nothing but hope and approval in her face. Jeremiah couldn't meet her eyes so he stared at his hands, ran his thumb over a cut on his palm.

"I'm not dating—"

"Do you want to talk about this?"

"No."

"Jeremiah—"

"No. I don't."

It was bad enough seeing Lucy when he came to pick up Ben, sitting cross-legged at Walter's feet beside Ben, a pile of reins between them.

He'd thought it was a one-off. There simply was no way Lucy was going to hang out with Walter and Ben every day. But yesterday, when he'd driven up, she was there laughing at something Walter had said. Her throat, pale pink and elegant, had been tipped back, her hair a dark spill over her blue shirt.

Ben and Walter were staring at her like she was the sun and they'd just come out of a cave. He'd known exactly how they felt. And he'd wondered if she was doing it on purpose. Some kind of ploy to get him to reconsider their breakup. A way to get under his skin.

"How is Ben doing?" Dr. Gilman asked.

Jeremiah didn't know how to answer that. There were no more tantrums. The running away had stopped, too. Yesterday his teacher had said that Ben was starting to take part in class discussions. Raising his hand even.

Which was all great, but there was this obsessive collecting of stories and pictures. He was like an emotional hoarder. It couldn't be healthy.

"He cries at night," Jeremiah said. "I can hear him through his door."

"Makes sense," Dr. Gilman said. "He's grieving."

"Yeah, but how long does this last?"

Dr. Gilman put down her notebook and stared at him. The intent in her gaze felt like a razor against his skin. Sensing danger, his balls curled up into his belly.

"Have you grieved?" Dr. Gilman asked.

"For my sister? Yeah. Of course." Cried like a baby through her funeral. Boxed up her clothes and sobbed. Had to call Cynthia to help him.

"No. Have you grieved for your old life? For the rodeo? For the life you lived before you took over caring for the boys?"

His stomach dropped and his brain felt too light. His skin painfully tight. Panicked, suddenly shaking with adrenaline, he glanced up at the clock.

"Time's up, Dr. Gilman."

"Jeremiah—?"

He didn't stop. Didn't listen. He grabbed his hat from the stand by the door and slipped out the door. But his stomach stayed in his leaden legs and his skin itched like it wanted to come off.

ANOTHER WEEK WENT BY and Lucy found herself, gathering more steam every day, pulling herself from the black hole the past year had buried her in. And every morning she woke up expecting this to be the day she would leave. To head, if not back to Los Angeles, then into some new direction on some new adventure.

But instead her eyes opened and she saw the familiar bedspread, the familiar sun falling through her window. The sound of her mother and sister talking in the kitchen. It all gave her that heady sense of home that she'd been missing for five years.

This, her heart seemed to say, *is exactly where I want to be. Here.*

It wasn't to say the situation was perfect. She needed her own space, an apartment, maybe in town. And she'd cut off her own arm for some sushi and a proper latte. But she had peace and quiet, privacy to work, wide-open spaces to walk. When her head got tired of designing— a heretofore unheard of balance in her life that was un- expectedly and deliciously satisfying—she had honest ranch work to do.

And for about ten minutes twice a week, she had Jeremiah.

Every morning, after deciding she wasn't ready to leave, she tested what remained of her feelings for Jer- emiah. Like lifting the lid off a rain bucket, she checked the levels and to her great pain and chagrin, the levels stayed the same. The infatuation wasn't ending. These feelings were not fleeting. Twice a week, her heart stopped at the sight of his truck in the driveway.

And every day—at least twenty times per day—when her mind was the most still, when she was in the gar- den or tearing apart her jewelry only to rebuild it with leather and metal from scraps of tack, she hoped Jere- miah was okay. If she couldn't be with him, she wanted the sacrifice to be worth something. If he was better off without her, so be it.

Thursday morning, she awoke and felt sick of herself.

The longer she lay there, the more it felt as if her chest was collapsing under the pressure of her yearning. Her longing to see him. Talk to him. *Maybe today he'd stay long enough to talk,* she thought, and then hated herself.

Honestly, this is not you. Do not let that man turn you into this. Get out of bed.

That seemed a bit extreme so she compromised by pawing around her bedside table for her cell phone.

Within ten minutes she'd called her real estate agent and told her to put the condo on the market in earnest. And sell it, sooner rather than later.

"What about your stuff? I put what was here in storage—"

"I'll come and get it in a few days."

Hanging up the phone on Los Angeles and her ties there felt liberating. As if she'd finally managed to get rid of the stony weight she'd been pretending wasn't killing her back. She could go and pick up their stuff and then she'd put that city in her rearview mirror for good.

Amber, she thought suddenly. *And garnets. Oh, my gosh, in a bridal tiara.*

Sitting up, she grabbed the notebook she'd been keeping by her bed and found a blank page. She found one of the ten charcoal pencils she kept close by and frantically started to sketch. With delicate points of amber and garnet, it would be as if golden red rain had been caught in the bride's hair.

Wow, she thought when she was done. *Expensive. One of a kind.* Meredith Van Loan came to mind again and she grabbed the phone. *It would be easy to call her. Just press the button.*

You need pieces to show her, she told herself. *You can't just call her and say, "Hey, I've got some sketches that I think you'd like."*

Nope. It wasn't time. She closed the phone, got out of bed and pulled on some clothes. She had a couple hundred dollars from the ill-fated taxi business. Perhaps it was time to see what she could scrounge together in terms of materials and tools.

Perhaps it was time to scrounge together a second chance.

JEREMIAH WASN'T SLEEPING WELL. He wasn't eating well, either. He wasn't actually doing anything well.

Lucy was a thorn under his skin. He'd narrowed their contact down to twenty minutes a week and somehow those twenty minutes had become painfully paramount in his life.

Bullshit, he thought, wishing that denying it made it less true. With his stomach in knots, he drove over Friday afternoon to pick up Ben.

Ignore her, he told himself. *Just ignore her.*

But she made herself impossible to ignore, sitting right there when he drove up. She wore tight jeans and a silky shirt that had no business being so close to a barn. And what was she doing with Ben and Walter, anyway? If she was trying to torture him, she was succeeding.

He slammed the door behind him, probably too hard, if the looks on everyone's startled faces were anything to measure by. As he stomped up to them, his evil mood grew blacker. Lucy must have picked up on his viciousness because she stood and headed into the barn.

Walter stood, too, looking like a man who had no need of a nine-year-old nurse.

"Ben," Walter said. "Help me inside, would you?"

"Ah, sure," Ben said as he stretched the reins he'd been working on into the grass to dry. He stood, taking Walter's elbow. "I'll…I'll be right back," he said to Jeremiah.

"Fine," Jeremiah snapped, and then got ahold of himself. "Sorry, Ben, yes, go on. I'll wait here."

It was foolish, crazy even, but it suddenly felt as if the entire universe was conspiring to throw him into Lucy's orbit. And he was no good at resisting. Terrible at it.

Ben and Walter crossed the rutted parking area and Jeremiah resisted his base instinct for exactly ten seconds before spinning on his heel and stomping into the barn. He found her in the cool shadows of the tack room, her back to him; she stood at the sink, rinsing out rags. Torn in pieces by his instincts and demons he could only stand there for a second before finally barking, "What are you trying to do?"

Water sprayed the wall and she whirled, furious. "Good God, Jeremiah, why are you sneaking up on me?"

He glared at her and despite his better sense stepped farther into the room. "Why are you hanging out with Ben and Walter?"

She turned off the faucet and faced him. Water splats had turned her white shirt transparent in places and it clung to her, revealing the lace at the edge of her bra, the pink skin of her stomach, the shadow just under her collarbone.

Lust did not improve his mood.

"Did... Is Ben upset about it?" she asked.

"No. I am."

She blinked. "Why?"

"I—" *I don't want to see you. I don't want to be reminded of you. I'm tired of having you in my head.* "I just think it's suspicious," he said. "You don't spend any time with Ben when we're sleeping together and then, when we're not, you're suddenly sitting beside him at Walter's feet two days a week."

"Wait a minute...you think it's about you?" The gentle way she said it proved what an idiot he was, but he was committed to this path.

Her eyes narrowed before she wiped her hand off on her thighs and started to walk past him.

Let her go, he told himself, his hands. *Nothing good will come of touching her.* But when she was just past him, he turned and grabbed her elbow.

Her palm connected with his cheek and his whole head snapped back under the force of her blow. There was a breath—a moment for reason to prevail, for sense to guide his actions—but instead he grabbed her shoulders, yanking her against him and his lips smashed against hers.

She fought and he tried not to like it. He tried to let her go, but the best he could do was lift his lips from hers and press his forehead to the top of her head, his hands still holding her in an iron grip.

"I'm sorry," he said. "I'm sorry. I miss you. I can't... I see you and I miss you and I can't remember why it's a bad idea to kiss you or touch you. I'm sorry. I am—"

She leaned away from him; her eyes, wise and knowing and feminine, searched his and saw all his cracks and weaknesses.

"You're a mess," she whispered, and all he could do was try to laugh, but it came out sounding like a groan. Her arms lifted and he let her go, because he wasn't the kind of guy to kiss a girl against her will, or...well, he didn't used to be.

But then her arms wrapped around his neck and she was kissing him again and it was sweet. It was warm and tender. Caring. It wasn't a kiss between strangers acting on their casual attraction. It was the kiss of friends, acting on their feelings.

And he liked it. Opened up to it like the land to the rain after the dry season. Then the sweetness turned to heat and she pressed those curves against him and he stepped backward under the pressure of her body until his back hit the wall. He put his hands back on her hips, carefully, slowly, not sure if he had the right. But she curled against him in agreement, in total acquiescence and he slipped his hands up her back, one hand under her hair, the other just under her shirt so his fingertips could soak in the sensation of her firm, tender skin.

He wanted to spread her out on a bed and explore this skin of hers. Chart her sensitive places, the hidden coves, curves. He'd wasted every minute they'd spent together before because he hadn't done that, hadn't memorized her body as if it were a treasure map.

Her hand slipped under his shirt, her fingers skating across the skin of his back and up over his shoulders to hold him against her. Her strength formidable or maybe it just seemed that way because his was all gone. Powerless against her, he arched, dying to be inside her in any way she would let him. They held each other as close and as hard as they could, welded together by the heat and sweat blooming under their skin.

I'm sorry, I'm sorry, his kisses told her. *I'm sorry,* he tried to convey through his touch, his heartbeat. *You don't deserve this. I wish things were different. I wish I had my old life back and things between us could be normal.*

"Uncle J.?" Ben's voice ripped the air and he jumped away from Lucy like a teenager caught by his parents.

"Coming, Ben," he cried, embarrassed when his voice cracked. Lucy's smile was knowing and he kissed it, fevered and tortured. "Meet me back at the hotel," he whispered. "Tonight. Please."

Abruptly, her body stilled, filled with a sort of explosive tension, and he held his breath, wondering if he'd messed this up again. When she stepped back, her face was utterly composed and his heart sank. *Blown it* didn't seem strong enough.

"Go," she said, "Ben is waiting."

CHAPTER EIGHTEEN

LUCY WAITED UNTIL SHE was sure Jeremiah wouldn't look back, before leaning forward and resting her head against the wall of the barn. The rough wood hurt her forehead and pulled at her hair, but still she set it there.

Because you are a glutton for punishment. Standing in line for more misery. It would be so easy to go to that hotel.

Damn right, her body cried, still angry with her decision not to. Instead of having wild, dirty sex with a hot man—for whom she felt far more than she should—she was going to stay home on Friday night and watch her mother knit. Maybe make a few more little leather bracelets while waiting for her supplies to come in and Jeremiah to move out of her thought patterns.

But he wasn't going to move out of her thought patterns.

She loved him.

You're an idiot, she thought, rolling her head against the wood. *I love him. I love his mess and his heart and his body and his mind.* His past and his damage and his effort toward those boys. His charm and grin and the way he was trying so hard to be the man he needed to be. The way he couldn't see the forest through his own trees, but managed to call her on her bullshit even when it made him uncomfortable.

The way he needed to be loved and helped and cared for even while he fought against it.

She loved all of that about him.

He will never love you, she told herself. *Not like you love him.*

It was surprisingly easy to shrug off that thought. She'd never needed anyone's permission before. She'd never waited for someone's approval on her feelings.

None of that changed the reality that he had feelings for her. Conflicted feelings.

Maybe, she thought, *maybe he just needs to be shown the way clear of all of that conflict. Maybe he just needed to realize she wasn't a distraction.* She wasn't leaving. She could help, share his life. The boys and the ranch.

It wasn't either her or the boys, like he thought. He could have both. Granted, it would be nontraditional with her—she wasn't going to give up her career to fold laundry and freeze casseroles. But they could make it work.

She hoped they could make it work.

"I am going to get my heart broken," she said out loud, hoping that it might scare her off this ridiculous plan she had forming in her head. "Smashed into pieces," she told herself. "Obliterated."

Amazingly, she wasn't even nudged one bit from her plan.

"You're a fool," she said, just to make it clear.

Yep, a fool in love and a fool with a plan.

Heaven help them all.

"AARON! ANSWER THE DOOR!" Jeremiah cried, trying to keep Casey from burning himself on the ancient waffle maker. "Great, Ben, that's perfect," he said as Ben filled the waffle maker with batter they'd turned green with food coloring.

It was Sunday and the boys were acting like it was Christmas morning. Even Ben was in the spirit, standing on a chair, pouring ladle after ladle of green goop on the black patchwork griddle.

"Casey, watch this," Ben said, lifting the ladle high and dripping it over the hot metal.

On Ben's wrist gleamed a leather-and-silver bracelet Lucy had made for the boy. It was simple in the coolest way and would no doubt make him the hippest boy in third grade.

Casey and Aaron wanted ones, too.

So did Jeremiah. He wasn't a jewelry man at all, he just wanted a small piece of her to wear on his body.

"These are going to be the best waffles *ever!*" Casey screamed, and the batter on his mixing spoon splattered the kitchen wall. "Oops."

"Yeah, oops." Jeremiah laughed and swiped at the spots with a towel. The doorbell rang again.

"Aaron!"

"Yeah, I'm getting it."

He heard the door open.

"Lucy!" Aaron cried, and Jeremiah immediately dropped Casey back onto the ground. "Keep an eye on that," he said to Ben, and pointed to the waffle maker.

He stepped into the living room, half hoping he was imagining things. But there was Lucy, gorgeous in that yellow sundress with the cowboy boots. The same Lucy he'd left infuriated in the barn two days ago.

"Look, Uncle J.!" Aaron cried.

"I see," he murmured, feeling like the luckiest man on earth. "It's Lucy."

"No! It's doughnuts!" Aaron held a big box from the

Hole in One bakery downtown and was in the process of lifting out a giant bear claw. "Lucy brought them. How awesome is that?"

"Very awesome, but take that into the kitchen," Jeremiah said, imagining the box spilling to the ground. Adele would spend hours getting sprinkles out of the carpet. Aaron skipped out and cheers greeted him in the kitchen.

"What…what are you doing here?" he asked, once they were alone.

Lucy dropped her purse onto the ground, threw her keys on top of it and crossed the room to stand a foot from him. Purpose made her glow in that yellow dress.

"I'm no man's dirty secret, Jeremiah." She flipped a ribbon of black hair over her shoulder and lifted her chin like she was going into a fight. His body roared its approval.

"I didn't… That wasn't my intention."

"You said you missed me," she said, ignored his pathetic denials.

"I do."

She grinned like he was a slow kid finally getting an answer right—and that's about how he felt. He could not figure out what was going on.

"I miss you, too," she said. "A lot. And if you want to meet me in a hotel on Friday nights for a few hours, I'm all for it."

"You weren't all for it on Friday."

"Because I want more."

Terror lasered through his body. "More? More what?"

"Well, to start, doughnuts. This morning with you and the boys. And if that's too much, then tell me and I'll go. But then you and I need to stop seeing each other. For good. Make another arrangement for Ben and quit coming to the ranch. Because it's obviously too hard on both of us."

He didn't answer, he couldn't. Because it was too much. But she was also here. Right here, in front of him, and she was glowing.

Longing clogged his throat, burning away the resentful words that would make her walk right back out that door.

I want her to stay. I want her. But I can't have her. We've finally got something good going in this house, I can't mess that up.

"Jeremiah—" She sighed, as if she knew. As if she was fully aware of how delicate the balance was in his life, how impossible it was to maintain it with her around.

"Lucy!" It was Casey, rocketing out of the kitchen, a doughnut in each hand. He hugged her legs, chocolate and sugar glaze smeared her dress, but she didn't seem to mind. "Thanks for the doughnuts."

"You are welcome, buddy. We miss you around the ranch. Mom has all this banana bread and no one is tasting it."

Casey gasped and turned on Jeremiah. "See, I told you, you should take me to the ranch. They need me, Uncle J."

"Clearly." The wryness in his tone went right over Casey's head, but Lucy caught it and the look she gave him was unreadable.

"Hey, Lucy. Can I have a bracelet like Ben's?" Casey asked.

"Me, too!" Aaron charged into the living room, a doughnut in both hands.

Ben stood in the doorway, lingering on the edges, as if reluctant to get too close. But he was there.

Is it possible, he wondered, *to have both?* To have what he wanted and what would be good for the boys? And how long could he make that last?

How much time would be enough, with her? How much time to satisfy this craving he had for her?

He was frozen.

"Hey, Lucy," Ben said, waving the ladle, green spots landing on his shoes. Jeremiah didn't say anything about the mess, he was just so happy to see that little smile on the corner of the boy's lips.

"Ben, you're the best marketing tool a girl could have." From the pocket of her dress she pulled out two other bracelets. She handed the larger of the two to Aaron and then crouched to put the other around Casey's little wrist. He gasped as if the leather bracelet had magic powers.

This cemented it. Better than Christmas.

Strange. Things had been fun before she arrived. They were special, with the green food coloring and the waffle maker that didn't get pulled out of the cupboard all that often. The boys were laughing and having a good time.

But now there was something happening that took all the sharp edges off everyone in this house. It was as if all the dark corners were pushed back and deep breaths taken. It was special, yes, because it was so comfortable.

And comfortable hadn't happened in a long time.

There were a lot of questions Jeremiah wanted to ask Lucy about her plans. About her future. About Los Angeles. Just thinking about it made the comfortable feeling retreat a bit. The tension came right back into the corners, that space between his ribs.

Stop. He told himself. *Just give yourself a minute.*

"Do you want a cup of coffee?" he asked, but what

he was saying was, *Stay, just for a little while. Stay and make this house a home.*

"Is it good?" she asked, wincing like she already knew the answer.

"We're not without some comforts out here in the boonies," he said. "And I spent some time in L.A., too."

"Then—yes, please." Her smile was radiant.

"You want to see my room?" Casey asked, yanking her toward the stairs.

"Of course I do," she said. "I'll take room service with that coffee."

But these minutes of peace, they didn't come without cost. Not for the Stones. Not for him. Even as part of him was so happy watching her go upstairs, part of him could see the disaster that would surely come.

WALTER FOUND HIMSELF SHAKING with the need for a drink. His throat burned for one. His stomach ached. This thing with Ben, the way everyone was acting like he was cured—a different man—all of it made his sobriety seem ridiculous. He wasn't a sober man. He was a drunk.

It was the thing with the kid. It wasn't going to go well, in the end. Every time the kid asked for a story from the old days, Walter felt as if there was some nail being hammered in a coffin somewhere.

And Lucy, hanging around like that? Talking about the past, a past he barely remembered. That he'd squandered.

He liked those memories dormant. Drowned under the sea of booze. Having them bob to the surface was like being haunted by a thousand ghosts. Regret and nostalgia wouldn't let him sleep at night. What had he been thinking letting this kid be his "nurse"?

Every single thing Walter touched, he ruined. Why

did he think this would be different? Because he wasn't drinking? Because they'd asked him to help? Everyone should know he couldn't do this shit.

Christ, I want a drink.

He paced the house, hoping he could walk off the craving, but from the shadows just outside the brightly lit kitchen, he saw Sandra standing at the stove. Steam from whatever she stirred wreathed her head, turning her cheeks pink. Pink to match the blouse she wore, which floated around her like a cloud.

She lifted a spoon that dripped red sauce to her lips and took a taste. Her pink tongue darting out to catch a drop.

His control snapped and the need for a drink ran rabid through his chest, his head.

Yes! One of the hired ranch hands would have stashed a bottle in the bunkhouse.

Hell, why didn't I think of this earlier? Every voice in his head screamed in exaltation. He got as far as the front door and—nearly running—he paid no attention to how loud he was being.

"Walter?"

He stopped, barely swallowing the "leave me alone" he wanted to bark.

"Walter?" Sandra's footsteps echoed through the stone foyer as she came closer.

"Stop." His voice was a guttural moan. Of course she didn't listen. The stubborn woman.

"Are you all right?" she asked, and he felt, more than saw, her arm reaching for him. He turned and grabbed her hand.

Her mouth opened and there was a small gasp. He didn't know if it was because he was holding her hand too hard, or if she, too, felt the lightning and flare between their skin. Years of expectation and desire and thwarted feelings filled the foyer like smoke.

"Are you okay?" she whispered.

"I—" His jaw shook; his throat squeezed the words, not letting them out. "I can't do this."

"Do what?" He could tell in the iron edges of her voice that she knew what his failure was. He shook his head, wanting to keep his shame private. Wanting to carry it alone despite the fact that it was breaking his back.

"Talk to me, Walter." Her hand shifted in his grip, her fingers, strong and smooth and cool, linked through his. Their palms pressed together and he could feel her heartbeat through her skin, pounding against his. "You don't have to do this alone."

Blood churned through his veins, a storm of desire and longing. Unable to help himself, when he looked at her all the parts of himself—scattered and loose, small and large—suddenly gathered under the force of her magnetism.

He could lean on her. It was the fundamental truth about this woman. It was one of the things he loved about her.

When her other hand cupped his cheek, sensation tripped through him, ricocheted through his chest and around his head. Sparks grew into fires.

His fingers tightened on hers, and slowly he pulled her toward him. She stumbled slightly, off balance, unsure, and he ignored that, dropping his cane to wrap his other hand around her thin waist.

She was small, smaller than he'd ever perceived, because her personality was so big. Against him, she was tiny. Perfect.

"Walt—"

He kissed her. Pressed his dry lips to hers and he swallowed her gasp, tasted the tang of the tomato sauce in her, the sweetness that was her. She took another step toward him, a willing participant in a kiss he'd never in his life dreamed would happen. He stepped forward, too, meeting her in the fevered space between them.

Her tongue touched his lips and he groaned in surrender; everything he was—all the demons and the meager angels he carried in his soul—sighed in bliss. This was a moment he'd never allowed himself to dream about. But somehow it was exactly as he'd imagined.

He opened himself up to her, slipping his arm farther around her waist, bending her slightly backward so that he carried her sweet weight in his arms. She moaned and sighed against him, melting like butter in a pan.

There was no end point to this kiss—it could have lasted for another hundred years. He could have pulled the strength he needed from her, but he wanted to come to her better than he was at this moment. He wanted to come to her as a man on his own two feet.

Enough. Pulling away was awful, like stepping out from a warm house into the cold.

"Sandra." He sighed, kissing her cheeks, her forehead. He wrapped his arms around her, holding her close, feeling her breathe against him.

"Why…why are you stopping?"

He stepped back, his fingers lingering on her waist, loath to give up what he felt under her shirt, the firm tension of her muscles, the softness of her skin.

"There's something I have to do, Sandra," he told her. "And I could talk to you, but I want to…" He didn't know how to put it into words, this driving feeling to be better. To deserve what she would give him for no good reason. "I want to give you the reason to be with me. I want to be a man you can be proud of. A man I can be proud of."

She didn't lie and say she was proud of him, which he respected. It stung a bit, but he wanted honesty between them.

"Can I help you?" she asked, her lips moist from their kiss.

"You already have." He bent to get his cane.

"You're making me nervous," she said. "You're not drinking, are you?"

"I'm trying very hard not to," he said, and leaned forward—delighting that he had the right, relishing that he had her permission—and kissed her again. It was a quick taste of her lips, the impression burning even after he'd pulled away.

He found himself smiling into her worried face. At his smile she threw her arms around his neck, surprising the hell out of him.

"You're a good man," she whispered. "Please don't lose sight of that now."

She stepped back and walked, head held high, back into the kitchen. *What a wonder it would be,* he thought, *to deserve that woman.*

He shuffled the other way, into the den with the phone and the computer. After collapsing into the chair he leaned sideways to pull out his wallet and the slip of paper he'd tucked inside.

The paper was soft between his fingers. He read the words for the millionth time, and noted the time underlined twice at the bottom of the note. According to the clock on the far wall if he hurried he'd only be a little late. He grabbed the phone and took a deep breath before dialing.

"Hello?" Jack's voice cut through the silence.

"Jack, it's…" He realized with a spurt of the ridiculous that Jack might not recognize his voice over the phone. "It's your dad."

"So I gathered." Jack chuckled. "What's up?"

"Are you busy?"

"No. You okay?"

"I…could use a ride, son."

There was a pause, long and careful, and Walter decided to answer the question before it was asked.

"There's an AA meeting at the church tonight."

"You want to go to that?"

Walter nodded and then realized he'd have to actually say the words.

"I need to, son. I can't do this alone."

"THEY'RE OUT," LUCY SAID, staring at Casey and Ben curled up on the coach.

"*Shrek 3* has that effect on kids," Jeremiah said, unable to look up from her foot, which lay in his lap. He ran his knuckles across the sole and her toes curled.

By the time Shrek had found Fiona in the first movie, he'd given in to temptation and pulled her legs up into his lap and took off her boots one by one. Rolled her pink socks down her ankles and off her toes.

It had been hot, a delicious tease, and he knew she liked that. Liked sitting in the room with this family, while Jeremiah undressed the only part of her he could.

He'd made a joke about stinky feet and the boys had laughed, but he'd cupped his palm around her heel as if he were holding gold.

What are you doing, cowboy? he asked himself.

"The third one's not as good as the first two," Lucy whispered.

He grinned, but there was something building in his chest. Something ugly and dangerous.

"I bet you never thought you'd have an opinion on the *Shrek* franchise." He said it disdainfully, totally negating the fun they'd had. He was spoiling for a fight and she had to know it. But she stroked the sting out of every barb he sent her way, making it a joke.

"I don't know," she said. "I've always liked fart jokes."

Jeremiah laughed, he couldn't help it. Lucy laughed, too, and then quickly clapped a hand over her mouth, peeking over the edge of the love seat to make sure she hadn't woken the boys. They were still fast asleep, heads together on the same pillow in the middle of the couch.

"Is Aaron still on the phone?" she asked, and turned down the volume on the credits. Using his remote controls as if she'd been doing it for years. As though she had the authority. And she did—he'd handed it to her. Like he wanted to hand everything to her.

This shabby house, the three wounded boys, all his problems and worries—he just wanted to give them all to her.

Right, he thought, *and she's going to love that.*

Upstairs the hum of Aaron's voice was just audible.

"Good Lord," he said, "it's ten o'clock."

"Must be a girl."

"Heaven help us."

"Well, thank God you gave him that condom."

"Yeah, it's my phone bill I'm worried about now."

She curled her foot into his hand and he reciprocated by running his fingers across the sensitive skin at her toes. Her breath caught in her chest and he liked that.

He liked everything.

"This was a good day," she said.

"Was it?" He watched his dark fingers against the white of her skin.

End this, he thought. *It's going nowhere.*

"What's wrong?" She put the tips of her fingers on his shoulder.

Now that the boys were asleep and they were alone, it was as if the bell had been rung and the temper Jeremiah had been trying to control broke free of the gate. He could barely hang on.

"Why are you staying here?"

"Because we had fun—"

"No. Why are you staying at the ranch?"

He could see in her face she knew what he was asking. What he was really asking. She pulled her legs off his lap and curled into a ball at the end of the love seat. "Because it's my home, Jeremiah. My family is there, and I want to be where they are."

"Living in the same house as your mother? As Walter?"

"It's not ideal, but it's working for now."

"And when it stops working?"

"I'll move. An apartment in town, maybe the little house, I don't know."

"But your design—"

"I can do from anywhere, and frankly, I like doing it here."

Slowly, he rose to his feet. He knew the burning question was in his eyes. She stood, too. *This brave, foolish woman.*

"You're here, Jeremiah. And I like you. I...like what we have."

His laughter was bitter—it turned the air to sludge and she flinched.

"We have a hotel room—"

"Keep your voice down," she hissed, finally getting angry. He liked that. He wanted the fight. "The boys—"

"Right. The boys. Tell me—do you think every day is like this? Lying around watching movies? Walking down by the creek? You think this is what it's like?"

"No, of course not. I know—"

"Nothing. I haven't slept through the night in two years. There's more work than time. Ben's practically failing school. Aaron's hockey costs more than my truck. Casey sleeps with Annie's old towel. Ben cries at night. We eat peanut-butter-and-jelly sandwiches half the time because I'm so damn tired I can't be bothered to take food out of the freezer—"

"I want to help. I want to share all of that with you."

"Why do you want this?" He gestured to the room, the house, the sleeping boys. "You could have anything. Choose anything. Why in the world are you choosing this? Why do you want to be stuck here?"

She stepped back. Once. Again. "I don't feel stuck."

He laughed, bitter and sharp. "Now, you don't. A month from now, it'll change and you'll be gone because you can leave."

The couch creaked and both of them turned to see Casey and Ben blinking up at them. They heard. Of course they heard. He'd been yelling.

A cold chill danced over his skull.

"Where are you stuck?" Casey asked, and then yawned so big his jaw nearly cracked.

"With us," Ben said. His eyes returning to that old-man gaze he had so recently shed.

What... How do I make this right? How...?

Jeremiah looked at Lucy but she was as stricken and angry as the boys. "Ben," Jeremiah said, stepping toward the boy in a panicked effort to repair the damage of what he'd just said. "It's not like that—"

"Not like what?" Ben asked, standing. He wasn't yelling, or sneering. It was as if the poison of his petulance was gone and now he stood there a survivor of the inner struggle that had nearly killed him.

It was Jeremiah's turn to be sweating and shaking.

This isn't about Lucy, he realized. Not at all. This was about Jeremiah never understanding why someone would willingly choose this life when he'd had it thrust upon him.

"You never wanted to be here," Ben said. "We all know it."

"That's not true." Jeremiah scrambled for words but everything sounded like lies and he couldn't breathe. Not in the presence of the grown-up pain on Ben's face. "I do want to be here."

"You wouldn't choose us."

"Every day I choose you," Jeremiah insisted. "Every day I stay."

"You don't make it feel like a choice, Uncle J." Ben helped Casey to his feet, but the little boy tripped over the blanket and Jeremiah leaned forward to steady him. But Ben was already there to do it. He led Casey up the steps.

"You should just leave."

Ben was giving Jeremiah permission, calm and cool, as if he had no heart in it anymore. And then they were gone, up the stairs, and Jeremiah stood there, chest heaving, shoulders slumped.

Defeated.

LUCY SAT BACK DOWN on the couch and grabbed her socks. Her anger on behalf of those boys making her clumsy.

"I've made a mess," Jeremiah whispered.

"It's a bit worse than a mess," she said, stomping into her boots. "Those boys don't deserve your resentment."

"You think I don't know that? You think I don't wake up every morning—" his hands clutched at his shirt "—wishing I felt differently?"

She gaped at him, shocked to hear him say it so boldly. She'd had her suspicions, sure, but this was real. "Maybe you *should* leave," she said.

"Yeah, and what will happen to the boys?"

"There are a lot of people who would step up, it's that kind of community."

Immediately, he shook his head. "I'm not leaving my boys to be raised by some other family."

My boys—that was a first.

"Do you love them?"

"Of course I love them," he snapped, as if offended she would ask.

"Well, they don't seem to know that, Jeremiah. You could probably start fixing this disaster by telling them that." She grabbed her purse, swinging it over her shoulder.

In the far reaches of her mind she knew the pain that was coming her way. It was building force and steam. It had been a mistake to come here.

"You've got a good life here, Jeremiah. And what's going to ruin it isn't this place, or the boys—it's you. Figure this shit out before you put those boys through any more pain."

She walked toward the dark foyer, her boots clicking hard against the stone floor, each step the sound of something breaking.

He touched her shoulder and she whirled away, out of reach.

"Where are you going?" he asked.

"Back home."

"What...?" The poor man looked so lost, so alone, and she almost took pity on him, but he had some work to do, work that didn't involve her. "I want to ask if you'll come back, but it sounds ridiculous. I don't know why you'd want to come back to this mess."

"I...I like you. A lot. I like your boys and your mess. And I want to be a part of it. But you have some work to do. And more important, just like those boys, I want to feel chosen."

She left him standing there, in the foyer of his family home, lost and without a map. The pain was starting to settle in her chest, her arms were heavy, tears burned behind her eyes, but she kept walking. She got into her car and left Jeremiah behind her, hoping, hoping with all of her heart, that he would figure out how to come to terms with his own heart.

JEREMIAH STOOD OUTSIDE Aaron's door, his forehead pressed to the wood. The boys were all in there, talking. He could hear the muffled exchange, but no specific words.

He was trying to figure out what to say, how to make this all right, or if not make it right, make it forgotten, but he didn't know how. There was no work he could make them all do. No punishment. He had nothing left. No actions to pull them from the wreckage.

Tell them you love them. Lucy's voice rang in his ear, like the scent of her perfume lingered in his house. The ghost of Lucy was going to haunt him for a long time.

Until, anyway, he figured out what she meant about feeling chosen.

Tell them you love them. He'd start there.

He knocked and after a long silent moment Aaron finally turned the knob and opened the door a crack. He could see Ben and Casey sitting on Aaron's bed. Casey could barely keep his head up, but Ben sat there clear-eyed.

Somehow that boy had figured out how to pull himself from whatever brink he'd been near. And he found himself deeply envious of a nine-year-old.

You're amazing, Ben, he thought, and then realized the kid had no idea he felt that way. How could he? Jeremiah had never said it.

"Can I come in?"

Aaron nodded and stepped back. Jeremiah stepped into the den of an athlete, complete with hockey posters and dirty socks. He sat on the floor, cross-legged. The boys all looked at one another, unsure of what was happening.

That makes four of us, he thought. *Four of us.* He liked the sound of that—*the Four of Us.*

"I love you," he said, staring at his hands, but then decided the boys deserved better. He looked each of them in the eye.

"I love you," he said to Aaron, who blushed but smiled. "You remind me so much of your dad," he went on. "Easygoing and fun. Everyone liked your dad, just like they like you. He'd be so proud of you. I...I am so proud of you."

Aaron nodded, his eyes bright. "Thanks, Uncle J."

"Ben." The boy flinched as if Jeremiah had hit him and those eyes of his wouldn't meet Jeremiah's. "I love you."

Ben snorted.

"I do. I know it may not seem like it sometimes."

"Ever."

Jeremiah sighed. "I'm sorry for that. I'm sorry for a lot of things I've done wrong by you boys, but I'm most sorry that I've never told you how I feel about you. How much I care for you. I love you, Ben. You're so smart and intuitive—you're an old soul like your mom. Sometimes I look at you and I can see her so clearly, it's amazing. You're amazing."

Ben didn't say anything but his throat bobbed as he swallowed hard, staring at the Sidney Crosby poster.

"Casey, my little charmer. I love you—"

Casey hopped off the bed and curled up in Jeremiah's lap, finding the place he best liked to squeeze up next to him. "I love you, too, Uncle J.," he whispered, and put his head against Jeremiah's chest.

He gave himself a moment to soak in that love, to acknowledge it in a way that he never had before.

"You still want to leave," Ben said, his eyes unforgiving.

"I don't," Jeremiah insisted.

Ben and Aaron shared a long look and Aaron shook his head. "We…we don't know how to believe you."

"We think you're lying," Ben said in far clearer terms.

"You know I can't go back to the rodeo. My accident—"

"Doesn't mean you don't want to," Ben pushed.

Jeremiah searched and he searched and he took as long as he needed to try and find the answer that made sense, a way that he could convince Ben, but it was lost somewhere he couldn't get to.

"Have you grieved for your old life?" Dr. Gilman had asked, and when she did, he'd broken out in a cold sweat. The grief was in there somewhere. Somewhere he was a little scared to go.

"I think maybe we need to go see a friend of mine. Dr. Gilman."

"I don't like doctors." Casey sighed.

"She's not that kind of doctor. She's the kind of doctor that talks, helps people figure out their problems."

"A head shrinker?" Aaron asked. "That's what Grandpa calls them."

"Some people call them that, but Dr. Gilman has helped me a lot and I think she could help all of us…as a…as a family."

"We're not a family," Ben argued.

Solemn and sad, Jeremiah nodded in agreement. "Then being a family is what we need help with."

LUCY WALKED THROUGH the empty house and opened the fridge looking for a beer. Of course there was no beer. Not anymore. Once, the house had been dripping with booze and she hadn't cared one bit. But now, the one time in her life when she wanted to get rip-roaring drunk, the house was dry.

Figures, she thought.

She grabbed a Diet Coke and in the dark she sat down at the empty table. More like she deflated, right into the seat. A boneless slop in a yellow dress.

Now, she thought, staring at the silver can, lacking even the energy to open it, *how do I recover?*

From behind, she heard her mother coming out of the laundry room.

"Lucy?" Mom said, stepping into the dark room with a full laundry basket. "What are you doing?"

What am I doing? she asked herself. To her utter chagrin, to the bottom of her independent feminist soul, she shuddered. "I think I'm waiting."

"For what?" Sandra put the basket on the table.

"A man," Lucy answered with a groan.

"Is someone picking you up?"

"No. I'm waiting for a man to come to his senses."

"Ahhh... A woman's lot in life." Sandra smiled and reached into the basket, pulling out the little half curtain that used to hang in the bathroom window. *Mom is washing curtains at eleven o'clock at night?*

"Is it Jeremiah?"

"I love him, Mom." The words came out like a mourning wail and Lucy cracked open the can for a sip to drown out the sadness.

"And you think he loves you?"

'I think figuring out he loves me is so far down on his to-do list it will never happen. Not in this decade."

"And you're willing to wait that long?"

"No... I don't know. I don't know anything."

Sandra handed her one of the long sheers from the living room. "Help me hang this back up, would you?"

"Mom," she moaned, "I really don't—"

"Let me give you some advice, honey. Don't wait. Get on with your life. Work. Be busy. Because if you wait, you lose a little of yourself every day. You can hope this man you love comes to his senses, hope he does what he needs to do to deserve you, hope he returns your feelings in the way he should. But if you wait for it to happen, you're just wasting your time and yourself."

Lucy touched the silky edge of the drape—sheer and old, it felt like silk when it was probably just 1970s polyester. "Why are you hanging curtains at eleven o'clock at night, Mom?"

"I am hoping, too."

"Walter?"

"I know that bothers you, Lucy, but I cannot stop how I feel."

"It doesn't bother me, Mom, not like it did…but I just don't understand how you go from a man like Dad to a man like Walter."

Sandra took her end of the sheer and walked into the family room. Lucy, holding her end, followed like a fish on a line.

"Perhaps they are not that different."

Lucy snorted. "Dad was perfect—"

"Don't, honey. No one is perfect. No relationship is without its problems."

Moonlight fell across Sandra's face, and like the sheer, her expression was hiding and revealing at the same time. Luey wasn't going to pry—she liked her memories of her father, her memories of her childhood. She had no interest in changing any of that.

Lucy stepped up onto the chair beside the sliding glass door. Carefully she threaded the hooks through the slits in the tops of the sheers.

"So, we're not waiting?" Lucy asked.

"Nope."

"We're getting on with our lives and…we're hoping?"

"Yep."

"Then I'm going to Los Angeles to get our stuff."

"Sounds good."

"And I'm going to call Meredith Van Loan and make an appointment to show her my wedding jewelry collection."

"That's my girl." With that, Sandra started to pull the sheer back down, ripping holes around the hooks. "Take those off, will you?" she said. "I'm going shopping. This place needs an overhaul."

Lucy grinned and unhooked the sheer.

"That's my mom."

CHAPTER NINETEEN

JEREMIAH BOOKED A MEETING with Dr. Gilman for Monday afternoon. The boys went to school in the morning but he picked them up at lunch. He had apples and cheese for the ride over in the truck.

The boys were silent, probably nervous. Jeremiah could relate—he had cold sweat pooling in the small of his back. "I don't want her to shrink my head," Casey whispered from the back.

Jeremiah grinned at him in the rearview mirror. "She won't. Trust me. I've been going for months—does my head look any smaller?"

He took off his hat and Casey inspected it. "I guess not."

"You've been going for months?" Aaron asked.

"Saturday nights," he said. "When Grandma and Grandpa come over."

"I thought you were playing poker!" Ben cried.

"I lied."

"You shouldn't lie, Uncle J.," Casey admonished.

"I know, buddy, and I'm not going to anymore."

A few minutes later he pulled up to the red building, and the four of them walked up the sidewalk. As they pushed through the door, the little bell rang four times.

"Well, hello," the receptionist said, swiveling away from the computer to greet them all.

The three boys all said, "Hi, ma'am," but Jeremiah

wondered if he was going to pass out. It was so hard to breathe. His skin prickled and sweat dripped down his back. His nose was running like he had allergies.

"Go on back," the receptionist said. "Dr. Gilman is waiting for you."

Casey gripped his hand and Jeremiah led the boys down the small hallway to the back room, the sunlit office with the Kleenex and the couch. The place where he talked, the only place in the world where it felt all right for him to spill his guts and be afraid instead of pretending like he knew what he was doing.

This was the place where he was weak.

It's going to be okay, he told himself. *This is the right thing to do.*

Dr. Gilman stood up from her desk as they all walked in. The boys said, "Howdy," polite as ever, and Jeremiah hung up his hat. He grabbed Ben's baseball cap and Aaron's new cowboy hat and set them on the rack, as well. Casey shrugged off his sweatshirt and handed it up to him. Jeremiah set it up on the rack.

He tilted his head. That…that looked right.

The four of us, he thought. *A family. It begins here.*

FROM INSIDE THE BARN Walter heard the car door slam and he quickly walked out to see who it was.

Sandra was getting out of Mia's old truck, her arms full of catalogs and fabric samples. She'd been gone the whole day, not even there at breakfast. Which left him deflated over his toast since he'd spent the hours close to dawn figuring out what he needed to tell her.

She wasn't there at lunch, either, and his little speech was drilling holes in his head.

"Can I help you with those?" he asked.

She didn't spare him a glance and he wanted to kiss

his way across that stubborn chin of hers. But instead he grabbed the top two big books in her arms. Wallpaper samples.

Interesting.

"Thank you," she said stiffly, and Walter nodded, following her into the house.

Once in the kitchen, she dropped the stuff on the counter and he followed suit. Then suddenly, with their arms empty, his urge to touch her, to hold her, was strong. Too strong, and despite his speech and his intentions he grabbed her hand. Just that. Her fingers in his, tiny and fragile and perfect.

"I'd like to talk to you," he said.

She nodded, still unreadable. She was going to make him sweat—the realization almost made him smile.

"I am sorry about the other night."

She yanked her hand back. "I'm not interested in apologies. Or guilt. We kissed, Walter, it's not the end of the world."

"No. I'm not sorry I kissed you. Lord, never…never that. I'm sorry I ended things the way I did. I…I don't have much practice."

"Me, neither." Her smile was shy, sweet, and it sent a lightning bolt into his heart, kick-starting the old thing. "Perhaps we can practice together."

He wiped his sweaty hand over his pants, hoping it was worth turning away this second chance. "I…I would like that, Sandra, more than you know. But I've joined AA. That meeting you told me about down at the church."

Her mouth fell open, a shock that he utterly understood. But then she shook her head and that gape-faced shock changed into a transcendent smile. "I'm proud of you, Walter."

He smiled in return, "Thank you. So, ah...so is Jack. He gave me a ride. They have another group at the same time, for the family members of alcoholics. He went—said it was interesting."

"I'm so glad," she whispered. "For the two of you."

She wrapped her arms around him and embraced him with her whole body. And it was like stepping into warm water. It was perfect, just what he wanted, but he had to step away.

With his hands at her elbows, he moved back. "You, ah, you know how I feel about you. And that hasn't changed. But the thing with AA—I want to do it right. I want to keep making you proud, and Jack proud. I can't have a relationship like that. Like...the way I want... with you. Not right now. Not for a while."

She brushed hair off his forehead, her fingers cool. "Can we be friends?"

"Please."

"Then the rest can wait." She pressed one tender kiss to his cheek, a brand that would linger, marking him as hers for future use, and then she stepped back.

"But," she said, her tone bright and friendly, the Sandra of old, "we're going to have to stay busy. And I have the perfect thing."

He glanced at the wallpaper books and paint chips. She was going to get rid of the ghosts. She was going to brand this house as hers.

A fresh start all the way around.

"I'm so glad you're here," he said.

"Me, too. Now, let's get to work."

BEN LED THEM OUT of Dr. Gilman's. Jeremiah brought up the rear, feeling wrung out. Drained.

"That was good work today," Dr. Gilman told him at the door. "You should be proud of yourself."

"Because I cried like a baby?"

She smiled, indulgently, letting him use his jokes as a balm to his pride.

"Thank you," he whispered, wondering if it would be weird to hug her and then deciding he didn't care. He crushed the good doctor into his arms.

"Oh!" she cried, and then laughed, patting his shoulder. "You're going to break me."

He let her go, waved goodbye to Jennifer and ran to catch up with the boys.

"What did you think?" he asked, once they were all inside the truck.

"I liked her." Casey, the most easily impressed of the three, quickly gave his stamp of approval.

"She's nice," Aaron said.

"Do you want to go back?" Jeremiah asked.

"Yes," Ben said quickly from the back. Jeremiah turned in the seat to look at him, somehow not surprised. Ben's eyes were red from crying, as well. And for the first time since Annie's funeral the two of them had hugged. Jeremiah and Ben needed help with this stuff, somehow; while Casey and Aaron could process their grief and confusion, he and Ben got stuck in places. Lost.

"Okay." Jeremiah smiled and his heart soared when Ben's lips curved in response. He turned back around and started the truck.

Lucy is going to love this, he thought. He could see her face when he told her what happened, how... The thought sputtered out and he stared blindly out the windshield.

"Uncle J.?" Aaron asked. "You gonna cry again?"

Jeremiah smirked at Aaron's teasing but the boy just laughed.

"I think…" He stopped, started again. "I want to date Lucy."

"I thought you already were," Aaron said.

"Yeah, well, I might have blown that last night."

"You should apologize," Ben said.

"I don't think that will be enough," he said.

"Draw her a picture," Casey suggested.

"Flowers." Aaron nodded knowingly. "Girls love that."

"How in the world do you know that?"

Aaron shrugged—the sage Casanova.

"Let's just go see her," Casey said, and then he whispered to Ben, "they have banana bread over there."

"Good idea, Casey," Jeremiah said, and pulled away from the curb. He'd start with some groveling and go from there.

"WHAT DO YOU MEAN she's not here?" he asked Sandra a half hour later, his guts in knots. "Where did she go?"

"Los Angeles."

He stepped backward, down off the step. A breeze would have knocked him over. "She left? I thought—"

"She's just getting our stuff," Sandra said. "She's coming back."

Light-headed, he braced himself against the house. "When?"

"A few days. She was going to make some appointments."

Doubt clawed at him. She was going to get back to her life, back to the work that made her who she was, and she'd forget about him. About the boys. About dating a man with nothing to offer but a dirty house and a hotel room once a week.

Stop. He squashed those thoughts. *You have more than that. You are worth more than that, and the boys deserve better than your constant negativity.*

She'd said she wanted to be chosen, probably because she'd already chosen them, warts and all.

"What's your address in Los Angeles?"

Sandra blinked, a smile sparking across her face. "You're going down there?"

"I'm going to give it a shot, Sandra."

She ducked inside and came back out with a scrap of paper she'd written the address on and a few directions off the southbound highway. "Look for the balcony with the roses—you can't miss it."

"Thank you." In an expansive mood, he gave her a hug, which she returned generously.

"Do you want me to keep the boys?" she asked. "They're welcome—"

"No." He glanced back at the truck where the boys were all piled in the front seat staring at him through the windshield. "We're a family," he said. "We go together."

THE CONDO HAD SOLD a few days before, but she didn't have to officially move out until the end of the month. So Lucy grabbed some stuff from storage and moved back into her old bedroom for a few nights. All of their furniture had been moved out—the sleek modern replacements were a part of the staging. It was ugly and far, far from homey.

Meredith had reluctantly agreed to meet with her tomorrow. Lucy dug through her boxes looking for her notebooks. She still didn't have any samples, which probably made this appointment pointless. Meredith wasn't going to want to look at sketches. Meredith would probably laugh her right out of her gorgeous upscale boutique.

But Lucy was going to give it a shot. She sat on the floor, her sketchbook on the glass-and-iron coffee table that she would never have bought, not in a million years. And she redrew her original sketches in ways that brought out the detail, the brilliance, of each piece.

An hour later she turned on the lamp, contemplated dinner, but decided to finish the details on the amber-and-garnet gold tiara. Ten minutes later the scent of Mr. Lezinsky's cabbage rolls wafted up through the floor and her stomach howled in protest.

All right, she thought, and stood, cracking her back, shaking out her fingers. Since she was only in town for a few nights she was going to get her fill of Rosita's down the street. Her mouth watered at the thought of her carnitas and tomatillo salsa.

There was commotion outside her door and when she opened it, all she saw were balloons and legs.

"Hey, Lucy!" Casey ducked down below the red balloons and grinned up at her. "We found her!" he yelled at some other legs, and Jeremiah stepped forward, a bouquet of wilting convenience store roses in his hands.

In her chest, her heart was inflating like one of the balloons. Every second she looked at these men, it was in danger of getting too full, of popping. And yet she couldn't look away.

"Hi," Jeremiah said.

She opened her mouth but nothing came out.

"Can I let go of these balloons yet?" Ben asked.

"I'm letting go of mine," Casey said, and a silver Mylar balloon wafted into the condo. It read Happy Birthday.

Jeremiah winced. "We let Casey pick out the balloons."

"We brought chocolates, too," Aaron said, ducking past the balloons to come in and press a box of candy into her numb hands. "But Uncle J. wouldn't let us stop for dinner so I got hungry. The coconut ones are all that are left."

Ben finally stepped in, pulling the balloons in behind him. They crowded through the door, squeaking, but then they bent and shifted and squeezed in. He let them go and red, blue, green and yellow balloons floated past her head, bumping into her nose, her hair.

This is a dream, she thought. *I am dreaming.*

When they bounced up onto the ceiling, strings dangled down around them.

"What...what are you doing here?" she whispered, her eyes never leaving Jeremiah's face. He seemed different somehow, softer, as if something had melted, as if some invisible wall had been torn down.

He looked young, nervous.

I love you, she thought.

"We're on vacation!' Casey cried, and when he tried to bounce on the rigid couch, he winced.

"Vacation?" she asked Jeremiah.

"We went to a counseling meeting and then stopped by the ranch to see you. Sandra said you were here and, well, the kids haven't had a vacation in years. After their mom died I just kept them in school trying to keep things normal, but I think maybe...maybe they could use some fun. Just a week. Their teachers said it was okay. I thought maybe we'd go to Disney Land or World, or whichever is out here."

He was rambling and it was sweet and she was smart

enough to read between the lines, but she had her pride, too. Lots of it.

"But why are you here?"

He blinked and took a step forward, closing the door behind him, batting the gold strings away. "I choose you."

Her knees melted at the look in his eyes, the sweetness of his voice, but she was no fool and she kept her mouth shut, letting him get to the good stuff.

"If you're brave and crazy enough to choose me and the boys, I'd be a fool not to choose you. I would choose you no matter what my life was like. You're the most exciting woman I've ever known. The most beautiful and talented person I've ever met and I was a fool."

"You were." She nodded in agreement, though her heart was exploding with love.

"Glad we agree." He stepped closer, closer again. "Boys," he said over his shoulder. "Go into the other room."

"Are they going to kiss?" Casey asked, and Ben shushed him before pushing him into the kitchen where they'd probably be eavesdropping.

"I don't know what is going to happen in a few years or next week—hell, with these boys I don't know what's going to happen in ten minutes." His fingers cupped her cheek, brushed the hair behind her ear. Then he cradled her face in his big rough hands. "I've never been in love," he said. "So, I'm not sure if that's what this is. But I want you with me. For as long as you want to be there."

"That sounds like love," she whispered.

"You are the expert." He kissed her, as sweetly as a first kiss, as tenderly as the thousandth. "I love you," he breathed into her.

"I love you, too."

"Gross!" Casey cried in the kitchen "They're kissing!"

Jeremiah laughed, pressing his forehead to hers. "It won't be easy," he said, as if warning her.

She wrapped her arms around his neck, holding on as tight as she could. The ride would be bumpy, no doubt about it. But she couldn't imagine anything more fun, more exciting, more fulfilling, than taking this ride with Jeremiah and his boys.

"Who wants easy?"

EPILOGUE

One year later

"ASK ME AGAIN," Lucy whispered against Jeremiah's ear as he listened intently to whatever was happening up at the front of the church.

He didn't even turn. "Marry me."

"One more time." She grinned, she couldn't help it, and when he turned slightly murderous eyes on her she grinned harder.

"For the love of God, Lucia Marie Alatore, have mercy and marry me. Or at least answer me. It's been two days."

"I want to take my time. This is only going to happen once."

He shook his head, looking away. "Oh, come on, we're up."

He grabbed her hand and pulled her to the front of the church where Mia and Jack stood with baby Oliver by the baptismal font.

Lucy and Jeremiah said what they were supposed to say as godparents and Lucy fell even harder in love with Jeremiah, at the earnestness with which he agreed to care for this baby as if he were Jeremiah's own.

He knew better than to not take it seriously.

Baby Oliver was dipped into the fountain, cold water trickled over his head. Oliver wailed and behind her she heard Sandra, Walter and the boys laughing and sighing with their own love that they had for the new baby.

"Yes," she said in the noise, squeezing Jeremiah's hand. "I'll marry you."

He grinned, but didn't say anything for a long moment. Then he lifted her hand and kissed it, closing his eyes to savor the moment.

BACK AT ROCKY M, Jack and Mia were having a small party at their new house, which had been finished in Mia's seventh month of pregnancy. Or, as Lucy liked to put it, demon stage two. Mia had not been a happy pregnant woman.

"I swear to God there will be blood if someone doesn't get me some cake," Mia muttered, stroking Oliver's head as she breast-fed. Mia was the most untraditional happy new mother Lucy had ever encountered. Not that anyone expected anything different.

"Do you have any idea what my nipples feel like?" she'd said at one point. "You try being happy with these nipples."

"I'll get you some cake," Lucy said, unperturbed by her sister. She really couldn't be perturbed by anything anymore. Not even when she stepped out of the nursery to find Walter and her mother necking like teenagers.

"Really?" she asked as the two jumped away from each other. No one was quite sure what was happening between Walter and Sandra, but Walter had gotten his year sobriety chip a few months ago and suddenly he and Sandra couldn't keep their hands off each other.

It seemed she'd moved in with Jeremiah just in the nick of time. She had no desire to share her mom's love shack.

"You know, Walter," she said with a grin over her

shoulder, "the least you could do is make an honest woman out of her." She caught their startled faces before heading into the kitchen.

Where, of course, her own little family was doing their best to polish off the cake. "You better save some of that for my sister or there will be trouble."

The boys all looked panicked and quickly put their second helpings back on the platter. They all knew better than to get in between Mia and cake.

Jeremiah tugged her into his arms. "When do we tell them?" he asked, knowing the boys could hear. She wrapped her arms around his neck and kissed a little of the blue frosting off the corner of his lips. "Let's make them guess."

"We're getting a dog!" Casey cried. He'd been on a real dog kick ever since Sandra and Walter had bought a new pup.

"No," Jeremiah said firmly. "No more dogs."

"They're getting married, dummy," Ben said, and Aaron looked up.

"I thought you guys already were."

"What?" Lucy cried. "When?"

"You guys took that trip to Vegas..."

"It wasn't Vegas—it was Sonoma," she said. "And I was selling wedding rings, not getting married. Do you guys really not listen when we talk to you?"

"We listen." Aaron shrugged. "So you're getting married?"

This really was not the kind of reaction she was hoping for. She wanted some yelling. Some hugging.

"You guys are bummers."

"Who is getting married?" Mia said, stepping into the kitchen. She handed Oliver off to Jeremiah, who for whatever reason was like the baby whisperer when it came to that kid.

"We are!" Lucy said. "We're getting married."

Mia shrieked and Jack ran in at the sound. "What's going on?"

"They're getting married!" Mia cried, her eyes alight, and Jack turned to Jeremiah, clapping him on the back.

"Good news, my friend. Excellent news."

"What news?" Walter asked, walking in. Sandra followed, her lipstick suspiciously reapplied.

"We're getting married," Lucy announced, and finally the room erupted. Jack got out the champagne and poured glasses for everyone but Walter and the kids.

"To happy endings," Walter said, lifting his ginger ale. Her family, old and new, all looked at one another and smiled. They'd managed to create a family from the pain and tragedy of their pasts. They'd managed to forgive one another and move on to a place of happiness. These were the greatest blessings of her life.

Utterly unexpected, this family of hers. But she couldn't imagine one better.

She turned to Jeremiah, where he stood holding a sweet sleeping baby in his arms. "I love you," she said.

He grinned, kissing her lips. "I love you, too." But when he glanced down at that baby he sobered. "But…I think we have a problem."

"What?" she asked, incredulous. There were no problems on a day like today. It wasn't allowed. It was a rule of the universe.

"I think I want a baby."

Uh-oh.

* * * * *

HEART & HOME

COMING NEXT MONTH
AVAILABLE JULY 2, 2012

#1788 UNDER THE AUTUMN SKY
The Boys of Bayou Bridge
Liz Talley
One night with Louise Boyd and Abram Dufrene wants more. Then he finds out she's the guardian for a recruit and his job as coach is on the line. Yet walking away is impossible!

#1789 ISLAND HAVEN
The Texas Firefighters
Amy Knupp
Weeks before paramedic Scott Pataki's escape from San Amaro Island, Mercedes Stone shows up with the half sister he's never met. But he's determined to leave, no matter how tempting it is to stay.

#1790 THE OTHER SOLDIER
In Uniform
Kathy Altman
Corporal Reid Macfarland can't live with the mistake he made. But if he can convince a soldier's widow, Parker Dean, to forgive him, maybe Reid can learn to forgive himself.

#1791 HIDDEN AGENDA
Project Justice
Kara Lennox
Jillian Baxter is undercover on her first assignment. But she can't keep her cool when she learns her new boss, Conner Blake, is the boy from her past responsible for the most humiliating incident of her life.

#1792 THE COMPANY YOU KEEP
School Ties
Tracy Kelleher
Surely Mimi Lodge and Vic Golinski have put their past behind them. But when they meet at their college reunion, it seems the sparks are flying just as high!

#1793 A SON'S TALE
It Happened in Comfort Cove
Tara Taylor Quinn
When Morgan Lowen's son goes missing, Caleb Whittier finds himself reliving the nightmare of a similar case. This time he'll do all he can to make sure this boy comes home.

You can find more information on upcoming Harlequin®
titles, free excerpts and more at www.Harlequin.com.

HSRCNM0612

REQUEST YOUR FREE BOOKS!
2 FREE NOVELS PLUS 2 FREE GIFTS!

Harlequin®

Super Romance®

Exciting, emotional, unexpected!

YES! Please send me 2 FREE Harlequin® Superromance® novels and my 2 FREE gifts (gifts are worth about $10). After receiving them, if I don't wish to receive any more books, I can return the shipping statement marked "cancel." If I don't cancel, I will receive 6 brand-new novels every month and be billed just $4.69 per book in the U.S. or $5.24 per book in Canada. That's a saving of at least 15% off the cover price! It's quite a bargain! Shipping and handling is just 50¢ per book in the U.S. and 75¢ per book in Canada.* I understand that accepting the 2 free books and gifts places me under no obligation to buy anything. I can always return a shipment and cancel at any time. Even if I never buy another book, the two free books and gifts are mine to keep forever.

135/336 HDN FC6T

Name _____ (PLEASE PRINT) _____

Address _____ Apt. # _____

City _____ State/Prov. _____ Zip/Postal Code _____

Signature (if under 18, a parent or guardian must sign) _____

Mail to the **Reader Service:**
IN U.S.A.: P.O. Box 1867, Buffalo, NY 14240-1867
IN CANADA: P.O. Box 609, Fort Erie, Ontario L2A 5X3

Not valid for current subscribers to Harlequin Superromance books.
**Are you a current subscriber to Harlequin Superromance books
and want to receive the larger-print edition?
Call 1-800-873-8635 or visit www.ReaderService.com.**

* Terms and prices subject to change without notice. Prices do not include applicable taxes. Sales tax applicable in N.Y. Canadian residents will be charged applicable taxes. Offer not valid in Quebec. This offer is limited to one order per household. All orders subject to credit approval. Credit or debit balances in a customer's account(s) may be offset by any other outstanding balance owed by or to the customer. Please allow 4 to 6 weeks for delivery. Offer available while quantities last.

Your Privacy—The Reader Service is committed to protecting your privacy. Our Privacy Policy is available online at www.ReaderService.com or upon request from the Reader Service.

We make a portion of our mailing list available to reputable third parties that offer products we believe may interest you. If you prefer that we not exchange your name with third parties, or if you wish to clarify or modify your communication preferences, please visit us at www.ReaderService.com/consumerchoice or write to us at Reader Service Preference Service, P.O. Box 9062, Buffalo, NY 14269. Include your complete name and address.

HSR11

*Harlequin® American Romance® presents a
brand-new miniseries* HARTS OF THE RODEO.

*Enjoy a sneak peek at AIDAN: LOYAL COWBOY
from favorite author Cathy McDavid.*

Ace walked unscathed to the gate and sighed quietly. On
the other side he paused to look at Midnight.

The horse bobbed his head.

Yeah, I agree. Ace grinned to himself, feeling as if he,
too, had passed a test. *You're coming home to Thunder
Ranch with me.*

Scanning the nearby vicinity, he searched out his mother.
She wasn't standing where he'd left her. He spotted her
several feet away, conversing with his uncle Joshua and
cousin Duke who'd accompanied Ace and his mother to the
sale.

He'd barely started toward them when Flynn McKinley
crossed his path.

A jolt of alarm brought him to a grinding halt. She'd
come to the auction after all!

What now?

"Hi." He tried to move and couldn't. The soft ground
pulled at him, sucking his boots down into the muck. He
was trapped.

Served him right.

She stared at him in silence, tendrils of corn-silk-yellow
hair peeking out from under her cowboy hat.

Memories surfaced. Ace had sifted his hands through
that hair and watched, mesmerized, as the soft strands
coiled around his fingers like spun gold.

Then, not two hours later, he'd abruptly left her bedside,
hurting her with his transparent excuses.

She stared at him now with the same pained expression she'd worn that morning.

"Flynn, I'm sorry," he offered lamely.

"For what exactly?" She crossed her arms in front of her, glaring at him through slitted blue eyes. "Slinking out of my room before my father discovered you'd spent the night or acting like it never happened?"

What exactly is Ace sorry for? Find out in
AIDAN: LOYAL COWBOY.

Available this July wherever books are sold.

This summer, celebrate everything Western
with Harlequin® Books!

www.Harlequin.com/Western